SUSIE GOE...

by

ROGER QUINE

CHIMERA

Susie Goes to the Devil first published in 2002 by
Chimera Publishing Ltd
22b Picton House
Hussar Court
Waterlooville
Hants
PO7 7SQ

Printed and bound in Great Britain by
Cox & Wyman Ltd, Reading.

SUSIE GOES TO THE DEVIL

Roger Quine

This novel is fiction – in real life practice safe sex

'Are you truly ready for forgiveness?' he asked, reaching out to Susie and pulling the tight panties higher, stretching them, squeezing the wet softness within.

'I'm ready,' she said, and meant it, because she too was about as ready as she'd ever been.

The vicar looked at them again, gazing from one to the other while his left hand absently stroked the huge erection that still poked proudly from his underpants.

'Repent then, and show your sin!' he shouted, and stepping back he whirled his right arm like a windmill and the leather belt whistled through a semicircle and lashed across two sets of buttocks with a stinging *crack!* And both girls squealed as their flesh quivered and a red line appeared across both bottoms as if branded there, and he grasped himself harder in his left hand.

Chapter One

*He saw the legs first, long and lean and smooth, and drew
closer for a better view, hissing through his teeth in surprise
as his eyes picked out the sharp white V nestled snugly
between the very top of her thighs. Her skirt was up around
her waist and he drew in his breath sharply once more as he
realised he was looking at her underwear. He inched closer
still, leaning forward in his seat as he peered downwards,
his mouth beginning to sag open as he stared at her knickers,
tight between her thighs. Her widespread thighs: she'd
shifted in her seat, opening her legs invitingly, exposing
the tight curve of white panties as they dipped downwards,
cupping her perfect mound in a skin-tight casing.*

Maybe it was the warm spring sunshine, the uneventful
routine of driving, or just the persistent rumble of every
westward mile that helped the horror of the last weeks and
the New Believers recede into the background of the English
countryside. But whatever the cause, the effect was
undeniable and now, after an hour or so driving, the whole
thing had faded to little more than a vague memory, perhaps
no more real to her than to anyone else who read about it in
the Sunday newspaper. Now it was just as if she and Sophie
had never taken part, and all the things that had happened
had happened to someone else. The Susie she was today,
heading west along the motorway, was untouched, a
different person altogether. Fresh and innocent as she'd
been before, she was just a pretty, cheerful blonde girl with
something alive and restless shining in her eyes, revealing a
deep, glowing hunger, a yearning that was matched by the

warm glow in her knickers.

High up in the cab of his lorry he had a perfect view down into the little car as it droned steadily along in the nearside lane. Being French, he'd looked down into the car by force of habit, hoping as always for a glimpse of thigh. He was often lucky in this, and sometimes even luckier, catching a rare glimpse of stocking top and suspender. Once before he'd seen that Holy Grail of the truck driving voyeur, a pair of knickers, but that had been back at home in France, where driving positions were reversed and he could look into the passenger side of the cars passing below him, where such sights were more likely to be found. Here in England he saw mostly hard shoulder and grass verge, since he so seldom overtook a car, and when he did it was usually because the driver was old enough to be his grandmother and moved just as slowly.

But this was different. This was a lithe young woman in her twenties, with shapely, parted legs, sexy little knickers and a hand that was gently stroking the inside of her thigh, reaching higher and higher with each caress!

Yes, incredibly, the warm wet welcome was still there, fresh and demanding and as undeniable as it had been every day of her life since – well, since her schooldays and Miss Piggy's cane. Susie let herself linger on the memory of those few minutes bent across the school desk, when she'd been forced to slide her fingers in and out of her tender young body while the vast form of the gym mistress laboured away behind her, caning and masturbating with a deadly rhythm that spoke of years of practice. The memory was the first of many along the path that brought her from girl to woman, and the real miracle of that blooming was that somehow she had developed the sexual appetite of a full-grown and voracious woman but had lost none of the innocence of her youth.

He couldn't get any closer, and he didn't need to. He could see everything. He just held the vehicle steady and hoped she'd remain unaware of his presence, staring avidly from above as the delicate fingers stroked the front of the white panties, pressing into the softness within. He could almost feel the warmth rising from between her legs, almost feel the heat inside her gusset, the moist, wet gusset, the material getting wetter as the flesh inside gradually parted in arousal, opening the way into her body.

If she'd thought about it, and she seldom bothered to, Susie would have been almost as surprised by the demands of her own body as she had been when still a teenager experimenting for the first time. And maybe she would have realised that it was the survival of her youthfully innocent sexual greed that made her such an irresistible magnet for men – and women. But she didn't notice, or even care that much, but regarded the phenomenon of her almost permanently aroused body with frank acceptance. Even now, after she had been so horribly abused by the New Believers, Susie regarded what was taking place between her legs as a brand new and highly interesting occurrence, which deserved to be treated as unique.

Because there was definitely something happening in her underwear, and it had never been possible for Susie to ignore such things, or leave them unattended to for very long. So, after glancing sideways at her sleeping sister, Susie moved the hand that had been pressing into her lap, plucked the hem of her skirt between finger and thumb, and raised it higher up her thighs, exposing the lean limbs and the taut muscles that drew the eyes down into the valley between them.

The lorry that had been alongside for some moments swayed and jerked slightly, and Susie realised it was foreign, and that from his seat on the left hand side of the cab, the driver could probably look right down into the car; could probably see her thighs, slender and tanned, and the idea of an unknown man – an exotically *French* unknown man – watching while she pleasured herself, caused a fresh flood of warm wetness to seep from her body.

Keeping her foot on the accelerator, Susie spread her knees wider and let her knowing fingers dip swiftly and easily between her thighs, stroking and caressing, until they'd encountered the stretched smoothness of her knickers, and the warm softness that swelled within them.

Her finger pressed downwards, pushing the material deeper, making the shape of her firm mound and soft valley in white cotton; he could see it with total clarity as he grasped himself, one hand clutching at the thick pole that stood up inside his greasy overalls.

The fabric was already moist and at the first touch of sensitive fingers she felt it become wet, as her body flowered and warm juices seeped between the opening folds of flesh, soaking her knickers and making it easy for her fingertips to trace the outline of the widening cleft in the clammy warmth. Playing for her audience, she let the motion continue beyond the point at which her body cried out for more, until she couldn't hold back any longer without moaning aloud.

Her hand continued its lazy stroking movement, and so did his as he stared, mesmerised, and his patience was more than rewarded as the finger pushed ever inwards and the white material slowly disappeared, until it was just a narrow band of white that cut her in half. He was literally dribbling now, strands of saliva hanging from his lower lip as he stared in disbelief. Incredibly he could see the pinkness of the neatly shaved mound and the darker, rosy wetness inside her as the wrist arched and the finger straightened, before it sank slowly past the band of white and disappeared all the way inside.

Susie plucked at the elastic of her knickers with two elegant fingers and pulled the material aside, stroking the warm slickness of her own body, teasing herself with her fingertips and her fingernails until she could control herself no longer, and with a soft moan she raised her bottom so she could slide a finger into the welcoming heat and wetness.

Sighing happily, she let her weight sink down again, forcing the finger deeper, flexing it slowly and luxuriously as her thumb began a swift, delicate flirtation with the tiny bud of her clitoris, stroking, rubbing and flicking, spreading the syrupy wetness around it, making the sensations deeper and smoother.

He could almost hear the sigh of satisfaction that accompanied the arching of her body to meet the intruding digit, and he could almost hear the soft wet sucking noises as that finger began to slide in and out, glistening with moisture each time it reappeared. Fumbling frantically he undid the buttons of his overalls, dragged the grubby underpants aside and pulled himself into the open so he could match her, stroke for stroke. Especially now that she had two fingers at work, one either side of the tight line of white, pulling it tighter as the fingers sank, releasing it as they surfaced, glistening wetly in the sunshine that illuminated the interior of the car, little diamonds of moisture that sparkled in the light. Holding the wheel steady and holding his breath, he stared transfixed as the languid movements of her arm and wrist grew more staccato, and the muscles of her thighs pulled tightly as she flexed her hips upward to meet the thrusts. His hand moved faster and faster inside the cab and he began to gasp, feeling stupid for his fear that the sound of his breath might alert her to his presence and spoil the show she was unwittingly providing.

9

Susie opened her legs as wide as she could, and slid down in her seat as much as she dared while still being able to see enough to keep the car pointing in the right direction. She arched her body and spread herself apart with two fingers so he could see how wet and ready she was, and then she slid one finger inside, slowly and luxuriously, wriggling it around as it sank deeper and deeper into the heat and wetness.

She smiled, a pout that revealed a glimpse of even white teeth, and added a second finger, revelling in the sensations as it spread her wider and filled her, wriggling alongside its companion. She didn't know if she had a G-spot, and quite frankly she didn't care. But she knew what felt good, and this certainly did. Sometimes she needed to tease and tickle her little button, and that would provoke rapid orgasms of brief delight. Other times, and this was one of them, she liked to make herself come with her fingers inside. It took longer, but it was infinitely more fun along the way and the climax, when it came, was far better, longer lasting and of frightening intensity.

Knowing that was what lay just a few minutes ahead, she revelled in the early signs of that powerful rush of pleasure, the glorious sensations that were building steadily between her thighs, a warm tightness that gripped her groin and spread up into her body in long slow pulses that were getting ever stronger and faster. She delighted in pleasuring herself for her own sake, of doing what pleased her for the pure fun of being pleased. Right now it pleased her to know she was being watched, pleased her to know the lecherous driver high above could look, could dream, but could never touch. Knowing she was going to excite him enough to make him come in his pants – that was her pleasure, her power, and her restoration.

Her back arched, her hips bucked and her breath rasped

in her throat, and she knew the driver would see and know she had climaxed, and that heightened her pleasure still further. As the climax reached tidal wave intensity the shuddering spasms that gripped her released more than the usual tensions. They washed her clean of the past few weeks and set her free, to be herself once more, and the knowledge that she was once again in charge of her life added a special force to her climax. Her delight was so extreme that she allowed her display to go on longer than necessary, holding her thighs apart and spreading the soaking fringes of her body apart so the foreign lecher could see as much as possible for as long as possible.

'Yes,' she murmured drowsily to herself as she still teased the soft wetness, 'I'm back.'

Eight feet above the lorry driver's pumping wrist did its work, and with a Gallic grunt he ejaculated over his overalls, just as Susie gathered her composure and pointed the nose of the little Peugeot westward, towards Kingscombe.

Chapter Two

The gravel crunched comfortingly under the tyres as the
little Peugeot stopped outside the cottage that Susie
remembered so well. She smiled fondly at it through the
windscreen as Sophie squealed in delight.

'Oh Suze, it's lovely, isn't it? Just perfect. No wonder
you liked it here so much.'

And Susie realised she had been talking about it in glowing
terms for the last half hour – and that she'd meant every
word.

The village atmosphere, the welcoming smiles, all of it
seemed safe, secure and friendly. Even the vicar was only
an amiable eccentric with a penchant for having sex with
his female parishioners after he'd spanked them very
soundly. It seemed a pretty harmless foible to Susie, as
quaint as the village itself, a very British form of
misbehaviour. She smiled a little at the recollection of his
florid countenance. Then she remembered his admirably
impressive equipment and the smile grew a little wider.
Incredibly she felt a stirring below her waist, as if her body
had remembered too, and was moistening in anticipation
of renewing its acquaintance with his long, hard thickness...

Susie shook her head to clear it and tried to pay attention
to what Sophie was saying.

'How long can we stay here?' she was asking wistfully,
and Susie felt a flood of affection; Sophie was younger by
a couple of years, had always seemed vulnerable, and had
certainly been through the emotional mill just lately.

'Oh, at least a week, I should think,' Susie replied

protectively as they climbed from the car. 'It'll probably take that long to get accepted again and get myself back on the invitation list to his private meetings.' She smiled meaningfully and the two of them giggled together as they walked to the front door.

'Then just one night of hard work?' laughed Sophie, raising an eyebrow.

'Well, hard in one sense, but not in another, if you see what I mean,' said Susie, feeling again a fluttering below the waist as her body anticipated the sensations of the vicar's attentions and prepared itself in readiness.

Concealing the sudden pang of desire, she joined in Sophie's laughter and linked arms with her as they went inside, where Susie took a deep breath and felt herself relax. The journey down had been a cleansing process of sorts, but this was different; this was a homecoming, and Susie felt a deep sense of comfort from being back in this little cottage once again.

'Are you sure you'll be okay?' asked Sophie, concerned. 'I mean, so soon after – well, you know.'

Susie did know exactly. 'Yes,' she sighed, 'I do know. But it all seems so distant now.' She was talking over her shoulder as she took Sophie into the neat spare bedroom. 'This is yours.'

'Oh, fabulous, and what a view!' exclaimed Sophie in delight, and she was right. England looked delightful as it sprawled beyond the window, green fields dotted with piebald specks as the herds munched their peaceful way through another uneventful day where nothing much happened except the grass grew and the flowers blossomed in the bright sunshine.

'Well, if there's anything I can do to help...'

Susie smiled and embraced her sister. 'You just rest and enjoy the scenery,' she said, 'and let your big sister get on with her job. No,' she raised a hand to forestall the argument forming on Sophie's lips, 'honestly Sophe, I'll be fine. After that lot back there,' she jerked her head to indicate the general direction of the New Believers and the recent past, 'after them, the spanking vicar of Kingscombe seems fairly harmless. Don't worry, he's just a cheerful old pervert. It won't be a problem.' She could tell Sophie was unconvinced and hurried on. 'Apart from anything else, it's my job. It's what I do.'

Now she wasn't entirely convinced herself. Nailing the New Believers had been a very necessary thing and she was glad to have done it. Luring a randy vicar onto the front page of a national newspaper for no crime worse than screwing a bunch of even randier women who were at least as keen to be shagged as he was to shag them… it hardly seemed like a worthwhile occupation, not a very worthy cause.

'And the sooner I take care of the vicar, the sooner we can go home and take care of Hugh.'

Sophie frowned at the mention of his name, and then brightened at the prospect of revenge. 'Yes, and I won't let you do it without me,' she said with feeling. 'He's the bastard that got me into all that trouble,' she meant the New Believers, Susie knew, 'and it's time I got my own back. Although,' and she gazed earnestly at her sister, 'I don't quite know how we're going to pay him back.'

'Don't worry, we'll think of something.' Susie wasn't as confident as she sounded. Hugh would be expecting a payback and he'd be ready for it; he was a devious so-and-so and he'd been ready before when Susie tried to catch him out. This time she'd have to be twice as clever, or offer him something so tempting he'd abandon caution in favour of selfish, egotistic greed. Luckily he wasn't short of either characteristic, but the downside was that Susie

14

could only think of one thing that would tempt him enough to override his strongest natural instinct, the one for self-preservation, and she wasn't sure if Sophie was as ready for that as she thought she was. Sure, she was ready for revenge, but whether she could play the part of the bait with enough conviction, whether she could let Hugh come so far into the trap that he couldn't escape – that was something else. Because to get him into that position meant Sophie would have to put herself in a difficult position too, almost certainly with her knickers down and her legs apart.

But despite her concerns, and her sudden, newfound discomfort over the job she was there to do, trapping the vicar, and despite knowing that doing so would almost certainly involve her dropping *her* knickers and spreading *her* legs, Susie was still glowing with the same inner calm she'd felt growing inside as they drew nearer and nearer the village, and still felt at home, happy to be in familiar surroundings, and the sensation was much enhanced when Sophie not only loved the cottage, but loved the village too.

They went for a walk, buying bread and milk, sugar and coffee, visiting different shops, saying hello, starting the cover story at once, introducing Sophie as the sister recovering from illness, which is what Susie had told everyone only a few weeks earlier when she'd set off on her quest to rescue Sophie from the New Believers.

It didn't take long for the village grapevine to react, and the phone on the small table by the bay window of the little cottage was ringing inside the hour, and barely minutes later there was Stephanie, the woman who'd paved the way when Susie first arrived posing as Caroline, young newlywed minus a City husband. It was Stephanie who'd been the vicar's closest ally, who had come to visit and sounded Susie out and made sure the vicar's advances would fall on fertile ground, so to speak. All very polite and

15

subtle, but pimping, nonetheless. And it seemed she still enjoyed the same privileged position within the flock, and still had the same responsibility for procuring recruits to it.

'How are you, my dear?' she quizzed, as she took the opening of the front door as an invitation and walked straight through into the little lounge, hardly awaiting the answer to her question before asking more. 'What have you been up too... is your husband with you... oh, just your sister, I see, well you will be sure to bring her with you when you come – you *are* coming tomorrow night, it *is* Wednesday, after all...'

It was part question, part order, but Susie demurred. She didn't want to rush into things. It wouldn't do to be seen as too eager, and she'd hardly had time to recover from the journey and get the equipment ready, and in any case, she liked it in Kingscombe and wasn't in a hurry to leave. If it took a few days to build up the relationship with the vicar again, then that was a few days rest for her as well as Sophie.

'Don't rush it,' the editor had said, 'take your time and don't hurry.' And Susie had every intention of following those orders to the letter.

Stephanie was fluttering around with apparent excitement, although Susie got the distinct impression that she was less pleased about Susie's return than the vicar, and she remembered how jealously she'd guarded her special relationship with him – 'Andrew', as she constantly pointed out, thought of Stephanie as 'essential' to his work.

'I bet he does,' Susie said to Sophie after she'd gone, 'who else is going to pimp for him the way she does?' and they started giggling again.

And she *had* been doing that, enquiring almost without preamble if Susie would be going to church on Sunday and then re-stating the invitation to the vicar's special meeting the following evening. 'He is most anxious to know,' she said, a wistful look in her eyes that mixed sorrow with something closer to jealousy, 'and when he knows there are two of you... are you a churchgoer?' she asked, turning suddenly to Sophie with a look that implied she'd give up ten years of her life if the answer was no, and concealing her disappointment at the affirmative by the narrowest of margins.

But she brightened visibly when Susie told her that Sophie was still recovering from illness, and probably wouldn't be ready to leave the house for a week or so. 'Well I expect the vicar will be upset. I'm sure he'd have been delighted if you'd both been able to come.' She sniffed happily as she took her leave.

The two girls looked at each other and started laughing, and Susie was cheered at the sight of Sophie's clear blue eyes alive with delight; the healing process had clearly begun. The laughter died and they looked at each other, before embracing, a firm clasp of love and friendship.

'I love you,' Susie whispered, and squeezed her sister, not quite sure what she meant exactly, and feeling Sophie's uncertainty too as their lithe bodies moulded perfectly together, their slightly parted lips almost touching... and then Susie pulled away slightly, breaking the embrace.

'So do I,' said Sophie, and they both laughed again, clumsily trying to camouflage the embarrassment of the moment.

That evening they cooked together, watched TV and drank a bottle of wine before retiring to their rooms. Some time after midnight, wide-awake and unable to sleep, Susie heard her sister cry out.

It was probably a bit of a nightmare, she told herself, but went to check anyway.

'Sorry,' Susie whispered in the shadows, 'didn't mean to wake you, but I was worried. Thought you might be having a bad dream.'

'Not while you're here.' Sophie held out her hand, and Susie took it as her sister raised the covers invitingly.

The vicar smiled benignly at them in the street next morning, roaming freely over Susie's body with his eyes as he gushed platitudes, and then looking equally greedily at Sophie.

'And this must be your delightful sister,' he said, and once again Susie decided it was too complicated to explain that though they looked like twins and had been brought up in the same family for most of their lives, Susie was her mother's daughter and Sophie her father's, and they weren't actually sisters in any sense but the genuine bond which had grown between them over the intervening years. 'Better than sisters,' they always said. 'We're friends because we want to be, not because we have to be.'

Instead she just nodded confirmation, and the vicar's piggy little eyes glinted hungrily as he looked swiftly from one to the other, as if trying to choose between them, or decide which was the prettiest, hardly listening at all as Susie explained that her sister had come down to Kingscombe on doctor's orders, to aid recovery from an unspecified illness.

'I shall pray for you,' he said, as if he was bestowing a divine blessing, holding Sophie's hand in his. 'In fact, I shall be delighted if you'd come along to my meeting this evening so I can minister to your needs in a more personal way.' He stared at Sophie without a trace of shame in his rheumy eyes, affecting not to notice as Susie bristled at him.

'That's kind,' said Sophie, allowing her hand to stay in his. 'I do feel it would be nice to have someone looking after me.'

'Oh, I shall take very good care of you,' he assured her, 'as I'm sure your sister will tell you,' and Susie was amazed that Sophie had failed to spot the leer on his face or the noticeable growth in his trousers. 'I'll take that as yes then, shall I?' he pressed, bustling on without waiting for an answer. 'I look forward to seeing more of you later. Both of you,' he said, turning the leer towards Susie.

As he walked away she almost stamped her foot in anger. 'Oh, Sophie!' she exclaimed. 'Why did you have to encourage him?'

'Me? I didn't... well, all right, I suppose I did a bit,' she admitted, without seeming particularly repentant. 'But it's like you said; he's just a harmless old dodderer, really.'

'Oh yes,' snapped her sister, 'a harmless old dodderer with a ten-inch prick and a vicious leather belt, both of which he's planning to use on us later.'

'But that's what you came here for, isn't it?'

'It's what I came here for, yes. But I don't want you involved.'

'Oh, come on, I can look after myself.'

'You're supposed to be resting, or whatever.'

'I am rested.'

'Well do some more of it.'

'I'd rather help you.'

'And I'd rather you didn't.'

And they walked back to the cottage in silence.

Later, sitting in the cottage, Sophie said, 'Look, I'll just come along and keep an eye on you. Let him do his stuff with you – which is what you'd planned – and then afterwards we can just make our excuses and leave.'

Angry as she was, Susie couldn't repress a smile.

'You're my sister as much as I'm yours,' said Sophie,

'and I want to take care of you as much as you want to take care of me. I'll just be there to look after you.'

'As long as you remember that, then,' Susie conceded sternly, secretly touched by her sister's care, and also relieved that she wouldn't have to face the vicar alone.

'You mean I can come?'

'Yes,' said Susie, and though she was pleased her sister would be with her, she was also worried that she might come to further harm. But after all, she mused as they prepared for the evening, he was just a harmless old codger – even if he did have a dick the size of her forearm. And once again she felt the pulse in her groin quicken and the temperature in her knickers increase.

That evening the two girls prepared for battle in much the same way as they had prepared when younger, when they went hunting together in the pubs and nightclubs around their home. It was a familiar ritual and it still had the same old connotations of excitement, and the tension in the cottage grew strong and palpable as the time grew nearer.

They began by washing with care, sharing the bathroom, comparing make-up, perfume and the implements of their hunting, soft brushes, sharp scissors and glittering tweezers, doing sisterly things for each other as they made themselves ready.

'Help me with this,' Susie asked, indicating between her legs and offering her razor.

Sophie hesitated, staring at the neatly shaped oval of pink flesh, at the soft lips uncurling slowly to reveal the glistening inner surfaces. She licked her lips, a swift, nervous flicker of her tongue, and then, still staring in fascination at Susie's groin, she nodded uncertainly and knelt between the widespread knees, taking the razor from Susie's hand. Hesitantly at first, and then with growing confidence, she began to shave the smooth curves, trimming up to the edges of the short-cropped triangle of blonde fuzz with a trembling hand.

Being so meticulous, Susie had been shaving between her legs for some time, leaving only a small V of soft curls. At first she'd merely been pleased with the fresh feel and appearance that resulted, but quickly discovered how much nicer it felt when she touched herself, which was at least once a day... if not twice or three times, in truth. Now, not only was she still pleased with the way she looked and felt, but she enjoyed the act of shaving for its own sake. The sensation of the razor scraping gently over her most sensitive skin was always delightful. And this evening, supplemented by Sophie's fingers gently spreading and pulling, the pleasure was almost too much to bear, and Susie could feel the heat simmering between her thighs, knew that Sophie could not miss the slowly spreading lips and the warm liquid that seeped from within. And the wetter Susie became the more Sophie's hands trembled, until at last she said in a shaky voice, 'I'm done.'

'Sit here and I'll do you,' offered Susie.

'No, it's okay.'

'Go on, it's much easier than doing it yourself.' Sophie hesitated a moment longer. 'It's okay, I won't cut you,' Susie reassured.

There was a moment of stillness before Sophie nodded. 'Okay,' she whispered, and almost reluctantly, she took Susie's place in the small chair and let her knees fall a few inches apart.

'Come on, then.'

Still reluctant, she spread her thighs and Susie knelt between them, pushing her sister's knees aside, and as she shuffled closer she saw why Sophie was so reluctant; if Susie had been aroused by Sophie's ministrations, the effect

21

was doubled on the younger girl. The soft pink lips were spread apart, glistening thickly with warm syrupy juices that sparkled and glistened as they trickled across her flesh, inviting – no, begging – a probing finger or tongue to slip inside where it was warm and dark. Sophie's eyes were wide and apprehensive, awaiting a reaction.

Thinking rapidly, Susie lifted the razor and with two fingers held Sophie's flesh, feeling the warm slickness, feeling her flinch away from the touch with a little gasp.

Then there was silence, apart from the soft rasping of the razor as Susie trimmed the short blonde hair away. The gentle pressure of her fingertips mingled with the tickling scrape of the blade, and each touch or stroke heightened the sensitivity between Sophie's thighs, and a glittering trail of moisture ran from the lower curve of her opening, coating the taut skin of her bottom as she moaned softly in time with Susie's steady strokes.

'There,' Susie said as she finished her work, brushing the last few stray hairs away tenderly. 'You're perfect. You look perfect and you feel perfect, too.' Suiting action to words, she traced a finger to the outline of the glistening pink lips, and then found it slipping deeper and deeper, as if drawn by a power greater than gravity, until the humid softness clasped the elegant digit fully and Sophie sighed deeply.

Susie gazed dreamily as a second finger slipped in beside the first, spreading the softness wider, opening the little mouth that clasped and sucked as her two fingers stroked in and out. 'Perfect,' she whispered again. 'Good enough to eat.' Slowly she bent her head, lower and lower, until her mouth closed over Sophie's hot, soft lips, feeling the tickle of the short blonde hair above and the secreting warmth of the moistness below.

'Ahhh,' Sophie sighed, as a clever tongue probed lovingly

at the hard bud, and Susie began to suck gently, dropping the razor to the floor as her hands slid around Sophie's body, grasping the firm bottom and pulling it towards her, lifting the molten honey pot to her hungry mouth as Sophie raised her knees and spread her thighs as wide as they would go, welcoming Susie's busy tongue into her body.

Later, after Sophie's whimpered squeals had drifted around the room and gradually subsided, the girls bathed and dressed, ready to meet the vicar.

At Susie's instruction they dressed demurely, but Sophie especially so, since she was supposed to be keeping the low profile, entrusted with ensuring the tiny concealed lens was always pointing at Susie and the vicar. When Susie considered he'd done enough to be defrocked, hopefully before she suffered the same fate herself, they'd make their excuses and leave in the approved fashion. Sophie was somewhat peeved by her role in this, and peeved also to find that Susie had the coffee-coloured cashmere dress that was tight and clingy, and a bit too short, unavoidably revealing a glimpse of stocking when she sat down, easily revealing a flash of white silk if Susie chose, without making it appear deliberate.

Sophie's clothes were plainer; a straight black dress that made her blonde hair glow, but down to the knee, and worn with low heels. To compensate for her lack of visible glamour when compared to her sister, she also put on black stockings, her own late addition to her wardrobe, along with black knickers and a sheer black bra that had an almost unbelievable effect on her already voluptuous proportions. It wasn't that she planned to do anything naughty, just that she was going out with her sister and whatever the plan and however low-key her role was meant to be, Sophie just didn't want to look anything less than her best. Or, in this case, less than Susie's best.

Which was quite stunning. The tan dress was one thing, revealing more than it concealed as it clung to her shapely thighs, narrow waist and full breasts. But underneath Susie wore white, and if the purity of her underwear didn't make the randy old sod jump on her, she'd thought earlier as she stood looking at her reflection in the mirror, then he was not the dirty old man she thought he was. Especially looking as good as she did, she reasoned, turning a little away from the mirror and easing her panty-clad bottom out provocatively, presenting two firmly rounded buttocks that were as peachy as peachy could be... even if she did think so herself.

With the handbag camera safely in Sophie's control, loaded, tested and rolling with two hours of battery and tape, they set off towards the vicarage. Walking along the quiet village street, Susie felt the first twinges of trepidation, together with the first warnings from her body as it responded to fear in the usual way, with a warm seepage of moisture into the folds of flesh squeezed gently together by the embrace of white silk, that was steadily getting more damp and more see through with every step she took.

Chapter Three

Susie wasn't scared of what might or might not be about to happen, she told herself as she rang the doorbell of the vicar's cottage, just nervous about what the outcome might be. What could go wrong? She'd asked herself the same question many times walking through the village, and the answer was always the same; what could go wrong was that the vicar might suspect something, or see the camera or find it accidentally, guess what they were up to and throw them out of his home, and then there would be no story on Sunday. That's all that could go wrong and that didn't really matter, wasn't really anything to worry about in the greater scheme of things.

No, what made the butterflies flutter and her juices flow was that it would all go *right* – very right. In which case the vicar would pull her panties down, punish her severely with his leather belt, and then… and then she shook her head to clear the images of her bent over the large table, and though her eyes were focused on the front door of the vicarage, she could still feel the treacherous desire between her clenched thighs.

Then the door of the vicarage opened to reveal, not Stephanie, but the vicar himself, white hair sticking up wildly, a dark flush on his red-veined cheeks, and a greedy glow in his watery eyes. Looking at him, Susie felt the gentle fluttering of the butterflies double their speed, and the warmth in her panties told her that her body was still responding to the situation in its normal way. It was a condition that was easily mistaken for passion, and which had all too often got her into trouble in the past. It was magnified when – as now – she sensed some form of sexual activity was imminent, and that her partner – in this case the vicar – would assume she was aroused and react accordingly. It was a condition that might be considered a drawback in private life, but it was a bonus in her line of work, since her natural response to fear meant she seldom had to fake arousal when the job required it, even though she was not aroused – if it was possible to be *un*-aroused when ones knickers were soaked with warm honey, she thought wryly.

Still conscious of the damp silk as she moved, she obeyed the vicar's invitation to enter, leading Sophie towards the back room, with the large wooden table she remembered so well. Susie was surprised the vicar had opened the front door himself, and was secretly pleased at the implication – that there had been a change of plan and no one else was on the guest list for the evening, apart from her and Sophie.

But she was wrong.

She opened the door and was confronted with a scene of debauchery that belonged in a strip joint, not in a country vicarage.

Amanda.

On a straight-backed chair in the centre of the room, with a pouting smile and heaving bosom, Amanda sat with her short skirt rucked up, her knees apart and her knickers glistening in the light, for all the world as if she was posing for Sunday's front page.

This, Susie knew, was the woman who had first rung the paper to inform on the vicar's activities. At the time she'd seemed quite shocked by the depravity she'd heard of, especially incensed since a man of the cloth performed it, and even more shocked when the vicar suggested she might even like to join one of his special evenings. And she knew what that meant. There had been enough gossip for even such an innocent newlywed such as she to understand that the vicar was ministering to the purely physical needs of the young and attractive women of the village.

And so she'd rung the paper and denounced him.

At their first meeting, when Susie – aka Caroline – had remained firmly incognito, she'd quite seen the vicar's point when he'd propositioned Amanda; early twenties, long legs, bottom like two halves of a basketball, breasts ditto, waist about twenty inches max, angelic face with little cupid-bow mouth, neat white teeth, inviting smile and eyes that were at least as blue as Susie's own. It was a body that would make a homosexual bishop try to put his hand up her skirt, never mind a randy vicar with an appetite exceeded only by the size of his dong. And top off the body with a dose of glowing and youthful innocence, all pure English rose, sweet twenty-one and never been kissed… *well*.

But this could hardly be the same person. She wore a dress crafted from diaphanous white silk that clung to her like a second skin, revealing more than it concealed. Like, for example, every bone in her ribcage, every tense of muscle in her flat stomach, the full firm swell of breasts that were supported only by a bra made of equally transparent sheer white, with bullet-hard nipples jutting through, dark and biteable. It clung also to the tops of her toned thighs, though it was gathered up by her parted legs, revealing a tiny pair of white knickers, as sheer and see through as the dress, allowing Susie to observe the neat, inverted triangle of black hair that ended where the furrowed entrance to her body began. The smooth pink curves of her shaven labia were as visible through her knickers as if she'd been naked under a searchlight, but the effect was a million times more stunning because it felt like peeping, catching illicit glimpses of forbidden fruit.

Susie felt herself growing hotter and wetter as she stared, wondering what had happened to Amanda in the past three months to wreak such a change, and wondering if she could believe her eyes. The gusset of her knickers was clearly wet, the parting they revealed in the soft flesh puffy and open, shining through the material – and when she rose, turning away to pick up her coat and bag, Susie saw the dark red lines across those firm young buttocks and knew at once that the vicar had only just finished ministering to Amanda's needs in his own special way.

'Do come in,' she sparkled brightly, eyes shining with that just-fucked look that Susie recognised at once. 'The vicar's just finished my instruction.' Her chest heaved and Susie eyed the dark tips enviously. 'Can't stop. Hubby's expecting me home, and we mustn't disappoint him.'

She tripped off into the hallway, pecked the vicar on the cheek, seemed not to notice the friendly caress of his livered hand on her round bottom, and disappeared from view, leaving Susie and Sophie just inside the room, speechlessly rooted to the spot.

'Come in, come in,' boomed the vicar heartily and inappropriately from behind them, but he held out his arms and swept them into the room, revealed in the light as somewhat more red in the face than normal, breathing a bit too heavily as well, as he smoothed his clothes and ran ineffective fingers through his hair, looking more like a mad scientist than ever.

'Such a sweet young thing, Amanda,' he enthused. 'Her husband is *so* pleased with the change in her since she started coming to see me.' He beamed enthusiasm and salaciousness in equal quantities. 'Used to be a miserable little thing most of the time, always a bit reluctant to enjoy all the pleasures God has made available to her. Quite spoilt their evenings together.'

His knowing smile was almost a leer, and Susie could hardly believe he was being so obvious about everything. Unless, of course, he assumed Susie had told Sophie exactly what to expect – which he did, judging by what followed.

'So he asked if I would have a word with her. I've managed to open a few doors for one or two other ladies in the community, as I expect you know,' he said to Sophie, 'and I know you do,' he smirked at Susie, 'and so I said I'd try with Amanda. She didn't want to come at first, but her husband persuaded her and now of course she comes all the time.' He was almost like a blue comedian, Susie thought, hoping most fervently that the audio was as good as the video and was recording every dirty, smirking word. 'Yes, I'd say she's a completely different girl now,' and he smirked again. 'Yes, I do believe I've saved the marriage with my special instruction. Now then... Sophie, isn't it?' And he held out a hand, almost embracing Sophie as Susie wondered about Amanda, obviously now on her way home to satisfy her husband with the ardour stirred up – quite literally – by the vicar. And she wondered about Amanda's husband, obviously as pleased with the arrangement as was his wife.

As the dirty old goat turned to Susie, with the same smug smile, she stared, horrified by the expression on Sophie's face. She was gazing at the man as though she liked and respected him. What was it he had over women? Surely the stupid girl could see what a detestable old lecher he was.

Gone now was Susie's earlier doubt about spoiling his mildly eccentric lifestyle. He wasn't just a randy old goat, he was a nasty, selfish, manipulative and ultimately destructive pervert pretending to be something he wasn't, and abusing the trust his position bestowed upon him. Now she'd had another encounter with him, she was in no doubt

29

at all about what she was doing, nor the moral rectitude of the situation. If the bishop wouldn't act, then the only way to depose him was to expose him – on the front page, to five million readers, this coming Sunday. Oh yes, she was desperate to wipe the self-satisfied smile off his leering old countenance with a nice big eighty-four point banner headline.

Blissfully unaware of her intentions, the vicar was proceeding towards his doom as fast as his randy little legs could get him there. 'Now,' he said to Sophie, her expression clearly not wasted on him, 'I wonder if you don't need my special care first?'

'Well, vicar…' Susie tried to interrupt, but he took no notice, fixing Sophie with his intense and overpowering stare. Susie had felt the force of it herself once before, and knew the effect it could have; she'd certainly given in to it without much resistance.

'I know you've been unwell, and you don't look as if you're a hundred percent fit just yet,' he continued, still gazing deeply into Sophie's eyes. 'So I think you need my help… and the Lord's, of course. It's a wondrous thing, how healing prayer can be. Shall we start with that first? I'll lead.'

Asking apparently harmless questions, with no earthly reason to answer in anything but the affirmative, is a well established technique that gets people into the habit of saying 'yes', while at the same time manoeuvring them inch by inch into a situation they would not have agreed to if asked outright. Susie knew it and recognised what the vicar was doing, and tried at once to intervene.

'I don't think Sophie's ready for anything hard just yet,' she said, instantly regretting the accidental *double entendre*. 'I mean, *difficult*,' she amended lamely.

'I think we'll let her decide when she wants something

hard,' said the vicar, pouncing on the opportunity, squeezing Sophie's hands and looking into her eyes with his own bloodshot gaze.

Susie could hardly believe he was so obvious about where the evening was heading – or at least, where he wanted it to head – especially since he'd hardly spoken to Sophie before, but once again she guessed he was basing his confidence on the assumption that Susie had explained the nature of these sessions to her sister, and Sophie's presence at his cottage signalled at worst mere acceptance or, at best, positive eagerness to take part.

And so he continued, addressing Sophie in the flowing tones of the practiced public speaker. Despite his ravaged appearance – he looked more like a low-rent Marquis de Sade than a vicar, thought Susie, as small fragments of copy composed themselves in her mind in preparation for the story – despite his looks, he had a soothing voice and a definite presence and, confronted with it, Sophie seemed oblivious to everything else.

'Sophie,' she said, but the vicar shushed her with a waved hand.

'Just relax and leave her to me, my dear,' he soothed, but Susie knew the calm tones were for Sophie's benefit, and the stern glare he shot over his shoulder was for hers. 'I'll take care of her,' he added, in a voice redolent with authority, and against her better judgement Susie felt herself slightly overwhelmed by his presence.

'Now Sophie,' he droned on, talking of her pain and illness and the well-being of healing and the warm comfort of surrendering your destiny to yourself and yourself alone, and as his fingertips pressed lightly against her temples and massaged, slow circular movements, Sophie relaxed before Susie's eyes, and the melodious tones of the vicar's voice soothed her too.

'Kneel,' he said to Sophie, and she did, placing the bag on the chair by her side, quite high enough to do the job as long as it was pointing in the right direction, but without peering obviously at it Susie had no way of knowing which way it was pointing. And anyway, the vicar, still massaging Sophie's temples with his fingertips, was speaking to her.

'Kneel beside your sister,' he said to Susie, and she did as she was ordered. 'Now, repeat after me,' he said, and began a slow incantation, his hands still circling on either side of Sophie's head. And as he chanted Susie felt herself becoming more and more attuned to the rhythms of his speech and the cadence of his voice, listening as he intoned the words of love, healing and forgiveness which we all desire, and feeling the warm glow of contentment within her core as she relaxed.

It was having the same effect on Sophie, she could tell, only more so, as her sister's eyes grew wide and bright and her mouth opened slightly, tongue moistening her lips as her chest began to heave and the vicar drew her further and deeper under his spell, the massaging fingertips circling lower and lower, soothing Sophie's cheeks, and then the sides of her neck, her shoulders, thumbs coming into play, circling, pressing into the muscle, relaxing, moving on, hands creeping lower, massaging her upper arms, squeezing them in his palms as the thumbs reached outwards in large circles, sending waves of pleasure through Sophie's body as they came tantalisingly closer to nipples whose outlines could now be seen through the black dress.

And Susie wasn't the only one to have noticed that Sophie was almost in a dreamy trance of delight. The vicar knew too, and Susie saw with fascinated horror the huge bulge appear as his trousers tented, thrust forward by the enormous growth within. Sophie had seen it too, watching it as the cobra watches the snake charmer's pipe; fascinated,

32

mesmerised, hypnotised as it grew, already impossibly large but still getting larger.

'Do you want to feel the power of God's love?' he asked of Sophie, who was staring at it through lowered lashes, trancelike.

'Y-yes please,' she whispered, instinctively licking her lips.

'Do you want to feel the power of God's love in you tonight?' asked the vicar, and Sophie hardly paused before she answered.

'Yes,' she sighed, 'oh, yes.'

'Do you want to feel the power of God's love in your body tonight?' he asked again, and once again Sophie sighed her reply like a lovesick schoolgirl.

'Oh, please,' she begged.

'Are you ready to let the power of love enter you tonight?' asked the vicar.

'Yes, yes, yes,' said Sophie, apparently failing to notice that God was no longer part of the proceedings.

'Are you ready to feel the power of love inside you tonight?' he asked, and Sophie's chest heaved as she nodded.

'Are you willing to give yourself completely to love?' asked the vicar, and Sophie's breath quickened in her throat, her breasts swelling, and her voice was low and husky as she answered.

'Yes, I am.'

'Say it,' commanded the vicar. 'Say after me: I want to feel it.'

'I want to feel it,' Sophie gasped obediently, one hand clutching at the black dress where it covered her groin, knotting the material with fierce fingers.

'Say you want to feel it inside you.'

'I want to feel it inside me,' she breathed, as the vicar's

hands settled firmly over her breasts and the bullet-nipples pressed into his palms as he squeezed and kneaded.

'And are you ready to surrender yourself to the power of love?' he asked, his eyes closed in concentration as his fingers sought the two erect centres of Sophie's breasts and pinched them, prompting little gasps and sighs.

'Oh yes, I'm ready,' said Sophie, pressing her flattened hand against her groin, hips beginning to sway and rock.

'Say you're ready to surrender to love,' ordered the vicar, letting one of her breasts free as his hand rose to his waist and the fingers began to pluck at the fastening of the leather belt.

'Oh, I want to surrender to love,' sobbed Sophie, as her hand squeezed and her fingers curled, searching urgently between her legs.

'Are you ready to give yourself to love?' asked the vicar harshly, his own breath ragged and fierce as he undid his trousers, allowing a thick black pole to spring into view as his massive erection thrust his underpants out, making Sophie's eyes widen in shock and greed.

'I'm ready to give myself to love,' she whispered as her free hand reached up and hesitantly grasped the black shaft, then confidently squeezed and began to rub, sliding the black material up and down in short and jerky movements. 'I'm ready,' she said again, both hands still busy, one for her and one for the vicar.

Looking at the expression on Sophie's face, like a child in a sweetshop who's just been told it's all free and all for her, Susie knew she was telling the truth, and she knew the vicar would know as well. Sophie was about as ready as a girl could be.

'Before you can feel love you must feel remorse,' said the vicar, in a voice hoarse with emotion. He grasped Sophie's wrist and raised her to her feet, turning her towards the table, guiding her, leaning her over the polished wooden edge.

Susie knew what was happening, knew she should intervene, but remained immobile, silent, watching. It wasn't just that she wanted the story, wasn't just that she didn't want to give the game away. That was part of it, but the bigger, most compelling thing was the power in the room, the crackling charge of sexual energy that zapped and sparked and leapt from person to person. Susie was spellbound by the drama between Sophie and the vicar, enthralled by tension as they moved inexorably closer to the moment of fulfilment, and entranced by her own mounting desire, juices flowing hotly between her thighs as she waited impatiently to observe that moment, to watch as Sophie's tender young body was spread open and revealed to the vicar's gaze before he penetrated her with his immense maleness and ravished her succulence.

Which was almost visible now, as the vicar lifted the hem of Sophie's dress, pulling it up over her taut rump, exposing the supercharged eroticism of stocking-tops and suspenders, the narrow V of black that bisected the two halves of her bottom and became a thin black line that disappeared between the two rounded swellings as it cut her glistening peach in half, leaving its inner pinkness and the gathering moisture to sparkle in the light. It was an intoxicating sight, and the vicar was unable to prevent himself from leaning heavily against it as he tucked Sophie's dress up around her waist, the thick shaft that jutted from his open waistband slotting neatly between the curves of her bottom.

'Are you ready to feel the power of the Lord?' he asked, rather unnecessarily, Susie thought, since she was fairly certain Sophie could feel it already.

'Yes, I'm ready,' replied Sophie, her voice muffled

because one side of her face was pressed against the wooden table.

'Are you *really* ready?' asked the vicar, as he reached for Sophie's hand and pulled it back, pressing it down between them, standing away from her so he could see what he was doing, guiding her hand until it was pressed over her own pink opening. 'Make yourself ready,' he said harshly, but Sophie, who really was *really* ready, needed no telling, and was already stroking herself luxuriously, raising up on tiptoe as her fingers separated the wet flesh, spread it wide, caressed it and teased it, before sliding slowly into it until she stood there with her bottom lifted, her wrist bent and her fingers spread out wide like the wings of a butterfly, except for the middle finger which bent and disappeared into her body.

'Now…' breathed the vicar, turning towards Susie, shirttails hanging loose, held aside by the strength of the huge erection that speared from his gaping fly, swelling inside his black underwear, 'what about you, my dear girl? Are you ready to feel the power of love as well? Do you need it too?' As he asked, his voice hypnotically low, he pulled his belt from its loops.

'Yes, I need it,' whispered Susie. It was the only possible answer, because she had to have the pictures and the story, and because she was almost as mesmerised by the power of the vicar's personality as Sophie, and because she was so aroused by the imagery of her sister and the vicar, and the knowledge of what they were about to do, that her white silk panties were shamefully damp.

The lost look in her eyes was unmistakeable, and fired the vicar to even greater heights of desire. 'Do you want to feel the power of love in you tonight?' he asked, as he stepped closer, unzipping the creamy cashmere dress with his free hand, freeing it from her shoulders and watching

36

as it fell to the floor.

As his eyes feasted on the smooth curves of her shapely body, the firm swell of her breasts inside their flimsy covering, and the unmistakeable sheen of her freshly-shaved skin, pink and smooth within the near-transparent panties, Susie saw his erection twitch, an involuntary spasm of excitement, and she felt her own body mirror the movement, a thrilling surge of excitement and need as she imagined it thrusting inside her.

Then he roughly grabbed her arm and propelled her towards the table, hurrying now because he could hardly wait, almost forcing her down so she bent over the polished wood beside her sister, instinctively adopting Sophie's pose, face sideways on the tabletop, looking towards her, with her feet apart and her bottom raised. Sophie felt Susie's stockinged leg against hers and smiled, eyes half-closed and moist lips parted slightly by desire. Behind her, Susie sensed the vicar's eager movements and heard the rasping of clothes being hastily removed.

'Do you crave the power of love inside you now… *really* crave it?' The vicar's voice was a harsh croak as his trousers fell to the floor.

'Yes, I think so,' confirmed Susie, taking a firmer grip on the far edge of the table, and settling her tummy against it in preparation for his thrusts.

'Oh yes,' said Sophie dreamily, spreading her body wide with two fingers so he could see just how much she craved it inside her.

'Are you ready to feel the power of love right now?' He stepped from his trousers, standing close behind her with the belt dangling in one hand.

'I'm ready,' sobbed Sophie.

'I'm ready,' said Susie, quite certain that the pose she was in gave the vicar a perfect view of her wet sex lips, through white silk panties made transparent by her lasciviousness.

The vicar's heart was hammering as he stared at Susie's vulnerable body, hammering harder as his gaze shifted to Sophie's gleaming wet pinkness and the shiny finger that slithered in and out.

'Are you prepared?' he roared, and freed the giant erection from the opening of his underpants, letting it pulse in front of him, the bulbous purple tip shining and smooth.

'Oh, yes please,' cried Sophie, looking over her shoulder at the object of her need, bobbing just inches from where she desperately wanted him to put it.

'Are you ready to repent?' The vicar caressed Susie's bottom with his free hand, making her flinch at his touch.

'Yes, I...' she whispered.

'Are you ready to repent?' His hand reached across and brushed Sophie's tight rump before dipping down to the irresistible honey pot she was so lovingly stirring for him.

'Ohhh yessss...' she sighed, as a fingertip nosed the soft lips aside.

'Are you truly ready for forgiveness?' he asked, reaching out to Susie and pulling the tight panties higher, stretching them, squeezing the wet softness within.

'I'm ready,' she said, and meant it, because she too was about as ready as she'd ever been.

The vicar looked at them again, gazing from one to the other while his left hand absently stroked the huge erection that still poked proudly from his underpants.

'Repent then, and show your sin!' he shouted, and stepping back he whirled his right arm like a windmill and the leather belt whistled through a semicircle and lashed across two sets of buttocks with a stinging *crack!* And both girls squealed as their flesh quivered and a red line appeared across both bottoms as if branded there, and he grasped himself harder in his left hand.

'Repent, you sinners of the flesh!' he shouted as the belt cracked down again, his left hand pumping vigorously as his eyes roamed across the taut buttocks and soft wet pinkness nestled between.

'Repent, oh harlot!' roared the vicar, and he laid it on again, a stinging blow that drew another weal and another squeal. 'Painted whore!' bellowed the vicar as his left hand pumped faster and his right arm tried to keep up the pace.

Whack! Whack! The belt was swinging and striking with an unerringly repetitive rhythm.

'Say after me: I repent,' he panted.

'I repent,' the girls repeated, but there was no mercy from the vicar.

Whack! Whack! The leather resounded across four delicious buttocks, the cheeks aglow with rosy flame and the soft wet centres on fire with molten lust.

'Say again, I repent my sins!' he demanded, and though both voices obeyed at once the belt landed again, crisp and precise.

Whack! Whack! It stung Sophie's bottom and Susie's bottom almost at the same instant, so their squeals were in perfect unison once again.

'Repent your wickedness, repent ye harlots!' boomed the vicar, and his arm swept down and the belt slashed and the girls wailed.

Again and again the broad leather landed across the two girls, almost always striking both together, making them jerk in unison, an experience so arousing that the vicar's face was as purple as the rounded tip of his erection, the veins in his temples and throat almost as gnarled as those that knotted the length of his jutting shaft. His eyes were almost bursting from his head as his arm and hand blurred into a frenzy of blows, the belt swooping over his head and thrashing across the buttocks of the two sisters sprawled over the table in front of him, the effort so great he no longer had the strength to preach at them.

But the more he whipped and the more the girls wailed and the more they repented, the more aroused they became, and he gawped with rabid lust at the thin strip of black material that was now embedded in Sophie's pussy, glistening wet, her swollen lips split like a juicy fig.

'Repent!' he managed to croak, and as the belt swatted the material got wetter, the black slash grew narrower and more pinkness was revealed as the gusset pulled deeper into Sophie's writhing body.

At last the vicar's weary arm slowed, the lash of the belt grew weaker and in a heaving voice he asked, 'Are you ready to feel the power of love?'

'Yes,' whispered Susie, her voice undeniably husky with desire.

'*Please*,' begged Sophie, unashamedly peeling the black material from between her sex lips and holding it aside invitingly.

The vicar stepped closer, dropping the belt to the floor and taking his erection in both hands, pointing it as he leaned forward until the huge purple knob was touching Sophie and her quivering body froze, waiting… waiting… until finally he leaned over her deliciously vulnerable form.

Susie raised herself onto her elbows, and as she stared in awe the vicar fed his cock into her sister, making the inches disappear from sight one after the other – three… four… five… six… seven… eight… nine… until it was completely embedded in her, as easily as pushing a hot knife into butter.

Sophie sighed deeply and relaxed, slumped on the table as the vicar began to pull slowly out of her, easing himself bodily away and then falling forward again, pushing in and out with wet sucking sounds that grew louder and faster as his movements quickened and Sophie's juices increased in response.

Susie pressed her palms against the table and lifted herself further back; she'd seen the vicar in action before – and felt him of course – but she'd forgotten quite how large he was, how impressive his dimensions. Sophie was experiencing it all for the first time, and clearly enjoying it as she raised herself on tiptoe, lifting her bottom higher and back, pressing onto the pumping shaft, urging it deeper as her breath became a series of ragged sobs in time with each aggressive inward thrust.

The vicar seemed to notice Susie moving for the first time, beady eyes swivelling towards her in a face that was bright red and dripping with sweat that fell from bushy eyebrows, from the tip of his plump and purple nose, and from the fleshy chin, the droplets falling like warm rain on Sophie's buttocks. He was clutching them in his liverish hands, one set of stubby fingers clamped around each perfect globe, but he released one and reached for Susie, laying his hand firmly on her bottom, stroking the warm flesh inside the tightly stretched white silk panties, fingers searching inwards and down until they probed the narrow valley between her buttocks.

Instincts took over as she too lifted onto the balls of her feet and bent forward again, raising her bottom and spreading her thighs. The vicar's fingers found the heat inside the white panties and the wetness that soaked them, and began to hunt, pushing and probing excitedly, spreading the slick wet flesh apart but unable to force any deeper because of the tight material that was stretched over her opening, and they began to scrabble, as if digging their way through.

Susie's hips were beginning to thrust up and down as if she could help him force his way through her panties by

41

pressure, but she knew it was never going to happen, so she reached back and pushed the white silk panties down over her bottom, slackening the material that guarded her, letting the vicar's fingers push it deeper. He gave a sudden snort of satisfaction as his digits sank into the welcoming warmth, and pushed harder, thrusting the wet material into her body.

The sudden invasion felt good, but it was not enough and it was not what Susie had intended or needed. With a squeal that was an even mix of relief and frustration, she pushed the panties lower until they were dragging against his hand and he finally got the picture, releasing the pressure and allowing her to pull the wet material aside. Then his fingers thrust back again, and with a grunt of triumph he pushed easily into the scalding wet flesh, making Susie gasp as the knuckles thudded against her.

Now the vicar was leaning back, watching his own handiwork as he thrust in and out of both sisters, shoving his huge erection into Sophie and thrusting two fingers into Susie, making both girls gasp with each rhythmic penetration.

Then the movements stopped suddenly, and there was a moment of silence broken only by three gasping sets of lungs, then with a wet plop the vicar extracted himself from the girls, shuffled sideways, and rested something that felt like a hot rubber ball between Susie's soft and parted lips. 'Now you can feel the power of love,' he croaked, and as Susie gasped he pushed his long, purple-tipped shaft deep into her body.

'Aaah...' she gasped, as ten solid inches of rigid flesh sank inexorably into her pretty little pussy, until his grey pubic hair rasped against her scalded and punished bottom.

'Ohhh... aaah...' squealed Sophie, as her moan of disappointment was uplifted by two fingers that replaced

42

the emptiness, spreading her tight opening wide as they wormed into her and wriggled around.

The vicar quickly settled back into rhythm, pumping in and out of the two girls, making them gasp in harmony as his own breath tore and laboured in his lungs and his face reddened dangerously as he looked down to where his thick erection spread Susie's pussy into a perfect O, like a little round mouth that clasped wetly as the shaft pistoned back and forth, smearing its welcoming wetness along the glistening length.

The effect on Susie was growing as the fleshy rod pounded unstoppably, a steady, unbreakable rhythm that all her squirming could not change. No matter how much her hips writhed as she tried to make him go faster and deeper, the vicar just pumped steadily in and out until she thought she'd scream in frustration. And then she realised that the steady beat was having a pronounced, inexorable effect and there was a slow building of pressure in her sex, a continual rise of pressure, and her movements ceased, and she was still for a few seconds until she felt the beat and matched it, circling her hips in perfect time as she helped herself towards a beautiful crisis.

The vicar understood the signals and suddenly sidestepped again, pulling free of Susie and leaving her cold and empty as her sister sighed beside her, wriggling her bottom backwards along the shaft the vicar prodded against her.

Two fingers plunged into Susie's body and began pushing in and out, spreading and sliding, and slowly her body caught up with the movement and she relaxed, letting her pelvis rock and circle, and soon she was gasping again with each thrust and hearing Sophie gasp too. And then suddenly her back dipped, her head and shoulders lifted, her mouth opened and she was perfectly still. Even the vicar froze too, motionless except for the huge shaft that pulsed inside

Sophie, and she squealed several times before slumping again onto the table.

The vicar still had two fingers inside Susie; two fingers that kept perfect time with the spasms of his climax, and each time he sprayed a viscous jet into Sophie the fingers inside Susie convulsed and relaxed, and the extraordinary sharing of her sister's orgasm and the vicar's climax made her come again as well, and she shuddered like a rag doll as intense sensations ebbed and flowed once more.

The two girls had hardly fallen silent when the vicar withdrew his fingers from Susie and his now floppy semi-hardness from Sophie. 'Caroline,' he said, and it was a moment before Susie remembered that was her alias and realised he was talking to her. By then he had raised her weary body and turned her to sit on the table edge. 'Sophie,' he said, turning her, pressing one hand on her shoulder, pushing her to her knees between Susie's listlessly parted thighs, her face inches away from Susie's hot wetness. 'I'm sure we can make enough of this to satisfy your needs as well,' he said to Susie, and as he pressed Sophie's face between her sister's thighs he pulled Susie's head forward and down. Instinctively she opened her legs and opened her mouth, and as Sophie's tongue began to lap tentatively between her soft folds, probing into the dark warmth, Susie obediently took the engorged helmet of the vicar's still impressively large penis into her mouth and began to suck, tasting the spicy perfume of her sister's pussy mingled with the thicker creaminess of the vicar's ejaculation. And as she sucked she felt the fleshy column thicken and grow between her lips, stretching them, her jaw beginning to ache.

'Amazing,' she whispered, truly in awe of his stamina as she lifted her head and straightened up, holding the throbbing length and stiffness in her two hands.

'It truly is a miracle,' he agreed, and smiled as he curled a fist around the base, holding it still and straight, and shuffled forward, easing Sophie's head to one side so he could slide his length alongside her busy tongue, filling Susie with its hugeness as it sank deeper and deeper and deeper. 'Now, my children,' he said, and guided Sophie's head back into place.

Chapter Four

'Good work, Susie,' boomed the editor. 'Great story, excellent pictures. Excellent. My word, yes. Very detailed, very... er, very incriminating...'

'Right,' she said brightly into her mobile phone, pretending not to notice the way his voice tailed off into a guilty silence, and trying not to sound as nervous as that detail made her feel.

'Yes, we'll do a big splash on the front page, use one of the spanking shots – just him and the stockings and a bum. And then we'll do another splash in the centre, lots of pictures – no faces apart from his, of course, but a lot of the stuff with both of you in is just too good to leave on the bench.'

Prolonged silence meant he'd said his piece, and there were no more surprises. As if those weren't enough. Though to be fair it was not really a surprise. Susie had made him promise not to use Sophie in the story, and especially not to use any pictures of her. But she knew well enough that they'd use the best pictures, regardless of who was in them, and if that meant putting her sister on the front page and therefore through the emotional wringer, then they'd just go right ahead and do that. They had no compunctions about hurting people or destroying their lives, even if those people were innocent. Not if it sold a few thousand more papers. But this did not sound too bad, though she'd have to see the paper herself to know just how economical the editor was really being with what passed for the truth from his narrow perspective.

'As long as we can't be recognised...' she began, but the editor was ahead of her on that one and interrupted brusquely.

'No faces, no clothes, no jewellery, no nothing that could be used. Just two bums bent over the table. You could be any pair of bimbos for all you can see. Don't you worry about it.'

'Fine then, fine,' she said, not sure about being called a bimbo, nor quite as reassured as she tried to sound, and knowing she would not be able to relax until she had the paper in her hands and saw the pictures that had been used.

'I'll get them to email the layouts later on,' he said, thinking ahead of her, 'probably tomorrow. And then we'll give the randy old goat the phone call at about half-five.'

Sunday paper protocol dictated that all victims of such a front page exposé got a warning in the shape of an opportunity to say their piece, but they always received it as late as possible or polite on Saturday, in order to reduce the chances of a slick lawyer being able to dig out a helpful judge and get an injunction to stop the presses.

'Okay, fine,' she said, cutting off the call, still not reassured by his promise of an email. She was more worried, if anything. Layouts could change right up to the last moment before the presses began to roll – afterwards, if it was really important. Cigar chewing men with rolled-up sleeves and big braces tend not to run about the place shouting 'hold the front page!' but nothing is ever set in stone unless it's on the street. A layout could be made in two minutes and changed in half that, so offering to send it sounded more like a smokescreen than a demonstration of good faith. But Susie was determined not to let her sister see her concern, especially since she seemed more relaxed now they'd got back home.

They left Kingscombe the morning after their encounter

with the vicar, and headed homewards, stopping for breakfast on the M5 and handing the little tape to a bike courier before filling up with petrol and setting off again. On the journey Susie had promised Sophie that when the tape arrived the techies would read her note and erase the pictures on the end of it, with the two of them and the vicar, and that the story in the newspaper would only use pictures that showed the vicar spanking Sophie, and that her face would be cropped out or deliberately blurred. Now she was reasonably certain that the picture desk had done as predicted, and that neither of the two girls would be identifiable or, therefore, embarrassed by the publication of the story.

Their mother was delighted to see them and was especially overjoyed to see Sophie, and their lengthy reunion gave Susie plenty of time to sit down with her laptop, hammer out her story and email it to the office.

Next day, Friday, after a restful morning and a lazy afternoon, they set out to find Hugh and take their revenge, although their plan wasn't exactly well formed. They had both realised from the start that if they suggested a whips and bondage lesbian oriented threesome, or anything remotely similar, Hugh would spot it for the trap it was, and avoid it with his usual smug panache. Then Sophie suggested that they should hire a hooker, or maybe two, but anyway use someone completely unknown to Hugh so he wouldn't suspect. But while she was still working out the details, Susie had a brilliant idea.

'Tell you what,' she said hurriedly, her mouth racing to keep up with her brain, 'what we'll do is this. After we've tried to get him to come home with us, and after he's turned it down because he knows it's a trap, one of us can go to the loo and the other one can pretend to be lusting after his

48

body.'

Sophie looked puzzled.

'I'll just tell him I'm still swooning with lust after his erotic games,' said Susie, without being too specific and detailed, 'and I'll tell him that no one has been able to satisfy me since. He's bound to fall for that.'

Sophie agreed at once. 'Conceited bastard thinks every girl in the world wants him. And he thinks that no one who's experienced his perfect body could ever be happy with anyone else.'

'Exactly,' Susie said emphatically, shifting in her seat, acutely aware of the warm dampness in her knickers, aroused by her memories of Hugh's comfortably large erection and his inventive way with dildos, whips and women. 'He'll fall for it straightaway,' she continued, as her body flowered in anticipation of something her mind told her she didn't want, 'and he'll invite me back to his flat.' The warm seepage gathered momentum, as her reflexes overruled conscious thought and informed her that Hugh would be welcome between her legs at any time, preferably now, but in any case quite soon.

'And then what?' asked Sophie harshly, as if she understood only too clearly what was going on between her sister's thighs. Which could only mean that she was experiencing a similar reaction, thought Susie.

'And then comes the clever part,' she announced triumphantly. 'While *I'm* in the loo, *you* can tell Hugh you've been pining away for weeks and that you're desperate to get him back in your knickers.'

'But I'm not!' she denied, a little too insistently.

'I know that, and you know that. But Hugh doesn't know that. In fact, Hugh will be quite sure that you are already, even before you tell him. He'll believe it without a second's hesitation. And even if he stops to think about it – which he

49

won't – but even if he does, then the fact that we're cheating on each other will easily convince him it's true.'

'And then?'

'And then he'll invite you round to his flat as well.'

'And then?'

'And then if one of us doesn't get some good pictures of him dressed up as a nun or something he'll get off scot-free.' Sophie looked unconvinced. 'Look, it's easy,' Susie went on undaunted. 'We'll both take the handbag-cam and film him, erase anything incriminating and show the tape to all his mates as in Plan A.' She sat back happily, trying to ignore the burning heat in her groin.

'Yes…' Sophie agreed at last, 'yes, that'll work. The little shit will be so desperate to get our knickers off he won't stop to think; his whole life is ruled by what goes on in his trousers.'

'Exactly,' Sophie concurred.

But in the event, none of it mattered because they soon found that Hugh wasn't around, and hadn't been for a month or so; he'd got himself a new job that frequently took him away from home for long periods, and he showed up only occasionally in the pubs and clubs that used to be his regular haunts. So, disappointed for more reasons than either of them was prepared to admit to the other, they went home early and retired to their respective beds, both of them burning with frustrated lust.

Searching the pubs for Hugh, Susie's knickers had been a pool of liquid lust as she anticipated her evening with him, knowing in her heart – and her sex – that there would be quite a lot to erase on *her* tape, and most of it would almost certainly be after Hugh had done enough to make himself look ridiculous. Climbing into bed alone she had not yet admitted this to herself, but she was soon obliged to face facts. Her hand reached down, stroking the smoothly rounded shape of her groin, feeling the light dusting of pubic hair beneath the flimsy material, and the material was wet and warm, clinging to the hot flesh within. Susie had always loved the feel of her own body, and always loved the feel of herself through knickers made warm and wet by her juices. She imagined the effect it would have on Hugh when he felt between her thighs and found her panties drenched with lust, her body smooth and slick and ready.

She lay flat on her back in bed, knees drawn up and parted, as her nimble fingers dipped into the scalding wetness, trailing across the burning flesh, wishing the pictures in her head were real.

Sophie too had found the prospect of her reunion with Hugh disturbingly erotic, and the red panties she had been wearing as they searched the pubs and clubs that evening were still dark and warm when she closed the bedroom door behind her, sticky with a desire for Hugh that she found disturbing; she was supposed to hate him and her conscious mind really did. But her subconscious, and her body, still responded to the animal attraction of his smug self-confidence.

She too lay on her back with her parted knees drawn up, pulling the wet strip of red material up into herself, tugging against the elastic and releasing, a steady pressure that always produced the same effect. And this time as it happened, and her body arched as the spasms gripped her she stifled her cries, a small choking sob the only evidence of her release.

But she needn't have worried. Susie didn't hear, because she was gasping too, hips grinding up and down, muscles in her stomach taut as three fingers spread and penetrated, the gentle sucking sounds drowned by her breathless gasps of pleasure.

The paper with Susie and Sophie's pictures appeared on Sunday morning, and the layout was exactly the same as the one Susie had received in her email. She tried not to let her relief show, because she still didn't want Sophie to know she'd been afraid it could have been worse. But Sophie seemed to be unworried by the whole affair, and Susie was forced to the surprising conclusion that she had recovered more or less completely from her ordeal at the hands of the New Believers.

But the pictures, though indisputably of the vicar spanking Sophie and screwing both girls while they were bent across the table, were only recognisable if you'd been there. Susie knew it was her and Sophie, and Sophie knew it too. But their faces were invisible, except for one shot where Susie had turned to stare at the vicar penetrating Sophie, but movement blurred her face and she was unrecognisable even to her mother, who still believed Susie was merely a secretary.

'Great work by the techie,' said the editor when he rang to congratulate Susie on the story, and although she was relieved to see the result, she knew there would have been the usual Friday night viewing party, and everyone in the building would have seen the full length, uncut version of the movie. She'd heard about these 'screenings', which were supposedly for the benefit of those members of the editorial staff writing captions, headlines and fillers, but she'd never been to one. Just as well, because she'd starred in a few of them by now, and she knew what everyone else knew; namely that the audience had expanded way beyond the original concept, and most of the people in the plant would have been there, from the machine minders to the security guards, and from the truckies to the accounts clerks. It was bad enough knowing that the barrel-chested guard who checked her security pass on a Saturday morning had spent Friday evening watching her being screwed bandy, without actually being present while he watched. The idea sent a cold chill down her spine and a hot thrill through her underwear.

And there was another hot thrill in her knickers as Sophie put down the phone with a look that was part apprehension, part triumph and part something else.

'He's back,' she said in a flat tone, and Susie knew who she meant.

'Good,' she responded, hoping she sounded defiant and brave.

It was there all day, a tingle of anticipation that couldn't be ignored and would not be stopped, no matter how many times she locked herself in the bedroom and set her fingers to work.

When they first caught sight of Hugh in a crowded bar, Susie's heart gave a little leap and her sex clutched tightly; she was as nervous about this as she had been about any of her professional undertakings. And this was just Hugh, the arrogant bastard boyfriend who'd messed up her sister's life with his silly video. On the other hand, he'd outsmarted Susie as well, and not just with swapping tapes on her. He'd psyched her out too, either by clever guesswork or perhaps just discovering by good luck that her sexual appetite was large, varied and virtually unquenchable, and that it lay close beneath the surface, requiring very little encouragement before it was aroused.

'Play it cool,' she said through teeth clenched in what she hoped was an easygoing smile, 'just pretend you haven't seen him, and with a bit of luck he'll come to us.'

'The vicious shit won't be able to resist the opportunity to crow at both of us,' Sophie whispered back through her own smile, well aware by now that Hugh had outsmarted

53

her sister once already. And she was right, too, because the second he saw them at the bar his face lit up with a conceited smile and he began to shoulder his way across to them.

Susie couldn't believe his approach made her so nervous. The butterflies were out in squadron strength, the cold fingers were clutching up the length of her spine and her knickers were a swamp of hot desire, but she just didn't understand why that should be so. So she resolved to make herself immune to the effect he had on her – though she wasn't quite sure how to achieve this – and concentrate on revenge. 'Remember the plan,' she said through her smile, admonishing herself as much as Sophie, and as Hugh drew closer, Sophie inclined an acknowledgement with her head.

'Hello girls,' he said, beaming them his slimiest smile, 'have you missed me?'

Susie and Sophie both smiled back. 'Oh yes,' said Susie, 'we have. We've been talking about you quite a lot just lately.'

Hugh's smile grew wider and even more conceited as Sophie took up the story. 'I've missed you more than she has, of course. And I've quite forgiven you for your silly joke.' Hugh's smile grew, incredibly, broader still. Sophie hesitated, then in a lowered voice she added, 'In fact, the memory of it makes me…' she looked up through her eyelashes and simpered at him adoringly, '…you know, don't you?'

'Oh yes, I know.' Hugh was at his slimiest in moments of victory. 'But, er, which memories, exactly?' Sophie looked puzzled. 'Well,' he said nastily, 'was it just having sex with me you liked best, or was it being filmed having sex with yourself?'

'Oh no,' said Sophie calmly, 'it was the thought of all those blokes watching. I mean, how many girls can say they've made a roomful of pricks get hard?'

If Hugh noticed the *double entendre* he said nothing.

'I've missed you too,' said Susie, stroking his shoulder. 'You and your friend, Liz, of course,' she purred. Hugh looked down his nose at her, but Susie could sense his arousal, see it in his eyes. He wanted her. Both of them, in fact, and at this rate they might even get him the easy way. 'Yes, I thought that having another girl around and doing it all again could be so much fun. Don't you?' And she caressed her sister's arm meaningfully. Hugh's eyebrows rose and Susie could see he was tempted. In fact, a quick glance told her he was aroused, the front of his trousers swelling noticeably.

'I'd like that too,' purred Sophie, overdoing it a little.

'Mmm,' said Hugh, visibly tempted, 'I'll give that some thought.'

'What is there to think about?'

'Well, I'm not sure if I can be bothered,' he lied, testing their reactions, obviously pleased when they both bit their tongues and simpered at him. 'After all, what's in it for me?'

'Hugh,' said Susie in mock anger, 'surely you can remember that much?' And she let her hand brush lightly across his tented flies, pressing just hard enough to feel the rigid thickness inside.

'Mmm,' he said, clearly trying to sound disinterested, 'I'm not sure.' The tone of his voice was designed to provoke, and Susie just couldn't believe how smug the little bastard actually was. But she was playing a part, and continued to play it by the book.

'Well, if you can't be bothered,' she said, letting a trace of anger into her voice, just enough for him to think she'd failed to disguise it, 'I'll be back in a moment,' and she went to the ladies, still amazed at the wetness her body was producing in response to the arrogant prat. Nerves were responsible for some of it, but that wasn't all; there was something about Hugh, his voice and his imperious gaze, something was upsetting her biology and she didn't like it.

After she'd given Sophie what she reckoned must be more than long enough to put her side of the plan into action, she returned to the bar and was rewarded with a fractional wink from her sister, who then promptly excused herself. 'Hugh,' said Susie, wasting no time at all, 'why don't we go back to your place? Just the two of us? I don't care about Sophie, or Liz. It's just you I want,' and she impishly patted the lump in his trousers.

'Tomorrow,' he said carefully, but a little too quickly, as if he'd been thinking about the possibility, even expecting the question. 'Lunchtime? Say, one o'clock?'

Susie nodded, amazed it had been that simple and even more amazed to find she would have gone then, that minute, if he'd suggested it, even though the handbag camera was lying on the bed at home.

'Well,' he announced happily, 'say goodbye to Sophie for me. Must be off. Got something to take care of that just won't wait.' And he swaggered away, tapped a ravishingly pretty brunette who was wearing a fragment of material that might have been a handkerchief but certainly didn't qualify as a dress, and walked off without looking back, as if he knew she would follow him. Which she duly did, with every male eye in the place glued to a tiny bottom that rolled like two tennis balls on string as she trailed after him.

Susie raised an eyebrow as Sophie returned, not trusting herself to speak. Sophie's jaw dropped slightly and then set firm as she too struggled to disguise her anger. Or was it, Susie wondered, jealousy? Did Sophie share all the emotions about Hugh that had just rampaged through her body, leaving her wet, breathless, and resentful of the little slut he'd just waltzed off with.

'Smer... smer... smashing, isn't she?'

Of all the people in town, only one knew both sisters and had a stutter like a demented machine-gun. 'Hi Gary,' Susie said, without turning round to look at him.

'S-S-Susie,' he stammered. 'S-So...'

'Hi Gary,' Sophie interrupted him, sparing them all a long wait while he struggled with her name.

'Ber... Ber... Ber... Belinda,' he said, nodding at the doorway.

'His girlfriend, is she?' asked Susie.

'Ner... ner... ner... new job. Met her at wer... wer... wer... wer...'

'At work?' Sophie saved the day again.

'In the office, yes.' Gary looked grateful for the rescue. W had never been his strong point.

'What sort of job?' asked Sophie. 'Night work with young girls, is it, cash payments, no questions?'

'Secret.' Gary beamed proudly, either because he was proud of Hugh's job or because he'd managed the word in a single breath.

'Secret?' asked Susie quickly. 'What sort of secret?'

'Her... her... her... her...' Neither of them could guess what was coming next so they had to stand and wait for Gary to finish. 'Her... her... hush-hush!' he finally blurted, flushed with the effort, and clearly embarrassed at having taken so long to contribute so little. Susie felt sorry for him, as she had before. In fact, her abiding memory of Gary was feeling sorry for him, at least until the night she'd taken him to the bus shelter, and then she'd been quite surprised. Very pleasantly surprised, in fact. She shifted her weight from one foot to the other, the syrupy wetness in her knickers reminding her that there was still some unfinished business to take care of.

'So no one knows what he's up to?' she asked, suspecting that Hugh's new job was merely another figment of his depraved imagination.

'Ner... ner... ner... ner...'

'Okay Gary, we get the picture,' Sophie said.

'Only me,' he said firmly.

Both girls turned to him at once, Sophie resting one hand on his shoulder and pressing herself against him as Susie's arm encircled his waist. 'And?' asked Susie softly, letting the weight of her arm cause her hand to slip casually lower, until she was gently gripping Gary's bum.

'Car... car... car...'

'Course you can,' soothed Sophie, pressing closer, resting her hand on his chest as she looked up at him adoringly. Gary's eyes glazed over and his mouth sagged under the full impact of Sophie's admiring stare, and opened even wider as Susie's hand firmly clutched his bottom.

'Come on, Gary,' she breathed into his ear, 'let's go somewhere quiet and talk,' and her smouldering expression left him in no doubt that the kind of talking Susie had in mind would lead quickly to a repeat of his bus shelter experience, via telling her everything he knew about Hugh but wasn't supposed to say. The massaging hand moved a little lower, and Sophie's hand moved lower too, caressing the muscles of his abdomen as it stroked towards the waistline of his jeans.

He was bound to tell them. He knew it as well as Susie did, and with confidence rising she let her hand drop lower, so she was rubbing his thigh. 'Come on, then,' she encouraged, just as Sophie let her hand touch even lower as well, stroking the straining denim with a light touch that traced upwards along a thick and rigid bulge towards a rounded end that suddenly leapt under her fingertips.

Gary's eyes bulged and his face reddened. 'Ser... sorry,' he gasped, and then, surprising both girls, fled from the bar.

Susie raised her eyebrows at her sister. 'Was that...?'

'I'm afraid it was. Guess we're too much for him.'

'Or any normal man,' agreed Susie. Which made Hugh somewhat abnormal. But she knew he was, or he wouldn't have that effect on her. 'Come on, let's go,' she said, suddenly remembering that within the past ten minutes she'd been unexpectedly deprived of two opportunities to gratify the yearning in her knickers.

'No, let's stay,' said Sophie, looking along the bar to where a mixed group laughed and talked. They were more Sophie's age, her friends from school, probably, and she was welcome to them. Surprised at her impatience, and that she seemed to have lost her normal cheerfulness, the happy-go-lucky quality that had been her lifelong hallmark, Susie made her way home, drank a bottle of wine while watching a late night movie, with more subtitles than on-screen sexual activity, and went to bed frustrated, falling asleep with her hand still stirring unsuccessfully between her legs.

It was still there when she woke up in the morning. Sophie hadn't returned home all night, but Susie was neither surprised nor overly concerned. She'd obviously been with friends, and perhaps she didn't really want to go through with her solo meeting with Hugh. Anyway, without the handbag camera, which Susie had loaded and prepared for her own use, there wasn't much point in going at all. If she wasn't back later on, after she'd been to see Hugh, well, then she'd start to worry. Right now, all she could think about was what would transpire when she reached the creep's flat.

She was ready too soon, and arrived too early, so she forced herself to sit in the car in a lather of anxiety, trying to control the fluttering in her tummy and the warmth between her legs. But the fluttering threatened nausea by the time she climbed out of the car, prompted by an intense nervous excitement as she approached the front door and rang the bell.

Chapter Five

'Susie!' Hugh exclaimed with a smile, stepping back a pace and holding the door wider, obviously impressed by what he saw. And he could see most things, because she'd made certain he'd be able to, leaving her bra at home so that her breasts curved enticingly inside her T-shirt, and checking in the mirror to be sure that the lemon-yellow cycle shorts moulded to her curves. In fact, she looked like a naked girl who'd been sprayed yellow between waist and knees.

'I'm, er, going to the gym afterwards,' she said, by way of explanation.

'Let me take your bag,' he offered, and before she could protest he plucked it from her shoulder. The camera wasn't heavy, and she wasn't worried he'd notice it, but it was important that it should be facing the right way. Hugh dropped it casually on a side table and Susie was relieved to see the tiny lens still faced the room she remembered so well.

Quickly she took the chair beside the camera, obliging Hugh to sit opposite, where he'd be the subject of the pictures on the tape that was recording inside the bag. He smiled comfortably at her as he settled, causing the butterflies to flit and swoop in her tummy, and a warmth to spread in her shorts. 'So,' he said positively, 'what now?'

Susie had been hoping Hugh would take charge of the situation, and wasn't expecting this. 'Well,' she said brightly, 'you know.'

Hugh only raised an eyebrow.

'Well, I thought… it was so nice the first time, when we

both... you know.' She let her knees inch apart a fraction, giving him a teasing view between her thighs where the yellow shorts moulded to her like a second skin, where the soft folds of her sex had already started to swell and open, where the warm wetness had soaked and tinted the material, making it cling to her even more obviously.

A visibly growing lump in the front of Hugh's loose-fitting trousers rewarded her, and he shifted his weight in the chair. 'Okay then,' he agreed, 'you first.'

'Together,' she said, caressing one firm breast inside its white cotton covering, pinching the nipple between finger and thumb, 'let's do it together.'

'Like this?' Hugh stroked his own chest absently.

Pretending not to notice he was goading her, she carried on. 'Like this,' she said, opening her legs wider and putting her other hand down between them, surprised at the wetness under her fingertips as they stroked, enjoying as she always did the erotic feel of her own body inside a casing of wet, skin-tight material.

'Oh yes,' said Hugh, 'that's good. Go on.'

'Like this?' she asked, lifting her T-shirt, exposing one full, firm breast, offering it to him before her fingertips began to tweak and tease, sending electric jolts of sensation down into her lap, so she could almost feel them pulsing inside the yellow shorts through her fingertips.

'Yeah, that's very good,' said Hugh, 'don't stop.'

'Like this,' she said, spreading her legs as wide as they would go and letting her extended finger separate the two halves of her pussy, pressing up into the darkened wetness, spreading fiery sensations of delight in their wake.

'Oh, that's perfect, Susie, just perfect,' he breathed, 'show me more.'

The frustrated lust that had been burning between her legs for the past few days was now a raging torrent, and her hand left her breasts and delved under the waistband of her shorts. 'Aaahhh...' she gasped, as the cool fingertips touched hot flesh. 'Mmm,' she sighed, as they softly teased the swollen flesh aside. 'Now you,' she whispered hoarsely to Hugh, and as he began to unbuckle his belt and undo his zip Susie raised her bottom and peeled the shorts down over her thighs, kicking one ankle free, and placing the other foot up on the arm of the chair, spreading herself before Hugh's greedy eyes, letting her fingers open her secrets even further.

Hugh stood up to let his trousers fall, and as they dropped to his ankles that stiff pole she remembered poked out of his boxers, the glistening tip swaying gently from side to side.

'Oh yes,' she purred, 'like this, Hugh,' and she slipped two fingers into her body, feeling the tips of them push into the heat, opening the way as her knuckles opened her body wider and her palm pressed tight around the outer curves. 'Aaah,' she gave a short sob, and began to circle the fingers inside herself, working them around, winding them deeper and spreading herself wider.

Instead of grasping himself in a copycat of her actions as she'd planned, Hugh took a step towards her, and another. She should have told him to sit down and play the game; this afternoon's performance was supposed to leave the handbag camera with a film of Hugh masturbating, which she could show all his mates, but it was all going wrong; she should have stopped him before he moved, but she hadn't, and now he was out of the frame, standing close to her, standing between her widespread thighs with that thick stiffness just inches away, the skin gleaming with an oily sheen. She should have stopped him from kneeling between her legs, stopped him from grasping himself, aiming lower as he shuffled close. But she didn't. She just withdrew her fingers and placed her hands on the insides of her thighs, pushing herself apart as she lifted her hips, raising her body towards him.

'Susie.' His voice was monotone and low.

'Hmmm…?' she sighed, as the bulbous tip pulsed against her tender opening.

'I want you to do something for me.'

'Mm,' she sighed again as it pressed into her, just a fraction, no more, just enough for her to feel its weight and thickness resting against her.

'In the bedroom,' he said.

'Ooohhhh…' she gasped as he pushed forward, just enough to open her a little more, but still not enough to satisfy her.

'Come with me,' he said, and rose to his feet, leaving her frustrated and deserted. The plan was gone, finished, over. All Susie wanted now was to get that thing inside her and feel it pump in and out, and so she stood up, abandoning clothes, plan and dignity as she followed him to the bedroom door.

'I want you to help me make her come,' he said, and Susie was looking at a naked blonde tied facedown across the bed. She was kneeling at the side of it, hands pulled forward and strapped to the far side. Her ankles, pulled apart, were tied to the legs of the bed on the near side, exposing the firm globes of her taut bottom and the wet pinkness that separated them. Susie stared transfixed at the pretty little pussy as it glistened with juices, which had seeped over the clean-shaven skin.

'As you can see, I've already tried my best.' Hugh wagged his erection at her, and she realised why that too had been gleaming along its full length. 'But after her recent experiences it seems she just can't come unless, well, you know,' and he picked up a short whip made from black leather, with a soft loop at its tip. 'I think you know how to use this.' He smiled; it was not a nice smile. Susie was unable to speak, lost for words and totally flabbergasted.

'But... but... but that's...' she eventually managed.

'Your sister, yes.' His victorious smirk was almost unbearable to take. 'But I understand from Sophie that you two know rather more about each other than most sisters should. Not the sort of thing a girl normally likes to talk about, but I managed to persuade her to tell me a little.' Susie noticed the thin red lines across Sophie's bottom. 'But I'm no expert at this sort of thing.' He shrugged a theatrical apology. 'But I think you are. So perhaps you'd be so kind?' He offered her the whip once more.

'I can't,' she began to say, when Hugh stopped her with an upraised palm.

'Ah, there's no such word as can't. Let me encourage you.' And he lashed out, whipping Sophie so hard she screamed and jerked against the bed. 'See, I'm useless. If I do it, it's really going to hurt her.' Susie watched her sister squirm, a delightful wriggling movement that even she found attractive. 'I think you should be the one to do it,' he concluded.

Trying not to stare at the soft wet pinkness, trying not to notice the glisten of Sophie's juices, trying to ignore the warm wetness between her own thighs, Susie refused. 'No, I'm not doing that,' she said defiantly, shaking her head. 'I'm not helping you with... with this. I'll call the police.'

'I don't think you will,' he challenged with infuriating conceit, and picked up a remote control from the end of the bed. The portable TV sprang into life, and Susie was even more horrified than when confronted with Sophie. There was a video playing, but not just any video. It was the one she'd made only a few days before, of the spanking vicar of Kingscombe lashing Sophie's bottom while Susie looked on. Both girls were clearly visible, and she cringed, knowing what happened next, and sure enough the Susie on film turned to look down at the huge erection penetrating her sister, with a look of unadulterated greed that was breathtaking in its sexuality and clearly recognisable as her – Susie Wills.

'Goes all the way to the end,' he said unpleasantly, his voice dripping with self-satisfaction.

The bastards, she thought. There had always been rumours that the techies didn't just screen the tapes on a Friday night, but also sold copies of them, and now it seemed clear that the rumours were true. And somehow Hugh, of all people, had bought a copy.

'You bastard,' she said.

'Now, Susie, let's be sensible. I can let you have it. Right now, today.' She turned to him, hopeful, but knowing there'd be a catch. 'But you have to do something for me in return.' As he offered her the whip once more she noticed his erection still jutted proudly from his boxers, and guessed that Hugh was almost as aroused by exercising this sort of control, by forcing people to perform humiliating acts, as he was by sex itself.

She also noticed her own arousal had not exactly evaporated; in fact it had grown, and she knew it had grown because she was just as aroused by the situation as Hugh. He liked ordering people around, and she secretly admitted she liked being ordered around. She didn't know why. Perhaps it was something about the look in his eye, or the self-assured way he spoke to her, as if he expected to be obeyed, she didn't know what. But one thing was clear; she was losing control, losing it to Hugh, and she had to resist. 'But I can't—'

Swit!

Hugh lashed out with the leather-bound cane, and Sophie squealed in pain.

'Can't?' he said. 'You can't? Does that mean you want me to do it? And make enough copies of this for everyone in town to send one to their friends and family and still keep one at home?'

The look in his eye and the tone of his voice made her knees quake and flooded her groin with hot juice, so she couldn't speak. Her hand trembled as she fought to stop herself, fought to stop reaching out for the whip.

'Just *do* it, Susie.' Sophie spoke for the first time, in a voice that was low and husky, and Susie realised she was still in the grip of sexual arousal. She realised too that Hugh was probably right, and that Sophie wanted to be whipped.

'And... and I get the tape?' she asked.

'You get the tape,' Hugh nodded. 'And this, of course,' and he grabbed the rigid pole sticking out of his boxers and waved it at her, making her stomach knot eagerly.

The sharp stab of desire must have shown on her face, for Hugh smiled, cruel and triumphant, and held out the whip. 'Go on, then,' he ordered, and she meekly took it from his grasp.

Remembering her lessons at the hands of the New Believers, Susie knew exactly how to apply the whip so it would cause minimum pain and maximum arousal.

Swit! Her wrist was straight, the thin red line barely visible, the leather loop at the end nipping the vulnerable pinkness at Sophie's centre and making her cry out.

Swit! Once again, with the same result.

Swit! Susie struck a third time, fresh moisture leaking from the glistening pink flesh.

Swit! It landed once more and Sophie gasped as the loop dipped between the soft lips and the endorphins started to flood her bloodstream.

Swit! Sophie caught her breath, and then gave a deep sigh.

Swit! She sighed again.

'Six,' Susie said to Hugh, and he gestured at Sophie. 'Don't stop,' he commanded gruffly, and Susie, knowing her sister was not yet satisfied, struck again.

Hugh reached down and took Susie's free hand, curling her fingers around his erection, the thickness filling her palm.

Swit! She felt him pulse in her fist as Sophie squealed and her hips bucked on the bed.

Swit! The column of flesh throbbed again as Sophie moaned a mixture of plain and pleasure.

Swit! It was a long stroking movement that trailed the loop over the slick wetness of Sophie's open body, producing a quiver in the exhausted kneeling girl, and Susie gripped Hugh harder, before recommencing up and down strokes that rubbed the foreskin over the shining purple tip and then back down the stout length. As she raised her arm to strike again his fingers searched across her bottom, delved beneath the tight curve and found the warm entrance, wet and ready. As his fingers invaded Susie whipped her sister again and Sophie squealed, Hugh's erection jumped and his fingers tensed inside Susie, making her gasp as her fist pumped faster and faster up and down the length of his erection.

Swit! Sophie moaned, her hips beginning to rotate in slow, luxurious circles as the climax started to unravel. Knowing Sophie was on the brink, Hugh thrust his fingers deeper and harder, making Susie gasp as well as her body began to shudder and her pink sex lips gripped the two fingers inside her, leaving her gasping for breath.

Hugh waited until her crisis was over before prising himself free of her grasp on fingers and cock. Then he knelt between Sophie's thighs, guiding himself forward, spreading the little pink mouth as he pressed inwards, filling her with his thickness until he was completely inside her and she slumped into the mattress with a weary moan.

'Now,' he gasped at Susie, 'again,' and he began to grind in and out as Susie, disbelieving at first and then compelled by the eroticism of watching her sister being fucked by Hugh, raised her arm and whipped it downwards.

'Yes!' screamed Sophie, and Hugh went into a frenzy of pumping, the broad pole pounding in and out faster and faster.

Swit! Sophie cried aloud.

Swit! Sophie screamed in delight.

Spreading her feet wide for a firmer stance, Susie realised her free hand was between her legs and her fingers were seeking her entrance. As they slid easily into her hot body the whip slashed down and Sophie squealed again.

As Susie took a deep breath and lifted her arm, she stared, watching Hugh's thickness spread Sophie open, the eager lips sucking hungrily along its length as he pulled backwards, and then being pushed inwards as he slid it all the way inside.

Swit! Sophie screamed for the last time.

Hugh pulled from her and shuffled backwards on his knees, nodding meaningfully at her swollen pussy, offered up, waiting. Susie looked puzzled. 'Come on, then,' he ordered.

She still didn't quite understand.

'You know what I mean.'

She thought she did, but she wasn't sure.

'Kiss her better.'

'But…'

'Susie,' he looked meaningfully at the TV set, where the spanking vicar of Kingscombe was energetically pumping his enormous length in and out of a very recognisable Susie while he thrust a finger in and out of a girl who was clearly Sophie.

Obediently, Susie knelt on the floor behind Sophie, not as reluctant as she might have been, because she knew what was coming next. Her, if she was lucky, with Hugh's fat shaft up to the hilt in her pussy.

Sophie was hot and slippery with juice, and still on the very brink of an orgasm. Susie could tell at once, by the way her whole body jerked as Susie's tongue dipped into the soft opening and licked inside. As she spread her knees wider, straining to get her head lower so her tongue could find Sophie's clitoris, so she opened her own body to Hugh's gaze, lifting it up to him, ready.

Hugh had only just stopped fucking Sophie and had no time for ceremony now; Susie felt the breath burst from her lungs as he sank into her from behind, a prick the thickness of her wrist filling her completely with one heavenly thrust.

'Mmm,' she mumbled into Sophie's depths, and felt her sister respond, all three of them working to the same rhythm, moving together in perfect harmony until suddenly it was all too much for Sophie and her climax finally swept through her.

'Yes! Yes! Yes!' she squealed as she bucked, pulling against the bonds that tied her wrists and ankles, and her body shook from head to toe.

That was too much for Hugh and suddenly his steady thumping went into overdrive, short sharp thrusts that got faster and faster until they stopped altogether and Susie felt him thicken inside her as his muscles pumped jets of fluid along the length of his erection, and after each sudden expansion of the shaft came a hot spray deep inside, over and over again. That was what she'd been waiting for these last few days, and as Hugh's orgasm slowly died away her own took over and her muscles clenched around him, milking the last drop as she gasped her relief aloud.

'Oh, my God!' she called out finally, as she slumped over her sisters buttocks and Hugh fell heavily against both of them.

Sophie's departure had been rapid, with few words spoken to Hugh or her sister. She pulled on the clothes she'd been wearing the previous night and departed, rather shamefaced, Susie thought, and perhaps with good reason. Sophie had obviously been there with the sole objective of having sex with Hugh, but without the hidden camera there was no hope of revenge, so her motives had been selfish, and now rather embarrassing as well.

Susie had at least tried to get some pictures on tape that could be used against Hugh, although she'd failed dismally. Instead she had been forced to bargain with him for the return of the vicar tape, and he was still playing hard to get.

'Where did you get it?' she demanded. 'From the *Stab?*' The pub over the road from the office was variously thought to have earned its nickname either in reference to ancient hot metal printing techniques or, more likely, as a shortened version of a stab in the back, since most office politics were played out there.

'You sent it to me.' Hugh smiled his slimiest ever smile. Fully dressed, even in the revealing yellow cycle shorts, Susie felt as if she was back on even terms with Hugh, although she could still feel the ghost of his thickness inside her, and she was very conscious of a warmth between her thighs which owed more to his prolific outpourings than hers.

'I did? I don't think so.'

'Yes, you did.' His smarmy grin spread from ear to ear.

'No, definitely not.'

'Definitely yes, I'm afraid.' If it got any wider his evil smile would be visible from behind. 'You gave the tape to a bike messenger on the M5, and he gave it to me.'

'Why would he do that?' she asked, already believing that Hugh was telling the truth, since he knew so much about how the tape had been delivered to the office.

'Because it's his job.' He smiled that superior smile that everyone who knew him hated so much. 'I'm the new video technician.'

Susie sat down heavily on the couch, feeling her mouth gape in a useless series of fish-like movements. 'You?' she blurted. 'Why? How?'

'Because they like my work so much,' he crowed.

'Your work – oh no.'

'Oh yes.' He leapt to his feet, almost jumping for joy. 'They saw the tapes I made of you, right here in this flat – in that chair, even. The ones *you* gave them by mistake. And they were so good the editor got in touch personally to offer me a job.'

Susie had regretted the foul-up at the time, when she thought she'd given the editor a film of the vicar, but actually given him one of herself, sitting on Hugh's couch masturbating, after Hugh had somehow swapped them over. Now she regretted it even more, all over again.

'Yes, I've done some of my best work with you,' Hugh said smarmily, leering down at her.

'Some of your best...'

'Not as good as with that silly footballer, of course.'

The story had been front page news for a week – a week in which Susie had been otherwise occupied, with the New Believers, but she remembered it well enough. The crystal-clear still pictures had been taken from a secret video of one of the top division's finest new African recruits enjoying himself in a roomful of half-naked celebrity-crazed groupies. The pictures had included graphic close-ups of the sex act between him and all five of the girls, sometimes two and three at a time. The front page and centrespread story caused a sensation, largely thanks to heavily 'censored' pictures that left little to the imagination and no doubt about exactly who was doing what to whom.

'You did that?'

'Operated the camera myself.'

It had been a 'live' filming with remote control cameras, operated by someone who was at least as interested in the subject as the technology, according to one of the many lad-rag reports. The articles had elevated the footballer to superstar status among his fans, provided him with an endless supply of new groupies, and made glamour models out of two of the girls. The anonymous technician who had recorded the event received at least two man-of-the-month awards for his loving care in taking such detailed and revealing pictures, and now it turned out to be bloody Hugh!

After a few moments she got over the initial shock and anger, and as her rational mind took control once again she started to connect Hugh's sentences and make some kind of order out of what he'd been saying – and she didn't like what she'd heard.

'*Some* of your best work?' she asked carefully.

'What?'

'You said "some" of your best work. There's more than the one tape from here?'

'Two from here, if you remember.'

How could Susie have forgotten about Liz and the huge black dildo?

'And that's it?'

'No, not quite.' Hugh's smile was insufferably smug.

'There's one more.'

'One more?' Her mind raced. From where, and what could it be?

Hugh supplied the answer right on cue. 'I followed you – on the editor's orders. And I filmed you.'

'You... where? When?' It could only have been in the last few weeks, and for most of that time she'd been under lock and key. She couldn't think where it could have happened unless Hugh had been a New Believer as well – but surely she'd have seen him if he'd been there... wouldn't she?

'In the West End.'

'The West... oh no!' She put her hand over her mouth like an actress in a silent movie.

'Oh yes. I have a rather good – no, make that *very* good – tape of you being shagged stupid by some filthy old wino in a Soho back alley.' Hugh was unable to keep the triumphant tone from his voice, but his words, his attitude, the memories, and the knowledge that he'd been watching, all served to send flutters of liquid arousal coursing through her body and seeping into the yellow that clung damply to the flesh within.

'No...' She was horrified, too.

'Yes.' His face was flushed, his eyes bulged slightly and his breath quickened. Just telling her about the film excited him. She was sure it had made him hard again, and his next words confirmed it. 'The pictures are very, very detailed, thanks to my expertise in low light. You can see everything.' Hugh licked his lips, and now it was certain that the greatest part of his pleasure came from telling her, and seeing her reaction. He was enjoying her turmoil even more than he'd enjoyed seeing her have sex with the tramp. 'I didn't give it to the editor, of course,' he went on. 'Told him it was no good. But I lied. It's brilliant. I bet I could make a fortune on Friday night, flogging that after the screening.'

'You bastard!'

'So you say. But don't worry, Susie, I won't show anyone. It can be our little secret.'

'Well, if you aren't going to show anyone, give it to me,' she demanded.

'No.' He smirked again. 'I still like to watch it. It's very, very sexy. You're so rude, you know, especially in this film, when you're so pure and clean and pretty, and he's so old and dirty and smelly.'

'Yuck!' Susie was disgusted, remembering the rancid stink of the old man. And even more disgusted remembering how aroused she had become despite that, how much she'd wanted him inside her.

'Oh no, on the contrary,' he gloated. 'It makes me *very* stiff every time I watch it.'

'Every time? You mean you watch it a lot?' The idea that Hugh was so excited by her that he watched the film regularly produced another trickle of liquid fire between her thighs.

'Well, you know. It's my favourite. Works for me every time.'

Susie glared at him. The idea of Hugh masturbating while watching movies of her being screwed was immensely arousing, although she had no idea why it should be.

'Don't be angry,' he said, in what might have been intended to be a soothing tone but which still sounded like a sneer. 'It's a compliment. Anyway, I know the idea of people watching your films makes you wet your knickers, so you don't have to pretend with me.'

She hated Hugh, and not just for his smug expression, but because he was right, totally right, and she wished he didn't know.

'Anyway, you'd better get used to the idea, because I

expect we'll be seeing a lot more of each other. Well, to be honest, I expect I'll be seeing a lot more of you.' Now he really *was* gloating.

'Why?' She already knew the answer.

He smirked unpleasantly. 'Well, I'm sure we'll be working together soon. And you'll be sending me more of your lovely tapes – the ones I don't shoot myself.'

'Over my dead body,' she retorted.

'I think not,' replied Hugh. 'In fact, I think you'll do exactly what you're told. And enjoy it. You like doing what you're told, don't you, Susie? And you like being made to do what you're told.' It wasn't a question and she hated him even more for being able to see through her, and recognise parts of her character she hardly owned up to herself.

To emphasise his point, Hugh picked up the whip. 'Now, why don't you just roll over on your knees and stick that pretty bottom up in the air?' he said, and Susie found herself doing as ordered, without even stopping to argue or refuse. 'Good, perfect,' he said, and she knew it was. She knew the yellow shorts were stretched tight across her bottom. And she knew they were damp, soaked by the warmth of her body.

'My, my,' Hugh leered, confirming her fears as he traced the looped tip up the inside of her thighs and let it brush softly over the flowering lips, 'you *have* been a naughty girl, haven't you?' and the whip lashed down across her bottom, a thin line of scorching pain.

'Yes, I'm better at this than I thought I was,' he mused. 'Better than you thought, as well.' He sneered as the thin implement slashed again, and again. 'I drove your sister berserk this morning before you got here, but I wouldn't let her come,' and he whipped Susie again. 'And nor can you.' It stung across her buttocks again. 'Unless you'd like to pull those shorts down and let me see what I'm doing a little more clearly. Then I can guarantee a result.'

The thin leather bit into her bottom again, and without hesitation or knowing why, without even wanting to know why, Susie reached back and pulled down the cycle shorts, exposing herself to Hugh's lustful gaze, and his whip.

'Perfect,' he said in a throaty tone, and the stinging lash landed across her buttocks almost at once.

'Aaah!' she squealed, a mixture of shock and arousal catching her breath. The humiliation of her position and her obvious arousal because of it triggered distant memories. The lash landed again and Susie was back in the schoolroom, bent over the desk before Miss Piggy.

It stung her again, and as the burning welt began to throb she reached back between her legs, slipping two fingers inside her body, the circling thrusts combining with the next stinging whiplash and starting the first inklings of a powerful climax as her traitorous body leaked its syrupy wetness and her pulse began to thunder in her ears.

Chapter Six

The M11 stretched away northwards to Thetford and Norwich, but Susie hardly saw the countryside as it thrummed past the window. Spring was fully sprung, and it would have been a glorious sight if she'd been paying attention, but her mind was fully occupied, her mood a strange mixture of emotions.

Sophie had gone again. Finding the situation with Hugh all too familiar and unbearable, a feeling made worse by her shame at having been caught out by her elder sister, she'd left home once more, this time on good terms with her family, this time going back to university where she belonged.

'She can't get into much trouble there,' Susie reassured her mother, although in her opinion modern university students were a bunch of drug-ridden piss-heads who do far worse things to each other in the name of enlightenment and fun than the New Believers could have dreamt of, and Sophie's moral well-being was in greater danger at university than if she'd taken up a career as a stripping prostitute who did lap-dancing on the side.

But that was the least of her worries.

After that, with her mother safely out of the house, Susie phoned the office and had a half-hour argument with the editor about bloody Hugh, of all people, as she tried to persuade him to fire the scumbag or at the very least keep the two of them apart. Neither option appealed to the editor.

'Look, I know you two have a bit of history, but you're both grown adults and you have to figure it out between yourselves,' he said, in his best paternal and understanding voice. 'You're the best at what you do and he's the best at what he does. There's bound to be a little rivalry, but I want my best people on the top stories, so you *will* be working together most of the time.'

'But boss, he's a real creep,' she objected, feeling the anger rise in her chest and the temperature in her knickers climbing as well. 'I can't stand being around him,' she lied, for the truth was that it was the thought of being around him that she couldn't stand. Susie knew that when she and Hugh were face to face her resistance would melt and so would her panties, and *that* was what was making her angry.

'Look, you don't have to marry the guy, just live with him.'

'Do what?'

'Didn't they tell you?'

'Tell me what?'

'Sorry, I thought you'd called because you didn't want to work with him on this next job.'

'What job?'

'You don't know?'

'You're right, I don't.'

'He didn't tell you?'

'No, he didn't tell me.' In fact, Hugh had hardly been able to speak last time she'd seen him. After whipping her to a near frenzy with his leather cane he'd mounted her ferociously, still bent over on her knees, and thrust vigorously into her pussy till she thought it would burst. But instead he had, hosing her insides with burst after burst of molten semen while she screamed and gasped and moaned as she came again as well. But as Hugh fell exhausted, Susie rose shakily to her feet and left without speaking, mostly because she was too embarrassed and ashamed and didn't know what to say.

'The office didn't tell you?' The editor interrupted her thoughts, which was just as well, since they'd started a hot wetness between her legs.

'I didn't call the office. I called you.'

'Ah, I see.' Realising for the first time that he was telling Susie something she didn't know, the editor plunged manfully on. 'Well, look, there's a job in Norfolk, a wife swapping club. We need to get inside it and the only way we can do that is by joining it, and the only way we can join it is if you and Hugh go up there, rent a house and pretend to be married.'

'Pretend to be *what?*'

'Look, you heard what I said.'

'But wife swapping – it's hardly the sort of thing you want to put on page seven, still less use your best people for. I thought you wanted to save them for the top stories.' There was more than a hint of sarcasm in her voice and it was at least partially justified.

'True,' he agreed, admitting the point, 'it's not normally the sort of thing we'd bother with, but this is interesting because the informant says it involves at least one well known figure of the local community, maybe more.'

'They all say that.' Which was true.

'Yes, I know they do, but we believe this one.'

'Like hell.'

'All right, Susie, I'll be honest with you. Hugh doesn't know this and you can't tell him, but it could make page one.'

'Who is it?' Susie knew that if a little bit of Hicksville hanky-panky was on the front page then there had to be a national figure involved.

'I can't say, but it's big.'

'Isn't it always.' She was half-convinced now, and again

80

she was fighting her own feelings, battling against the half of her that had suddenly thrilled with excitement at the thought of going to live with Hugh, posing as man and wife, sharing a bedroom... the moistness in her knickers was almost irresistible, but only almost.

'We don't get on,' she made herself say, hoping the editor would continue to argue.

'You don't have to like the bloke, just pretend. Fucking hell, Susie, you don't even have to sleep with him. The whole object of swinging is to sleep with someone else, for crying out loud.'

Or being made to sleep with someone else because Hugh tells her to, her guilty body sang, as her free hand searched under her skirt, seeking out the warm wetness that seeped into her knickers. 'Well, send someone else,' her conscious mind insisted.

'I can't send someone else; it's too important and I need the best. And you're the best at... at... well, you know what you're the best at.'

She knew indeed, and she was very good at it with Hugh, said her innermost voice as the bubbling rebellion in her panties continued beneath fingertips that were wet and warm themselves now, finding the pliable flesh beneath, spreading and pushing inwards. 'Well, send another techie, then,' she countered righteously, already knowing what the answer would be, and knowing she was only putting up token arguments for form's sake.

'But I keep telling you, he's good. He's the best. And right now I need the best on this job. That's him. Hugh must be there. Think about all his work on the football story. He's an expert at hiding cameras and operating them 'live' to produce a result. I need him there, Susie, he has to go.'

The damp gusset of her knickers seethed with wet

enthusiasm. 'But, boss,' she protested feebly, 'if you get him to set it up for me, even I can do that much.' It was her weakest argument yet, and she knew it.

'You're forgetting this is wife swapping. You need a husband so he can swap you around with the other guys.'

Susie's fingers pulled the wet material aside and she let one of them slide into her waiting body, imagining it was some other guy, some complete stranger Hugh had given her to, someone to whom she had submitted willingly, eagerly. 'I bet they let single girls in. They always do.' Her voice was thick with emotion.

'But this is different. Thing is, the way we got into this was through a local camera club. That's where they, well, recruit new members.' He sniggered at his own witticism. 'Not only do they make contact with them there, suss them out and so on, but they also test them, make sure they're right.'

'Test them?' Susie sounded incredulous, and no wonder. For most swapping clubs the only test to pass is turning up at the right place at the right time.

'I know, I know. But we got this from a woman – of course – who told us the whole story and we believe it. This is a completely male dominated group, with strict rules.' Easing another finger in alongside the first, Susie thought she quite liked the sound of strict rules. 'They require women to be brought into the circle by a man, who offers her to the group. Her opinion on the subject apparently matters very little, and the women are always treated like objects and told nothing of importance.'

'Hmm…' Luckily the editor interpreted her sigh of arousal as a sigh of contemplation while she pondered his point, and carried on talking, giving her a chance to straighten her buckling knees and lean against the wall for support, placing her feet slightly apart and pushing her fingers deeper and deeper.

'You realise what this means, do you?' he asked, and she sighed again as the thrusting knuckles rubbed and spread her soft lips. 'What this means is that any information we get will have to be gleaned by a man – by Hugh, who's the ideal choice because he will also be able to use his particular skills with hidden cameras in order to get us the pictures we need to stand the story up.'

Susie slid down the wall, and was sitting with her feet apart and knees drawn up while her wrist and fingers pumped in and out. 'S-sounds like it could take w-weeks,' she said feebly, the breath catching in her throat.

'Weeks and weeks,' he confirmed. 'Months even.' Pushing her fingers faster and deeper she gasped at the thought of it, which the editor luckily took for a noise of dismay. 'Look Susie, that's the job, bottom line, take it or leave it.'

She loved it when he got stern like that, and felt the muscles in her tummy tighten and squeeze as her thighs clamped together, trapping her hand. She gasped, feeling the hot wet tunnel gripping and releasing her fingers over and over again.

'I know you're upset about it, but it's got to be done.'

She moaned softly, still unable to utter any articulate words.

'There's nothing else on the desk right now,' he added ominously.

'O-okay.' Relieved, she told herself she'd tried her best and that she did not have a choice. But deep down inside she knew she'd put up only token resistance and there was always a choice.

And even deeper down, she knew she was only there because she wanted to be. Right now 'there' was the M11 two days later, on her way to the house in Norwich that

83

Hugh had rented for them, with anger in her heart and – and this is why she was so angry – a fire burning in her knickers. Whenever she thought about Hugh she felt that way even though she disliked him intensely. And although she knew in her heart she should not, she still found him strangely compelling, and she found that very compulsion arousing. When Hugh looked at her in a certain way, and spoke to her in a certain way, with that tone in his voice and that look in his eye, her knees turned to jelly – and so did her knickers. In fact just thinking about it made her wet, and she squirmed in the seat. The effect in her panties was amplified by the fact that she knew she shouldn't feel that way, knew she shouldn't respond and definitely knew she shouldn't let him get to her. But he did, and what was worse, her conscious loathing of him produced the same familiar response between her legs that had got her into trouble so many times before, so she was trapped whichever way she turned.

So now, like a rabbit mesmerised by a stoat, she was on her way to join him. On her way, she thought as her heart jumped and her knickers moistened, to do as she was told. Whatever that may be.

The Norwich signposts came up swiftly, and she found it easy enough to circle the ring road and find the quiet suburb where Hugh had set up a house for them to live. It was just an everyday semi, with a small front garden and a drive that was full up with Hugh's car. So she parked in the road and struggled with her own cases, trying to ignore the simmering sexual tension, trying not to be excited or nervous about being with Hugh. He'd been there for a while now, which was why he'd been away from home so much. He'd been there most of the time, setting up the house on behalf of an absent wife who was soon to join him, drinking in the local pubs, establishing a bit of history and generally becoming part of the local community – and becoming a member of the local camera club.

'I've been to three or four meetings now,' he told her as they sat in the small kitchen with coffee, while he brought her up to speed on the background. 'Last one was last night, as it happens.'

'How did it go?' she asked, growing calmer as she began to concentrate on work.

'Well, the first time they all just talked cameras and photographed trees. Bit of a waste of time, really, and I thought I'd come to the wrong place. But it must have been some sort of probation period or something, because the second time was better. They had a "swimsuit" model that one of the blokes brought along, nice but nothing special, except she finally got her tits out. They liked that.'

'Suppose it made a change from landscapes and bowls of fruit,' Susie put in.

'Then the third one I knew was going to be different, because it was only a few people. There's about fifty or sixty members and about fifteen or so at any meeting, but this time they had the meeting at someone's house instead of the church hall, and only a few people were invited.'

'Including you?'

'Including me.'

'So what makes you so special so quickly?'

'Well, I told them I was more interested in video, really, and I let them know I had a fairly big collection—'

'You haven't shown them anything of me, I hope,' Susie interrupted like a flash.

Hugh sighed a long-suffering sigh. 'I'm not stupid.'

'Good.'

'No, I just let them see a few minutes of something I did with an old girlfriend.'

'Not—'

'No, not Sophie.' It was his turn to interrupt. 'I said I'm not stupid, and I'm not.' The similarity between the two girls was close; on video Sophie could easily be mistaken for Susie, and Hugh was astute enough to guard against such a mistake raising suspicions.

'Oh,' she said archly, annoyed at the sudden surge of jealous anger that matched the warm flush of arousal for intensity, 'so who was it, then?'

'Helen James, actually,' he said, with a gloating smile.

'You're joking!'

'No,' he said, smug as a cat with two bowls of cream, and why not? Helen James, aka The Fridge, the most famous virgin of the sixth form, was reputed to be so pure it had healed up! Never been kissed – never mind touched, or anything else.

'But she...' Susie was lost for words.

'I know.' He was so full of himself she thought he'd start polishing his nails on his shirt, the bastard. 'She got pissed at a party one night and passed out. Some of the lads thought it would be a good joke to get a camera and take her picture.' He shrugged as if trying to indicate that he was not one of the lads and didn't think it a good idea, but he couldn't erase his giveaway smirk. 'Several guys had their picture taken with her; a few of them pulled her skirt up and a couple had their hands in her knickers.'

'That's disgusting.'

Hugh nodded agreement, but his evil gloating was impossible to conceal. 'Disgusting. Yes. And of course, it was all over school the next Monday. Poor girl was distraught, naturally.'

'I can quite believe it,' Susie said, who thought this all had a familiar ring to it.

'So the guys offered to return the negatives to her.' Susie

raised her eyebrows, knowing there was more to come. 'On certain conditions.' His arrogant smile stretched right across his face, and she lifted one inquisitive eyebrow again. 'That she let them do it again, while awake.'

'You bastards.'

'Not me, Susie, not me. I didn't suggest it. Quite the reverse, in fact. I offered to get all the negatives back for her, without the need to let half-a-dozen grubby oiks into her knickers.'

'How many?'

'Well, um, I think there were eight in all,' he said.

'Eight?' She pulled a face of disgust. 'And just one knight in shining armour?'

'Well, not completely shining,' he admitted, though it was a boast more than anything else. 'I did want something from her in return.'

'You mean you wanted her to have it off with you as well?'

'Not as well, exactly,' he corrected. 'Instead of. Better just one of me than all the other seven.'

She glared scornfully. 'And how did you propose to get the negatives back for her?'

'I'd never given them away,' he said, 'only the prints.'

'Oh, you absolute *bastard*.'

'I know,' he said, trying to sound humble with his voice full of pride.

'And she fell for it, the stupid girl.'

'Oh yes,' he said happily.

'She let you… yuk!'

'Not at all. It was very good, actually. She enjoyed it. Let's face it, she was a different girl afterwards.'

Susie had left home around this time and didn't know what became of The Fridge, but it sounded as if Hugh might actually have introduced a bit of pleasure into her life after all, the cheating scumbag. 'And I suppose you kept the pictures, as usual.'

'Oh no, I gave them back as promised,' he said with mock sincerity. 'What would I want them for? After all, I'd got a bloody good film by then.'

'Oh, Hugh,' said Susie, shaking her head, 'you're the absolute limit.'

'I know,' he said proudly, misinterpreting the comment against his moral fibre as a compliment. 'Anyway, don't complain; that's what got me the invite to the special meeting,' he went on, 'so just you be grateful.'

'So what happened, anyway?' she asked, wanting to move on to the business in hand.

'It was at a big house on the way to Kings Lynn, and it was a proper glamour session. Just soft porn, really.'

'Oh, right up your street then,' she said.

'Oh yes,' he said with relish. 'The models are all amateurs, inexperienced, you know the sort of thing.'

Yes, Susie knew all right. It *was* right up Hugh's street. 'So how does it work?' she asked.

'The usual,' he said, as if everyone else in the world spent their leisure time in the same creepy ways he did. Now she knew why he'd spent so much time in London as a teenager.

'One of the members brings along a model, and we all take pictures of her.'

'And then you have a nice cup of tea and drive her home to her mum,' Susie finished sarcastically. 'Anyway, what sort of pictures?'

'Just lingerie, bit of topless, and some rather coy nudes. At least, that's how it was the first time.

'And after that?'

'Last night was a bit different,' he disclosed, the cheesy grin appearing once more.

'How so?'

'Everything, really. Except the place – it was the same house as the other times. But the atmosphere was different, like they were expecting something. And the girl was different, too, right from the start.'

'What sort of different? Professional?'

'Oh no, no, definitely not. Belinda, her name was, about your age, maybe a few years older, brunette, almost foreign looking, came with a bloke called Andrew, no introductions as such except her name and that she was our model for the evening, but I sort of got the impression she was his wife, or if not, then a very regular girlfriend.'

'What made you think so?'

'Oh, just the way they were together. Looking at each other at certain moments. Like she was constantly making sure he was okay with everything, or maybe as if they were just enjoying it together. But she wasn't just someone he hired out of the yellow pages or somewhere.'

Susie nodded. It sounded as if Hugh didn't miss much. 'Go on,' she encouraged.

'And she wasn't shy. She started off wearing much less, took it off fairly quickly, got her legs open almost at once.' His eyes gleamed with zealous fervour as he recalled the images and paraded them before his mind's eye. 'And then a couple of the blokes started *helping* her into poses, but it was just an excuse to feel her up, the usual rigmarole.'

'And she didn't mind?' asked Susie, who could feel the liquid evidence of precisely how much she would have enjoyed being in that situation seeping into her knickers.

'No, she clearly loved it.'

'And you still think she wasn't professional?'

'No. And I tell you what else about them, her and Andrew; he wanted them to touch her. He was the first one to start fiddling with her knickers, and he was the one who got the others on it as well, asking them to do it for him while he "framed his shot", the soppy git.' Hugh's scorn for someone less skilled than himself in the photographic arts was genuine enough.

'So he was giving the orders?' Susie's body pouted inside her knickers as she pictured herself reclining on a couch while several men took it in turns to grope her.

'Oh no, nothing like that. He was just getting off on it. It was his wife, I'm sure it was, and he was getting his rocks off making her lie there while he got other blokes to feel her up, and took pictures while they were doing it.'

'So what did Belinda do?' asked Susie, knowing what she would have done.

'She was on cloud nine as well. She kept looking at Andrew while these blokes were arranging her, and you could see she was getting off on it too. Next thing, hubby's got someone helping her off with her knickers, and before you could say "open wide" she's fingering herself like a mad thing. Not just posing, holding herself open, but diddling herself and shoving two fingers in, really enjoying it.'

'And what about this Andrew bloke?'

'Bright red in the face, could hardly speak he was having such a good time.'

Susie was having quite a good time herself, just imagining the whole scenario. 'What then?' she asked, hoping she didn't sound too eager.

'Then she made herself come, all gasping and heaving, and for a moment I thought Andrew was going to come as well. Funny thing, he wasn't watching her, he was watching everybody else. He wasn't even taking pictures of her, not like everyone else, all close-ups and details. He was doing big wide shots of all the blokes gathered round with their cameras.'

He did sound more and more like the husband, Susie

thought, although she'd been fairly certain as soon as Hugh mentioned it.

'And then, you'll never believe this, then, while she's still trying to get her breath back, and everyone else is shuffling their feet and looking at the carpet, bloody Andrew hands her a banana, and she went *mad*.' Hugh was licking his lips greedily as he recalled the moment in detail, gripped by the eroticism of it all over again. 'Fucked herself quite happily for a few minutes until it was of no more use, and then asked if anyone had anything harder.'

'And?'

'She was nearly trampled in the rush,' he said frankly.

'Who rushed?'

'Not Andrew, that's for sure. He used countless rolls of film taking pictures of Belinda getting shagged bandy by half the camera club and loving every second of it.'

'And you?' asked Susie. 'What did you do?'

'Well, I took pictures as well. That's my job.'

'And what else is your job?'

Hugh's smile was a picture of indescribable smugness. 'That's my job too,' he said, 'to join the club and gain their confidence. I thought it would look suspicious if I didn't join in.'

'Of course you did,' she said, in as scornful a voice as she could manage, although it was difficult to be superior with him when her knickers were on fire just thinking about it all, let alone actually being there. 'Stop the tape first, did you?'

'I didn't have a tape,' he said. 'Didn't seem much point when I was taking perfect thirty-five mil of everything that happened.'

Fair comment, she thought, disappointed; it would have been nice to think of his bum bouncing up and down for a change when the lads sat down to watch on a Friday night.

'All right, was she?'

Even Hugh had the good grace to blush slightly at the question and the memory.

'What next, then?' Susie didn't wait for the answer. Not that she was jealous. Oh no.

'We wait a few days.'

'For what?' She hated him, making her drag the information out instead of sharing it like he should have done.

'On Thursday night I'm taking a "model" myself, a girl who works with me, who's short of cash, and is prepared to do a bit of topless for a few quid – although I told them I think she's a dirty cow and she'll do a lot more if there's a bit of cash on the table on the night.'

'And who is this lucky young thing?'

'You, of course,' he leered.

'Me?' she tried to sound surprised, but there was a flash flood in her knickers and her pulse rate doubled.

'Yes, you,' he confirmed confidently. 'Who else?'

'I'm supposed to be your wife, stupid.'

'I know that.'

'So?'

'So I told them you're a college girl who needs the money, but if we play it right and react well together they'll think you're my wife, and I like to see you with other blokes for a cheap thrill but I'm not saying so because I'm embarrassed.'

'Like Andrew?' It was clever, and bound to work. 'That's good, Hugh,' she said grudgingly.

'Yes, it is rather,' he crowed, although it obviously wasn't his own idea.

But the next double bluff he pulled was all his own work. Susie wanted to shower and unpack, so they had the argument about the sleeping arrangements next. Hugh finally gave in, and agreed that not many visitors would be going upstairs and therefore it wasn't necessary for them to share a bedroom in order to maintain their deception. And since both bedrooms had double beds but only one had an en-suite bathroom and anything like a sensible lock, Hugh had already guessed that would be the one Susie chose, so he'd moved into the other and was now delighted to be proved right.

But more than his cleverness at guessing correctly prompted his delight.

In the few weeks he'd been there, he'd taken the precaution of wiring the house for sound and pictures, but though there were cameras in both downstairs rooms, he only had enough to do one bedroom properly, and allocated it according to his interpretation of what Susie would choose. *That* was why he was so pleased to have guessed right, and now he sat in his bedroom, which was also the master control room for his DIY closed-circuit system, ready to test it most thoroughly by filming Susie alone in the bigger bedroom.

He'd hoped to see her in her underwear, and perhaps naked. He had no idea how aroused she had been by their earlier conversation, nor how clearly she could picture Belinda with her knees raised, being solidly fucked by one stranger while another thrust his erect cock into her mouth, and perhaps another placed her hand around his thick shaft.

Hugh wasn't able to see those thoughts on screen, nor even interpret them from the look on Susie's face. But he was able to guess at them fairly accurately based on her behaviour.

There were several cameras in the bedroom, and Hugh was able to swivel and zoom all four of them. So he twirled the control wheel and gently steered the joystick until Susie filled the frame as she stood by the dressing table, stripping off her clothes. The lighting from the window was particularly good, so the tape was recording every detail of her naked body in pin-sharp detail.

There was another camera hidden in the light fitting above the shower, giving him an overhead view as she washed, and shaved herself carefully between her legs. Hugh made a mental note to find a waterproof camera he could hide inside the drain grating.

Patting herself dry with a large towel, Susie sat on the edge of the bed. She was caught in a crossfire of four cameras now, and Hugh was particularly proud of the two incorporated in the design of the knurled cast-iron bed frame, one in each of the posts at the foot of the bed.

Adjusting one of them now, he had a perfect frontal shot as Susie dried her legs, then her thighs, and then high up between them. She let her fingers stroke and caress as she checked her shaving for smoothness, and then she let them dip into the simmering wetness.

As she lay back on the bed Hugh was looking at a choice of four images of her, and all four were award-winning stuff. The first, from a camera above her in the ceiling, picked out the detail of her hard nipples, her slowly widening thighs and the patch of blonde curls that skimmed the pretty curve of her pubic mound. On the wall directly opposite the foot of the bed was another, concealed in the patterned cornice. On full zoom it was looking right between her legs, filling the screen with an intimate close-up as she trailed her fingertips lightly up and down, making a deep, inviting furrow in the glistening wet pinkness.

One bedpost camera was also on full zoom, watching carefully as the fingers spread and separated, delving deeper, digging into the warm welcome of her body, soft squelching and sucking noises as pin-sharp on the audio as the pictures were on video.

The camera on the other bedpost was slightly wider, framing the centre section of her body as one hand squeezed her full, firm breasts and plucked at the nipples with sharp movements, and the other hand...

Oh, the other hand!

Hugh flicked back to the wall camera, swiftly zooming out to see the big picture as Susie reached out to the bedside cabinet. He zoomed in on her hand to see what – only a hairbrush!

Tutting in disappointment that she wasn't going to continue with what she'd been doing, he was about to stop the tapes when he saw that her hand was not lifting, she wasn't raising the brush to her head, but lowering it to her lap. He followed her, medium shot, hairbrush, hand and lower arm all in frame as she reversed her grip and ran the blunted wooden handle up and down between the puffy wet folds of flesh and then slowly applied more pressure, making it sink deeper and deeper. She made a little sighing noise as the snout found its way past the soft lips and spread the tight opening of her pussy.

She sighed again as the dark wooden shaft sank slowly deeper, until it could go no further.

She sighed again as it slid out, shining wet with her juices.

She sighed more loudly as she pushed it in again, faster and harder.

Hugh stared intently, hands dancing over the control panel as he selected camera after camera, close-up after close-up, watching the neat pink lips sliding wetly up and down the dark wooden shaft until Susie's hips lifted from the bed, the muscles in her stomach gripped and tightened and she jerked, then slumped back onto the bed.

Hugh was delighted with the quality and technical versatility of his set up. It was crystal clear, pin-sharp, easy to use, quick to operate and gave wonderful results.

Whoever joined Susie in the bedroom, whether he was a fat sweaty amateur pornographer or the local MP with whips, spurs and blindfolds, whoever it was, Hugh would have him bang to rights. Another job well done, he thought, giving himself a well-deserved mental pat on the back.

And another fine tape of Susie to add to the collection, as well.

He was just going to stop recording and label the cassette when she started to move, so slowly at first he wasn't sure if he was imagining it. She'd been motionless since her orgasm and the handle of the hairbrush was still inside her, and he thought she was beginning to rock just a little, thought her knees were beginning to lift and her wrist just flexing ever so slightly.

The soft, sucking wetness on the audio channel was what confirmed it for him, and he leant over the control panel again, zooming one bedpost camera between her thighs for a detailed close-up and setting the other so it filled the screen with her face. It would be nice to capture her expression at the moment of orgasm, he thought. That would put the price up when he came to sell copies on Friday nights, but it was the thought of all those grubby printers seeing her so exposed and revealed when they watched her face as she played with herself that Hugh liked best. It was making her so vulnerable that really made him hard. He unzipped himself as the hairbrush started to move in a wide circle and her hips began to rock in a lazy, luxurious rhythm. He could easily manage the controls with one hand.

Chapter Seven

'All set?' Hugh asked.

Susie nodded, with a show of more confidence than she actually felt inside. Nothing to worry about, she told herself, she'd done this sort of thing enough times before. So why was the butterfly squadron at full throttle, why were the icy fingers clasping her insides with their iron grip, and why was there a warm flood soaking her knickers?

It looked normal enough from the outside, she thought, as she walked up the drive of the large detached house on the outskirts of the city, feeling her heart thundering in her chest, cold fingers of fear in her tummy and hot liquid arousal in her knickers. On the other side of the plain wooden front door was a group of men she'd never met before in her life, and within minutes she'd be lifting her skirt and opening her legs to their gaze – and what they saw they'd interpret as sheer arousal. They'd see her wet and ready and think she was just a randy little tart who couldn't wait to get fucked... and then they'd fuck her.

'Oh yes,' said the man who opened the door, 'you'll be Caroline. *Very* nice to meet you, my dear. *Very* nice indeed...'

He was fifty-ish, smooth, well dressed, clearly a man of breeding, a man from good stock, as they say. But there was something extra in his manner; not just the air of someone used to giving orders and used to being obeyed. Perhaps it was just the faint tension about him, as he looked her up and down and perhaps wondered what she'd be like. And in her turn Susie wondered what he'd be like, wondered if he'd be the first.

97

He ushered her through a doorway, and she saw the group of men sitting or standing around the room. Amongst them, casually dropped on the floor, there were soft bags and aluminium boxes, spilling out the matt black paraphernalia of photography. Here and there she saw one or two tripods, erected early, waiting. Waiting for her. Waiting to discover the secrets of her voluptuous young body.

Including Hugh and the man who'd let them in, and whose house she assumed this to be since he appeared to be in charge, there were seven men in the room. As she'd expected in such a situation they weren't young, but mostly middle-aged, with the soft paunches and red faces of those who can afford to drink often and eat well.

Except one. He was eighteen, maybe nineteen, a beautiful, tall black boy who seemed too shy to meet her eyes, and with a catch in her throat and another sudden flush of warm wetness between her legs she realised that he must be for her. Out of place as a photographer, he was obviously another model, and the rest of them, the overweight businessmen with piggy little eyes and probably piggy little pricks, they were going to take pictures of her with him. Well, at least he was young and handsome. She smiled shyly at him, but he just stared back, impassive.

'Now,' the host said to her, 'I believe Hugh has explained what we do here. We're just a bunch of enthusiasts who take pictures of various different subjects.' There were some repressed smiles as he paused before continuing. 'And tonight the subject is glamour, a beautiful girl... you.' His oily charm was condescending and unpleasant, as if he was paying her some kind of compliment by wanting to look up her skirt.

She peered around at the others, hoping to find a friendly face, but even Hugh looked – no, not impassive, or even aloof – he looked cruel and unsympathetic.

He frowned at her, nodding significantly at her coat, still buttoned up, and she understood at once. She hesitated for a second, making Hugh frown and nod again, and then her fingers opened the buttons and she slipped the coat off her shoulders, and his frown of annoyance changed at once to a conceited smirk of satisfaction as there was a collective and salacious murmur of approval around the room.

To be fair he had accomplished his remit admirably, and with the diagonally striped tie knotted loosely under the collar of her white blouse, she looked beautifully fresh and demure. The dark blue skirt was pleated and a modest few inches above the knee, but the effect was devastating, and as Hugh had predicted, her face almost devoid of make-up complemented the look to perfection.

As did her genuinely shy smile.

'Right then, picture time,' a voice eventually broke the spell that seemed to settle over those gathered, and as she realised the host of the group was talking to her, looking at her, waiting for her to take up a pose they could photograph, and that it would be the first of many on a dubious road, so she realised what she had known all along that this was part of her job. Normally the 'rules' meant that she, or whoever was involved in any particular job, should make their excuses and leave at the opportune moment. In the past Susie's complete inability to resist the demands of her body had meant she'd stayed, and ended up making excuses to the editor. On more than one occasion her own enthusiastic participation, complete with recognisable appearances in the subsequent photographs, had meant that a story had to be dropped or delayed. On any job she knew she was supposed to incite others and then leave the room before it was too late.

But this was different. This assignment required that she stay, that she not only allow herself to be seen in the pictures but that she should be the centrepiece of them. This naturally created a problem that, for the purposes of publication, could easily have been circumvented by a little judicious blurring. But that would only have worked if Hugh had been the one photographer in the room. Tonight there would be many images taken from different photographers, and there was no way they could allow them all to be circulated.

At first this had appeared to be the sort of stumbling block that could have halted the entire operation, but Hugh – of course – came up with a technical solution that had delighted the editor. He would use a set of lights with a special bulb and filter. Normal in appearance to the naked eye, they would turn all the pictures taken during the evening into a kind of green soup.

'Yours as well, though,' the editor pointed out.

'No, not mine,' Hugh countered, before explaining more. 'Because I know the lights are dodgy I can put a filter on the camera to correct it. No one else will use the filter because they won't know I've fixed the lights. So the only person with useable pictures will be me.'

The editor had beamed happily, Hugh preened himself and leered pointedly at Susie, and a knot of apprehension gripped her tummy.

Now he was leering in the same obnoxious way, and she could tell he was enjoying what he fondly imagined to be her reservations for what lay ahead.

'Just take a seat on the Chesterfield to start with, I think,' said the host, indicating the large leather settee against one wall, and around which everyone was now gathered in a loose semicircle.

Obediently she did so, smoothing her pleated skirt down over her black stockings with a shy smile, looking at the seven men who were hungrily staring at her.

To her left, a portly and red-faced man hid a slack mouth

behind a bushy black beard. He whispered occasionally to his neighbour, a small, dapper man with equally black hair and eyebrows, and thick black lashes that gave him an effeminate appearance totally at odds with the greedy lust that blazed in his eyes as he drooled over Susie, unashamedly trying to see how far up her skirt he could look from where he hovered.

Behind him, looking over his shoulder with only mild curiosity, was the black youth, only he was glancing up at her before looking down into his hands where he was making intricate adjustments to the complicated camera in his grasp. Clearly she'd got him wrong, and he was just another snapper.

And to prove the point he leaned forward, passing the camera to the man ahead and to his right. Dead centre of the group that clustered around Susie, this man was grey-haired and pasty-faced, skin glowing with perspiration as he licked his lips in a nervous movement and squinted through thick glasses that magnified his eyes to bizarre dimensions.

Hugh stood beside him; trust Hugh to have taken up a position which gave him the best view as well as putting him next to the host. She knew it was his job, to worm his way in and gain their confidence, but she also knew he'd be there even if it hadn't been.

'Ready now?' the host asked as he peered at her. Though he had no camera in his hands, and in any case bore the general air of one who left that sort of thing to others, he had nevertheless secured himself a prime position in the semicircle, since Susie sat on the settee at an angle and was turned to face him, and the man beside him, a gangly, cadaverous person of indeterminate age. Early thirties going on seventy-five, thought Susie, watching his angular frame as he strove to look casual and failed.

'Okay then.' The host had taken Susie's silence after his question as a sign of acquiescence. Or perhaps he just didn't care whether she was ready or not. He was, and that was all that mattered.

Feeling the temperature between her thighs rising as she prepared for what she knew was to come, she sat up straight, hands demurely in her lap, tilted her head down and her eyes upward, looking towards the cameras through lowered lashes. It was, as the lights around the room flashed with that strangely mechanical thump as they released their energy and then sang as they recycled, a classic pose that had become a bit of a cliché, but still amazingly effective.

'Tuck your legs under a bit, Caroline,' Hugh directed, 'and give us a fraction more thigh.'

Responding to her alias, and the way Hugh used it to make sure everyone guessed she was really his wife and not just an acquaintance he'd talked into modelling for cash, she bent her legs a little more and inched her skirt higher, giving them a little more of her sheer stockings, wondering what she looked like, wondering if they too were already aroused in anticipation.

'And head up,' called Hugh, and she pulled her shoulders back a little, letting the fullness of her breasts press against the delicate bra and cotton blouse, stretching the white material and filling it with a lushly rounded, hard-tipped promise.

'Oh yes,' drooled the bearded one, obviously a breast man and obviously getting a good profile from where he stood to her left, 'that's lovely.' And the flash *whumped* again in response to his shutter, sending a flush or sudden excitement through Susie's panties as she knew for certain that he at least was excited.

'Button,' called Hugh imperiously, and she would have spat at him if they'd been alone. He got a definite kick out of ordering her to do things she didn't want to do while she had no choice but to obey… like now. Sadly, she thought as she loosened her striped tie and unbuttoned her blouse so that it hung open to display her cleavage, she liked being made to do things almost as much as Hugh liked making her do them, and the liquid fire in her knickers was ample proof of that.

The flashes were blinding, as everyone fired off two or three shots, anxious not to miss their first glimpse of her mouth-watering breasts.

'Open your legs a little now,' instructed Hugh, deliberately expressing himself as provocatively as he could, trying to embarrass or shame her. Obviously he didn't realise that Susie needed no provocation, and in fact the bluntness of his instruction, the sheer rudeness of him calling it out like that, loud and clear so everyone could hear, added an extra thrill to the spice she already felt. With all eyes on her, the centre of attention, Susie obeyed, slowly, deliberately, moving her knees apart, letting them look between her thighs, and as she felt the cool air between them she knew they were looking at the sliver of white that covered her secret places, and she felt the warm wetness in her knickers as her body tensed and her heart leapt.

The cameras were clicking and whining as the lights flashed, and Susie adjusted her pose slightly, sitting square on to the group so they each got the same sort of shot. 'Just pull your blouse out now,' called Hugh, and Susie reached down to tug it from the waistband of her skirt, obeying without hesitation.

'Fine, like that,' said the host, and she stopped, leaving just one side hanging free, a dishevelled pose that went well with her flushed face as she pouted at Hugh.

Click and flash went the cameras.

'Bottom two buttons,' instructed Hugh, and she undid

103

them, letting the blouse drop away to expose her toned midriff, slowly, making them wait, the white cotton rustling seductively, feeling the tension rising in the room, feeling the tension rising in her sex as her aching body blossomed, and there was only her tie holding her blouse loosely together around her neck, and the cameras flashed several times as she sat with her knees apart, knickers clinging damply to her curves, breasts swelling inside the delicate bra, the outline of her nipples just visible, pushing outwards, two shadowy discs straining against the pure tight whiteness.

'Pull your bra down.'

Susie could see how much Hugh was enjoying making her expose herself to the men, but she was caught up in the tension of the moment too, and although Hugh was passing orders, the power was hers. Seven men were holding their breath as she did as she was told, pulling the edge of the lacy cups down, letting one budding nipple pop into view, stiff and solid like a rosy bullet, feeling the cool air making it stiffen and grow, sending a cold tracer into the pit of her stomach.

Dozens of frames of film wound through the motor drives.

'Touch it,' someone directed, their voice tight, and she cupped her breast, lifting it as the flashguns zapped her.

'Take your bra off,' said Hugh, 'but keep your blouse on,' and she did the trick every schoolgirl learns behind the bike sheds, undoing her bra and pulling it off down one sleeve, dropping it aside and resuming her pose, feeling her breasts pressing into the soft coolness of the white blouse, which gaped at the front, shaped invitingly over their rounded smoothness and hanging from their erect tips.

'Skirt up a bit,' Hugh continued, taking charge, and obediently she squirmed a little on the settee as she pulled it higher, and the cameras started flashing as the stocking-tops came into view, dark bands against the pale softness of her thighs.

'And more,' said someone else, and she slowly pulled it higher, watching their jaws drop a millimetre lower for every upward, teasing movement of the hem. But eventually it bunched up around her waist, and Hugh was speaking again.

'No, that doesn't look right,' he said impatiently. 'One of you sort it out.'

Susie had hardly understood what he meant when the bearded one was there at her side, fiddling with the hem, smoothing the pleats, taking liberties, sweaty hands lingering on her thighs, pawing and mauling as he shaped her skirt back down, which she could perfectly easily have done herself, as everyone knew.

'Much better,' said Hugh, as the bearded one at last finished molesting her thighs. 'Now, legs apart a bit more,' he ordered, and she let her knees drift wider, and wider, feeling the response in her sex as the soft flesh fluttered and swelled and the moisture seeped into the white material – the blatantly *visible* white material, because with her skirt resting above her stocking tops and her knees parted, there was no longer any covering at all, nor even a shadow to conceal her modesty, and they were all seven staring intently between her legs as they gazed at the object of their desire, revealed by the bright lights, warm and wet and pinkly swelling inside the delicate material, wet and clinging to every curve.

'Nice one, love,' enthused one of them.

'More please,' urged another, and she let her knees move again, until they were as wide as they'd go, and the cameras flashed as their owners crouched lower and took photographs of her soaking gusset, with its pretty pink contents clearly definable.

'Nipple,' said Hugh, twiddling his fingers in midair, and

she obeyed, tweaking the little rosebud between finger and thumb, spreading the fingers of the other hand on her thigh as if holding her legs wide apart, and the cameras flashed again.

'Oh yes,' mumbled the fat one, but they were all starting to glow now, faces redder, eyes bulging, upper lips beaded with sweat, like a pack at feeding time knowing a meal was imminent.

'Pull them tight,' said Hugh, and her body thrilled with electrical pulses. She knew exactly what he meant, and her hand reacted without her telling it to, grasping the flimsy white material of her knickers at the waist and pulling it gently upward, pulling against herself, pulling so it pressed against her, squashing against the slick pinkness, taut and revealing for the cameras to capture.

'Lift your leg,' said Hugh, 'foot on the couch.' Susie raised one foot, settling the heel on the edge of the leather seat, which revealed no more than before but pulled the white cotton tighter still, creating a taut curve of material that must have looked even more enticing, judging by the number of flashes it provoked.

'Wait,' said one, fumbling in his camera as he changed film, but Hugh did not want to wait – he was on a roll as well.

'Fingers,' he said, rubbing his crutch suggestively, and Susie released the taut material, her outstretched fingers reached lower, spreading across the front of the white V like a fan, feeling the inviting fullness that swelled inside, and the cameras flashed over and over again.

'Harder,' he said, the bastard, still trying to shame her and not knowing the waves of arousal his words induced as she obeyed again, feeling herself wet and squishy in the valley separating the two swollen halves, hot and slick as her finger traced a gentle line between the full curves of

106

her open body.

So many pictures were taken so continuously she was bathed in a constant stream of bright white light.

'Inside,' snapped Hugh, and seemed irritated when she didn't obey at once. 'Fingers inside your knickers,' he ordered again, and watched as her fingertips slid under the elastic at her waist, making irregular bumps as they pushed lower, partly visible through the flimsy white, searched lower still and found the sweet warmth and separated the puffy lips as the cameras flashed and recorded, seeing through the white material, picking out the detail as her fingers slithered across the sensitive pink wetness.

All except Hugh's camera, that is, which was aimed at Susie's face, the perfectly framed close-up recording the evidence of her arousal, naked and revealed.

'Spread,' he ordered relentlessly, flexing one hand in demonstration, and she fanned her fingers so the neat nails showed from around the edges of the material, and her knuckles made little bumps in the white which stuck wetly to the back of her hand.

'Good,' he breathed, nodding with satisfaction. 'Now, hand out, and pull it taut again.'

Gathering the material in her grasp, feeling it wet and slippery as she bunched it up, Susie tugged softly and felt her body open instantly, yearning as she pulled the white knickers into a narrow band which slowly disappeared, pulled into her body, exposing the soft curves of clean-shaven pinkness either side of it for the first time, and the avaricious cameras flashed furiously, feeding off such a spellbinding vision of purity and beauty.

'Tighter,' said Hugh, his voice strained, and she obeyed.

They knelt around her, the semicircle slowly shuffling nearer, as if the lenses of their cameras couldn't bring them close enough to the object of their desire, and they took

107

picture after picture, the savage flashguns making pinpricks of diamond light dance around the soft pinkness as the warm moisture reflected their blaze.

'Kneel,' said the host, and she turned, kneeling on the cool leather with her bottom raised towards him, knowing the narrow white strip was still pulled tight into her body, slicing between the two firm cheeks of her bottom and deeper still, into the warm and wet furrow.

'Get the skirt,' commanded Hugh, and immediately he with the beard again loomed close, lifting the hem higher over her bottom, arranging the folds and pleats artistically in a manner which apparently required him to stroke the firm curves of her bottom several times, sending small tremors of need through the swollen lips and clitoris that waited hungrily for a decisive touch.

'Perfect,' said the host, and Susie twisted sexily to gaze back over her shoulder at the array of rapacious lenses. The flashes flashed and the cameras whirred, and Susie stroked herself, one dainty finger sliding against the slippery wetness of the stretched material between her thighs, gradually pressing harder and pushing deeper, harder and deeper, in response to the pressure as her body moved to meet the finger, asking, begging to be entered fully, and she gazed at them over her shoulder with the most innocent, dreamy expression, the naughty schoolgirl caught in the act, as her finger wriggled past the damp strip of her knickers and sank luxuriously into her body.

The soft sucking sounds betrayed how wet she was, how ready she was, grinding her hips towards the camera, letting the lenses look deep, as if their unblinking stare could penetrate the slippery pinkness alongside her finger, and the very idea started a surge of pleasure that grew, the beginnings of a climax she knew would be long and deeply pleasurable, and as her hips drew those rhythmic circles she knew that everyone in the room could feel the tension rising, and knew it wouldn't be long before she squealed and shivered and came and came…

'Wait,' Hugh interrupted, and she savoured a spasm of intense anticipation as she let her finger stop moving. Here he came, she thought, her lovely black boy with the big cock.

But how wrong she could be.

Chapter Eight

Her emotions in complete turmoil, Susie could not think how Hugh had managed to hide it from her when they packed their things ready for the evening's task, but from his bag he produced an ominous looking bamboo cane, and once again, for a reason poor Susie simply could not fathom, the portly oaf with the beard was handed the privilege.

'Just lay it across her… yes, like that,' instructed Hugh, as the cane was rested lightly over her smooth and, she suddenly realised, very vulnerable buttocks. 'Perfect,' Hugh added, and his voice triggered a battery of flashes as they all took a cascade of pictures, bending and crouching to change their point of view, relishing each delicious image – each image which would, Susie realised, make it look as if she really was being caned.

'Just lift the edge of her skirt with the tip,' said someone else, and that meant the bearded one had to first pull it down a little, which gave him an opportunity to let the back of his clammy hand stroke across the curved white wetness that was her cotton-sheathed pussy, making her quiver with traitorous pleasure, though she hoped he was too much of an oaf to notice.

Then he stood back a pace, and the tip of the cane traced a slow line up the back of her thigh, touched lightly and briefly but very deliberately right in the centre of the white crescent nestled between her thighs like a quarter-moon, touched on the spot where her soft lips opened, and then carried on upward, catching the hem of her skirt and raising it as if exposing her for the first time, and all of them must have used a roll of film each within the next few seconds.

'Just do the cane thing again,' urged another.

'Yeah, and this time put a bit of pressure on, bend it back like it's just landed... *lovely*.'

'What about a bit of movement – like motion blur,' another suggested eagerly, and immediately the beard applied some light strokes across Susie's bottom, which didn't really hurt at all, but she squealed and they seemed to like that as they flashed away furiously with busy cameras. They also seemed to like the way the dampness had soaked her knickers so they clung to her pinkly shaven curves, revealing the rounded fullness and the warm valley that was opening deeper and deeper all the time.

'Now touch yourself again,' commanded Hugh, the order given without a trace of warmth or affection, as all his instructions had been issued so far, and she reached back between her thighs, letting her fingers stroke the scalding wetness of the soggy knickers, arousal heightened by the knowledge that they were once again transparently wet, and it was as if she could feel with her tenderly probing fingertips the curves and valleys they saw with their intrusive lenses.

And as the bearded oaf let the cane fall lightly across her rounded buttocks once again she realised she was in that position once more, bent over with her bottom bared and her body exposed, one hand reaching between her legs to stroke and caress while an audience stared as she was caned. As she saw the mental pictures of herself, pictures that matched the thirty-five mil images forming on the emulsion, Susie could feel her groin contract and relax, marking the imminent return of the climax that had been stolen from her a few minutes earlier.

'Let's have a couple of real ones, shall we?' Hugh

prompted in his commanding way, and smiled with satisfaction as the cane suddenly cracked down across Susie's exposed bottom, making her jump and squeal, the settee creaking as she writhed away from the cruel impact.

'Oh, yes!' someone enthused.

'Hang on,' called another, 'let me get the motor drive switched on.'

Susie braced herself as they all announced various states of readiness, and then the cane swiped across her bottom again, laying a thin red trail in its wake, as if the burning pain was actually visible on film.

'And another,' demanded the fat one, almost dribbling with excitement, and the thin line of heat seared across her quivering buttocks once again. Then it fell again, and again, ten or a dozen times, until Hugh waved a hand and brought the onslaught to a halt. There was a lot of excited chatter as they changed film, staring critically at Susie as they discussed poses, as if they were in an art gallery analysing an exhibit that couldn't hear or speak and had no sensibilities to be offended.

'What about this,' said the cadaverous one in glasses, generally silent up to now but suddenly becoming just a little animated. As everyone else stared curiously, he stepped forward like a wading bird on a windswept shore, Susie not sure if he was always so awkward of movement or if he had a straining erection that made him walk like that.

He took the cane from the one with the beard, who went back to his camera a little sulkily, and gave her an experimental prod with the tip, pressing it into the wet fabric, spreading her opening as he pushed into her, and suddenly the room was again ablaze with light. Even standing still the man looked awkward, almost embarrassed by the success of his pose, one arm extended, wrist turned upwards like a fencer, with the tip of his foil pressed against

112

a sliver of white material that was moving slowly in response to his pressure, slipping deeper between the puffy lips and into the heated darkness.

Susie arched her back, lifting her bottom and instinctively pressing back against the tip of the cane that grazed her clit, and the cameras went wild.

The thin, bespectacled man pressed even more insistently, and Susie felt the wooden tip sink further.

'Push a little deeper,' Hugh impelled. 'Deeper…' and as the cameras faithfully recorded each deliciously slippery moment, the tip of the cane and the band of saturated white cotton did indeed sink deeper and deeper, revealing her succulent shape to the greedy lenses and the eager eyes behind the viewfinders as the material slowly vanished from view.

Susie gave a quivering sigh of pleasure as the folds of her body were pressed apart, and the cameras whirred, their owners anxious not to miss anything. The thin man beamed a self-satisfied smile at the bank of clicking and flashing, but Susie was oblivious now, because the build up of tension had reached close to bursting point and she was only aware of the irresistible messages being transmitted from her clit, as the background sounds faded and even the flickering lights grew dim.

There were many pictures taken now, as she shuffled her knees and lifted her gorgeous bottom, as she felt her body opening in response to the increasing pressure as the tip of the cane probed deeper, thickened as it gathered the wet material and carried it into her, and she began to rock gently on her knees, sliding against the intruder, slipping it in and out, feeling the rucked material around the tip travelling in and out, sending gentle waves of pleasure through her body, in and out it went as the sensations lapped at the edges of her subconscious.

'Okay, let's lie down now, please,' Hugh intervened at precisely the wrong moment. Obviously he'd read her mood exactly, although how he knew so much about her was a mystery. But the nasty bastard had stopped her just before it would have been too late, left her dangling on the precipice once again, although one step higher than she'd been before, with the peak that much closer and her need to reach it that much greater.

'Lay still, Caroline,' he went on, 'Peter's just going to rearrange you a little.'

Was there a subtle emphasis in his words? It didn't matter, because Peter, the one with the effeminate eyes, was already beside her and interpreting Hugh's instructions very literally, helping her onto her back and slipping one finger under the edge of her knickers and pulling them slowly aside, awarding himself a real close-up look at her and the luxury of letting his fingers slide a little way inside her sex, just enough to feel the heat and moisture, just enough to make her gasp and flinch, as if the cane had landed across her buttocks once again. Then, with his other hand, he guided the bamboo tip into place so once again it was pressing into her, pushing the white cotton inwards as well.

He then stepped back and the cameras started clicking at once, while the tall one with the thick glasses again pressed the cane firmly downwards, spreading and opening her at the same time as her soft curves and slick wetness were exposed to the greedy eyes behind the viewfinders.

'Just get hold of it now, Caroline,' instructed Hugh, and he would have explained further had not Susie grasped his meaning and the shaft of the cane in almost the same instant, wrapping her hands around it as if guiding a lover's erection into herself, raising her hips and pressing in deeper to where it felt best.

The cameras whirred furiously as she began to flex against

it, and Hugh said sharply, 'Both hands now,' and once again she understood, laying one palm on her mound, spreading herself with fanned fingers, revealing her nakedness and her need as she arched against the thickly wadded tip, her fingers slithering on her own smoothly shaved wetness, teasing where the wedge of wet material was being pushed into her as her hips rocked up to meet it and her thighs opened wider, offering herself to them.

'Just a few more like that,' Hugh said, waiting for the group to take their last shots of that particularly alluring pose. 'Perfect... now then, legs a little wider, Caroline, and let's go without the cane,' and he looked around the group, seeing nods of agreement. 'Okay, Caroline,' he went on, as the ungainly member of the group withdrew the cane, the last inch or so shining wetly in the light, 'carry on by yourself, there's a good girl.'

'With yourself,' sniggered someone, but her hand was already there, fingertips slithering luxuriously over the scalding wetness and spreading it tenderly, teasing and tickling for only a moment before sliding steadily deeper until two fingers had completely vanished from view as the cameras flashed more rapidly than ever, not quite masking the long sigh of pleasure as her hips rose to meet the inward thrust.

'Marvellous,' someone croaked, voice thick with lust as Susie's fingers began their work, in and out, thrusting deeper, spreading herself, frigging herself, wanting them all to see her fingers sliding in and out, wanting them to imagine it was them, thick and erect, fucking her.

'Right, on the floor,' said Hugh, and he made Susie kneel, elbows on the settee, face hidden, bottom raised again, knees apart, and then he made her reach back between her legs, spread herself for the cameras, slip a finger inside for the cameras, slip two fingers inside for the cameras and then stop, just when her crisis was threatening again.

'A firm smack, I think,' she heard him say, and someone was kneeling beside her – him with the beard, portly and awkward, resting the flat of his hand on her buttocks, fingertips just millimetres from touching her pouting sex lips.

'Okay,' said Hugh, and the bearded oaf slapped her, making her buttocks bounce, letting his fingertips dip into the very edges of her honey pot, then further in towards the centre until his slapping was more of a rhythmic squeezing, the thumb pressed into her buttock, fingertips curled into her opening, slipping deeper and deeper until he couldn't be patient any longer and released his grip, sliding two straight fingers hard inside her with a sudden jab, making her squeal in surprise, keeping her squealing and trapped against the settee as he pumped them in and out and the cameras flickered their owners' approval.

'Thank you,' Hugh said flatly, 'that's enough,' and the fumbling fingers left Susie just when she was about to burst with the power of her climax, leaving her gasping, frustrated, her hips writhing against nothing.

'You'll want to take some pictures,' Hugh told the overweight oaf with the beard as he stood up. 'Fred will give you a break.'

Fred was only a couple of feet away and was beside her in no time, hand on her bottom, fingers inside her without ceremony or speaking.

'Ooh,' she gasped, and then again as the thin one, waved over by Hugh, sat on the settee, right next to where she knelt leaning on it, and without being told she knew exactly what was expected. She reached for him, fumbling with the zip, and as soon as it was lowered she rummaged inside the gaping shadows and found him pulsing there, then tugged into the light a substantial erection. Getting utterly carried away in the intensity of the moment, she rubbed up and down and the flashguns went crazy… and they went even crazier when she leaned forward and touched her slightly parted lips to the bulbous tip, then sighed faintly as the one called Fred changed position to kneel behind her, and at last she was filled with something thick and solid as his hairy groin docked slowly against her beaten buttocks. He began to pump briskly in and out and she braced her knees into the carpet, arched her back to raise her hips and urge him deeper, and just as he hit the perfect pace and she felt as if at last she would be released from her torment, he grunted loudly and hot jets erupted inside her.

As the cock in her fist pressed upward and widened her lips, filling her mouth, another erection prodded and poked between her thighs before penetrating her. Three staccato thrusts and she thought it would be her turn, but before she spiralled into a shattering climax she felt the throbbing column jerk and spasm inside her all too soon and he slumped, panting heavily and replete, to the floor.

Desperately she plopped the erection out of her mouth and dragged him by it, steering him around to carry on where the last had just failed, and he knelt between her ankles, his cock hard and thick and straight and sinking inside her, forging deeper, spreading her open and filling her until she gasped in delight and then squealed in disappointment as he too found the eroticism of the evening all too much and ejaculated too quickly.

But then the bearded one was there, ready and waiting, dropping his corduroys to reveal a stout erection with a bulbous helmet, as inflamed as his face.

'Yessss,' she urged, reaching back to guide him to where she wanted him, turning her bottom as the tall one shuffled away, waiting for him to enter her, quickly, not realising she was pleading. 'Please, now, now, *now…*'

117

But all she received was the very tip, for it was all too much for him too, and with a grunt of dismay he erupted and coated her pouting sex lips and the backs of her thighs and stockings, but got no further.

'Oh no,' she gasped in frustration, and reached back between her thighs to thrust two fingers into herself in sheer desperation, but they were an unsatisfactory replacement for the erect cocks she'd just been robbed of, and she looked over her shoulder ready for anyone, even Hugh. And as she did her hand slowed and her breathing calmed. The coloured lad had taken his jeans off and was unbuttoning his shirt, and from his groin jutted a smooth dark shaft that looked dauntingly impressive. Every camera in the room was aimed at Susie's bottom when he knelt behind her, hands on her flanks, turning her, angling her so they could all see.

'Ready, gentlemen?' he asked, in a husky American accent that almost made her climax on the spot. 'Then I'll begin.'

The swollen tip was shiny, large and round. The pale pinkness of her body clung around the dark shaft, the soft lips spreading wider as he sank deeper and deeper, until she mumbled a small cry of warning. His groin had not reached her buttocks, but a significant proportion of his cock was still in view, while the unseen remainder filled her completely. When he eased back that which had been inside her glistened wetly with her juices.

He eased almost all of it from her, so the bloated helmet kept her lips parted, clinging to him, waiting while the cameras flashed. When everyone seemed happy he nodded again and leaned forward, pulling out almost at once, then sliding back in, and pulling out; a long slow fuck that did the trick and her climax boiled over at last, a shuddering orgasm that wracked every nerve and every muscle until she was sobbing against the settee, impaled on his erection while he knelt impassive behind her.

As her spasms died away, but before her breathing had calmed, she heard Hugh say something and the potent lad lifted her easily, lay her on her back on the carpet and entered her again, slowly, possessively, penetrating her before pausing for the cameras. Then slowly but easily he rolled, taking her until she was astride him, knees on the carpet either side of his hips, able to move as she needed to, up and down as she liked until she felt herself coming again, letting herself sink slowly onto him as her body shuddered and her inner muscles squeezed around the thick column spearing up inside her.

'Okay,' said Hugh, and the youth rolled her over again, rising to his feet, positioning Susie on her knees with the enormous serpent pulsing right in front of her spellbound face, and when he came the viscous seed splashed into her open mouth, onto her cheeks and into her hair, and dripped from her chin onto her breasts and into her cleavage, giving the club members a final sequence of stunningly erotic photographs.

'She's absolutely perfect,' the host quietly complimented Hugh, nodding pensively. 'Perfect... just perfect.' But he did not say what he felt Susie was absolutely perfect for, though the calculating look in his eyes suggested he knew very well what he was talking about, and it wasn't just her qualities as a model.

Chapter Nine

'There, see him?'

Hugh was with the club member Susie had secretly thought a bit effeminate, and he most certainly could see 'him' as he studied the pictures of Susie spread-eagled on the settee.

All of his transparencies – like everyone else's – were green and blurred, which was just the way Hugh intended them to be. But all these pictures showed something on film that had most definitely not been present in the room at the time.

Hugh bent over the light box again, and applied the magnifying glass to eye and transparency. It was dark and corrupted, unusable to all practical intent, but still good enough for basic outlines to be discernible, though most of the detail was lost in the green fog Hugh's lighting had produced.

A group of men clustered around the settee, taking photographs of Susie who had one hand between her legs. All of that was okay, nothing untoward there. However, at one end of the settee stood the figure of a man who was not taking pictures, but apparently observing, and apparently watching Susie as closely as everyone else. Hugh knew there was no way in the world that this person had been in the room at the time, or he would have noticed him, not least because he was stark naked. And a magnifying glass was utterly unnecessary to know this, since he sported a substantial erection, far and away the longest, thickest and stiffest appendage Hugh had ever seen.

It was impossible to make out what he looked like; his features were distorted and blurred, though Hugh was sure he could see teeth, which suggested he was smiling. Sometimes he seemed to be wearing a hat of some sort, and sometimes Hugh concluded he was just the unlucky owner of a very pointed head.

It was all extremely vague, hardly more than a trick of the light, and Hugh probably would not have noticed the shape at all if it had not been pointed out to him. Indeed, he'd seen a few other pictures from the evening – just held them up to the light when other members had shown him their appalling misfortune with the green smears – and he hadn't noticed anything on them, although he hadn't been looking for details. In fact, he'd hardly glanced at them at all, just enough to make it look convincing. After all, he knew what was wrong with them, and none of the others had mentioned a shadowy figure.

In fact, Susie's effeminate one even said the others had strenuously denied the existence of such an apparition on their pictures. But no one would come round and show him, or let him visit with his pictures so they could compare.

'I'm sure they know something,' he said carefully, as if wondering whether Hugh was part of the conspiracy as well, or if he was an outsider too. 'I'm sure they all have the same thing and are just pretending they haven't,' he declared.

'Why would they do a thing like that?' asked Hugh.

'Money,' he whispered mysteriously, refusing to be drawn on quite how a series of spoiled pictures could have any kind of value.

'May I keep one for testing?' Hugh asked casually, but the sheets were snatched quickly away from him. 'Tell you what,' he said brightly, trying to appear nonchalant. 'Let me re-photograph them,' he offered, and was grudgingly given permission to re-shoot three pictures on his digital camera.

Once his sulking visitor had gone, muttering darkly about unseen forces and conspiracies, Hugh sat down at the computer and started work. Knowing why the pictures were green and cloudy was a help, but not a cure. Detail not recorded on the film at the time of exposure could not be restored or recovered because it just wasn't there. Dissolving the cloudiness and revealing information that was there could be done, but only if one knew what Hugh did about how the pictures had been spoilt. But uncovering that information, though it once again revealed enough of Susie and what was being done to her to interest a casual viewer, also removed all traces of the shadowy figure.

Any other pictures and Hugh would have expected the strange presence to be a product of the emulsion or the developing agent. But he'd carefully chosen three pictures from the start, middle and end of the roll just given him. So that was a no-no. And he knew that because of the way the discoloration had been produced it could not be a trick of the light, or a result of deliberate fogging. Likewise, extraneous shadows were ruled out as well.

Sitting back with a frustrated sigh, Hugh was baffled and angry. Being baffled by things photographic and technical was neither normal nor acceptable and he was not happy. Nor was his investigation over. Not by a long way.

Carefully considering his next course of action he decided that openness was his best ally, and he reached for the phone. Go straight to the top, he told himself as he dialled, straight to the very top.

Upstairs Susie stirred and rolled over; it was the first time she'd moved since climbing into bed some time around two in the morning, and if she'd been aware that it was now almost midday she would have understood why she felt so completely relaxed and rested after the strenuous activities of the previous evening.

Hugh didn't know if Susie asleep or not, but he did not want to be overheard, so he kept his voice low.

'I expect you know about the pictures,' he said carefully into the telephone. 'My pictures are also green.' He knew he could easily make that so to a few dupes if he needed examples of his disappointment. And disappointment was the emotion he tried to project, rather successfully, he thought. He wanted the leader of the club, the one who'd hosted the evening, to think of him as the upset husband who wanted a photographic record of the evening his wife was screwed by a group of strangers, but didn't get one.

It seemed to work; the leader shared his baffled sense of loss as best he could, even suggesting they should all get together and do it again.

'It won't be the same,' said Hugh. 'Nothing's ever going to be like that first shoot.'

'No, I do sympathise,' agreed the voice on the telephone. 'Why don't you pop over for a drink later, and we'll have a chat, see if we can't think of something that, um, restores the freshness of a first time.'

Susie was in the bath when Hugh slipped into the driving seat of his car, turning it towards the house on the outskirts of the city. Skirting the cathedral, through the narrow lanes that had survived the bloody history of the medieval town, leaving by the straight riverside road the Romans had laid two thousand years before, overlooked by the steep hill on which the rebels had fought, died and been executed hundreds of years ago, Hugh tried to cast himself in his appointed role, bravely trying to conceal his disappointment that he had no clear pictures of his wife being screwed.

'We can arrange another evening,' offered the club leader

sympathetically, once they were sitting in his gloomy study, 'but as you say; it's never the same. I think all our members would agree that there's nothing quite like the first time they saw their wife with another man. Or men, as in your case.'

Hugh was not sure if there was a small jibe in there somewhere. Had he noticed Susie enjoyed being used rather more than even the most ardent and understanding husband would have liked?

'Oh, I think we all guessed,' the leader smiled archly, answering Hugh's concerns, enjoying his own astuteness. 'And her real name…?'

'Susie.' Hugh smiled, trying not to smirk. He still had the power to reveal her any time he wanted.

'It never loses its appeal, of course, but the first time is something special. We may not be able to replace that, but we can perhaps offer something different to make up for it.'

Hugh raised an eyebrow, trying not to appear too eager, his cover story, his professional self and the real Hugh all in perfect synch on this one.

'I want to explain something to you, but first, before that, I would really like you to meet someone.'

He stood, opening a door, not the one through which they'd entered the study. He motioned and Hugh stepped through into a darkened room, with no windows, no lights, but a faintly pungent odour, rather like joss sticks.

Chapter Ten

'Bloody hell, it's huge.' Most of it was wet and shiny and glistened in the light, the remainder was dry, matt, smooth and brown. Hugh thought it was a great image. Even allowing for his egotistic delight in his own handiwork, the picture was good; he'd caught every detail with pin-sharp clarity, from the shiny wetness of the stretched pink lips that clutched eagerly around the dark shaft, to the arched tension of Susie's straining body and the young man's apparent aloofness as yet another orgasm rippled through her.

'Fucking fantastic,' Hugh murmured to himself, as he held down the mouse button and dragged the picture across the screen, examining it critically.

There was no need for him to be checking so closely, since all the relevant material was already in London. His filter had worked perfectly and his pictures were even more perfect. He'd shot everything on his new digital camera and emailed the best pictures the next morning while Susie was still asleep. Well, the best pictures for the paper, he thought smugly, the ones with the group of eager amateur photographers crowded round Susie's naked form while she played with herself, the ones with them reaching out to touch her with expressions of lustful desire on their faces, the ones of them screwing her and being sucked by her – all the ones with identifiable faces that would incriminate when they appeared on the front page.

But in between those 'working' pictures, Hugh had also taken shots for his private collection, where the subject of the pictures was not the group of men but the girl at their centre, in detailed close-up. These pictures of Susie being fucked would soon be appearing on numerous adult websites, with the faces suitably blurred or masked so there would be no comebacks. There was little money to be made in such a plan, but the power it gave him, the knowledge that Susie's pretty little pussy was exposed to the world, that her intimate moments of delight as her fingers gave her relief or the huge black erection thrust into her – this was his reward, this was his secret pleasure. And he was enjoying it now, poring over the computer screen, selecting the pictures *he* would publish, choosing the ones which revealed the most – not just her nakedness, but her character, her being. He could see the need, the lust, the pleasure, not just in her face, but in every line of her straining body. These were his best work ever.

'This is your best work ever,' stated the editor on the telephone, even though he hadn't seen the ones Hugh thought were the best ever. 'The pictures are perfect, the faces clear, and they're the right people, too. Just what we wanted; one of them is definitely the opposition candidate, and one of them we think is the mayor, false beard and all!'

Refraining from disappointing his boss by revealing that the bushy black beard was all real and therefore the person behind it was not the local mayor, Hugh basked in the warmth of the editor's approval for a few moments longer, before delivering his *pièce de résistance*.

'They've asked me to go back again,' he said. 'At the weekend.'

'You?'

'Well, us; Susie was quite a hit, actually.' Hugh was reluctantly forced to share the credit, but added nastily, 'Seemed to enjoy it as much as they did, if you ask me.

126

Couldn't get enough. I suppose that's why they want us back.'

'Back where?'

'To another of their little get-togethers.'

'We don't need it, to be honest. We've got everything we want with this lot. No need to stay around and repeat the exercise. Just pack your bags and come on home.'

'But it's not another photographic night,' Hugh argued. 'It's a party. A party with a difference, they told me. Fancy dress, no holds-barred and anything goes. At Mendlesham.' Hugh had deliberately waited with that one, before dropping it into the conversation like a well-timed bomb. There was a short delay before it exploded.

'Mendlesham?'

'That's what he said.'

'But that's… it's…' The editor's voice tailed away into silence as he contemplated the list of rich and famous people likely to be at Lord Crispin's weekend party, and then thought about the sort of compromising activities they might get up to if the party was as wild as Hugh had suggested it might be. Moments like this were what gave tabloid editors a hard-on, and he savoured it for some time, enjoying it rather more than his last visit to Soho's most sumptuous gentleman's club – of which he was a life member, naturally – until his pleasurable anticipation was interrupted by Hugh, adding more fuel to an already raging furnace.

'This might be the swingers' club we came here for originally,' he stoked helpfully, although he was sure the editor had already thought that far himself. But there was no point in taking chances. Not when he wanted to go to this party as badly as he did. The opportunity to indulge in his favourite passion – taking pictures of people indulging in passion – was almost limitless, and he wanted to go more urgently than he'd ever wanted anything else in his life.

'Okay,' said the editor slowly, and Hugh released the breath he'd been holding. 'We'll hold over the story for a week, while you two go to the party. As long as Susie doesn't mind, of course.'

'Oh no, boss, not at all. She loves it.' Hugh meant that remark quite literally, but the editor either didn't notice or didn't care. And so it was settled. They'd go to the party armed with all the secret recording devices Hugh could muster, and get as much dirt on as many people as they could manage in one evening.

Hugh switched off his mobile with a malicious grin, clicked the mouse button and watched a fresh picture unravel on screen. Flat on her back, legs wide apart, Susie was holding herself open with the outstretched fingers of one hand and aiming a cock between her thighs with the other. The expression on her face was one of desperate frustration, but in the next shot, with the stubby erection comfortably buried to the root, the frustration was gone, replaced by exquisite relief. In isolation neither picture was as expressive as the pair, and Hugh sniggered nastily as he gazed between them. 'Oh yes,' he said to himself, 'she loves it all right.'

What Susie didn't love, as Hugh discovered, was being told that it had been decided she would be reliving the previous night's experiences on a grander scale in a few days' time, and as a result she was irritable and he wisely refrained from pursuing the matter, switching into full oily charmer mode, fixing coffee and food and running her a bath – which he naturally watched in secret on his hidden cameras, recording it for posterity as well.

By late afternoon Susie was feeling more resigned to the whole plan and more receptive towards the instigator of it, following a long hot soak and something to eat.

Drowsily content she succumbed to Hugh's suggestion that they should attend the party on Saturday, mostly because of the lure of the celebrity guest list and potential for front page headlines. Or so she told Hugh, and to an extent herself, and if Hugh was fooled, deep down inside she wasn't. In truth, the prospect of being the centre of attention once more was not only arousing, but highly compelling.

She slept well again that night, eased into a peaceful slumber by the waves of pleasure produced by her gentle fingertips. Watching the bedcovers quiver, knowing what was happening beyond the reach of even his ingenuity and the best technology Japan had to offer, Hugh cursed silently, and for the first time in a long while looked through his library before selecting a video to watch. It was the day Susie first arrived in Norfolk, and Hugh settled back in his chair as her image entered the bedroom…

Next morning Hugh broached the subject of the party, and its particular fancy dress theme, which he'd so far failed to mention to her.

'A Roman orgy?' she asked, raising an incredulous eyebrow. 'In Norfolk?'

'Well, you know, Boadicea and all that.'

Susie had quite forgotten that the avenging Queen of the Iceni had been a Norfolk lass. Norwich, in fact, a woman spurred into violence by the rape of her daughters by some lecherous Roman tax collector.

'I thought you could be Cleopatra,' he suggested.

'Now that really *is* ridiculous,' she scoffed. 'She was Egyptian.'

'Yes, but she always wears a crown,' he said meaningfully. 'Very useful things, crowns… especially if you wanted to hide a camera.'

Susie saw the point at once. Togas and tunics provided

little in the way of hiding places for half a kilo of high-tech hardware, and few Roman noblewomen carried handbags. 'Surely just a little one, for lipsticks or something,' she protested, but Hugh would have none of it.

'Strict period costume, I was told,' he said adamantly. 'Strict period costume. That means no modern bits and bobs.'

'Well how are you going to hide one on your costume?' she demanded. 'Mark Anthony didn't carry a briefcase, did he?' Hugh smirked odiously, and she knew he'd done something clever. Fumbling among the rubble of a worktop strewn with electronic components, bits of wire and various tools, he produced a broad leather belt and pouch, from which dangled an authentic-looking Roman sword in a decorated leather scabbard.

'Recorder in the pouch,' he boasted triumphantly, camera in the hilt. 'He pointed to where three large jewels embellished the handle of the sword. 'It's the big one,' he said unnecessarily, because now she was examining it closely, Susie could tell that although two of the stones were coloured glass the largest of the trio was a plain, impersonal black: a lens. She handed it back without a word. It was a masterpiece of Hugh's art, she had to admit; invisible, simple and under direct control of its operator. By resting his hand on the sword hilt, like any swaggering fancy-dresser pretending to be a Roman general, Hugh could point the camera in any direction, at any subject, without anyone ever being suspicious. It was clever, but she couldn't bring herself to praise him.

'There's one in your crown, too,' he said, reaching for a shiny gold object hidden among the debris of his workbench. 'A bit heavy, but it's all self-contained. You can take it off whenever you like. Just remember to put it on something strategically positioned and point it in the right direction.'

'Where's the rest of it?' she asked.

'That's it. All of it. It's a self-contained unit and all you have to do—'

'No, not the camera,' she interrupted. 'The costume.'

'Oh, just get a big white sheet or something. You can fix it up.'

'What about you?'

'Me?'

'Your costume.'

'Got it already. From the hire shop near the theatre.'

'Oh, thanks very much,' she sulked.

It took an afternoon for Susie to complete her own costume, after an hour in the library looking for pictures of Cleopatra. But by the end of the day she had what she needed, and after only a brief outing on Friday morning she'd acquired her own stroke of genius – a dark straight wig with a fringe low over her eyes. Not only did it look good, but everyone would know it was a wig and not be surprised if she had to wear her crown at all times in order to keep her hair on. She thought herself very clever. Perhaps not as clever as the ornate golden object with its snake design, the neck and head raised to strike, the gaudy eyeball pattern painted on the cobra's outstretched hood acting as perfect camouflage for the well-positioned lens, but very clever nonetheless.

'I wonder what you'll see at the party,' she asked the cobra, lying back on her bed, holding the crown up high with one hand, pulling her skirt up with the other, seeing herself as she imagined she would be on Saturday night, white gown pulled roughly aside, legs held apart by eager hands, fingers touching, pushing, penetrating.

Pulling her panties aside she let her fingers trace a fiery path up and down the soft pink lips, feeling the heat, feeling the wetness, feeling them open wider, asking her to push deeper.

Frowning with concentration Hugh twirled the buttons on his control panel, switching from camera to camera, cutting between the wide shot of Susie on her back across the bed with her knees high and wide and the close-up view, frame filled with wet pinkness and thrusting fingers.

But as Susie's thoughts joyously travelled every known path of human depravity with herself at the centrepiece, revelling in the imagined sensations, Hugh's pleasure was slightly dulled by his own perception of what Saturday night had in store. He'd already received one phone call from a member of the camera club, asking if Hugh's pictures had also assumed a somewhat murky appearance, as if taken underwater. Secretly delighted at his own success, Hugh had managed to share the poor man's disappointment without giving the game away, but now realised that part of his Saturday evening at least would be spent comparing notes and recriminations with the other members of the club who were likewise distressed by their lack of photographic success.

Chapter Eleven

It was a different house this time. Hugh had driven them there, heading out of the city, out into the flat farmland with its ruined churches and dark spinneys of crowded woodland, through one or two tiny villages and then along a series of narrow lanes. They'd left late and now it was truly dark, despite the moon washing the fields with silvery light.

Filled with the dread excitement of adventures unknown, Susie sat in the passenger seat in silence, wishing the cold fingers of apprehension would stop their constant griping in her tummy and leave her with just the warmth of arousal between her legs, even though she knew it was impossible. Fear made her wet, it was that simple. No gripes meant no fear, and that meant no arousal.

Arriving at the house alarmed her still more. The sheer size of the place was intimidating enough, a rambling mansion overlooking a sweeping drive that was probably more than half a mile long. It was, as any estate agent might have said, a secluded location.

But at least she didn't feel nervous about her costume. She'd been afraid of looking – and feeling – silly, tripping up a suburban drive in full Queen of Egypt garb, but out in the countryside there were no nosey neighbours to see or care.

At the top of the steps leading up to the grand front door Susie was relieved to see two burly Roman soldiers, with helmets shields and spears, standing guard in a welcome confirmation that they'd come to the right place on the right night, and were not about to be greeted by mine host dressed in immaculate dinner suit and black tie. That was a relief, but she was still nervous as her gold sandals slipped a little on steps of granite, weathered by hundreds of years' service at the family home of the Crispins. Roundheads, cavaliers, Elizabethan courtiers, all had stood there before her, and somehow her unusual attire didn't seem too out of place now. The history of Mendlesham had at least halved the two thousand year gap between Susie and the queen she was dressed as.

The reception area was capacious and suitably devoid of anything that might have dated it, and the two doors that stood open led into a huge pillared hall, that to Susie seemed Roman in every way; in the interests of authenticity for the night it had in fact been stripped of furniture and decoration, and large swathes of cloth in cream and white disguised the area, so that it might easily have been the Roman palace it was intended to be. And at the far end a large fountain, apparently built from solid marble, filled one corner, with babbling water dribbling from the mouths of tiny angelic figurines. It looked authentic, but was surely made from plastic and specially erected for the party – which on its own spoke volumes about how much cash had been spent in the quest for authenticity.

On either side of the fountain stood an iron cage, and Susie was stunned to see that in each prowled a large black cat. Not a domestic black cat, but a sleek panther or a puma, or something like that. Their eyes were keen, missing nothing, and they occasionally sniffed the air as if ready to eat and hunting the scent of their next meal.

Around the room were low couches, like those she'd seen in history books of actual Roman mosaics, and low tables groaning with food; huge bowls of fruit, large hams, turkeys and roasts, vast choices of cheese and bread and jugs of wine or ale. Susie was lost in admiration for the attention to detail and the overpowering sense of realism the design and layout provided. This was a fancy dress evening like no other she'd ever been to.

'Ah, there you are.' It was the host from the other night, the actual Lord Crispin, welcoming them theatrically with open arms. 'Glad you decided to come. She looks perfect,' he said to Hugh, ignoring Susie almost completely, except as an object of admiration, just as he had at the photo shoot, just as if she was a fine piece of art or a well trained pedigree bitch of some kind.

Hugh accepted the compliment as his due, and leaned closer as the photo club leader began to speak in lower tones. 'Everything is as we said,' he murmured, and Hugh leaned even closer, so the rest of his words were lost to Susie. After a few seconds the man looked searchingly at Susie. Personal authority was a strange enigma, she thought, for he looked every bit as assured in a toga and laurel wreath as he had in his business suit. But then he fitted into his surroundings perfectly; the room was full of men in togas, women in plain white robes and soldiers in short tunics, with swords and sandals and plumed metal helmets. And among the throng, dressed in simple white tunics and carrying jugs of wine and plates of fruit, drifted male and female servants; slaves, she supposed, in the strict obedience to costume, custom and practice Hugh said was a mandatory feature of the evening.

She was surprised she hadn't been dressed as a slave girl herself, for it was exactly the sort of thing she'd expect to give Hugh a cheap thrill. Instead she looked and felt regal, her cream wraparound robe made from beautiful silk, the gold chain around her waist holding it in place with a loose knot and a single small pin, and not knowing what arrangements Egyptian women made about underwear, she wore only the briefest white panties.

She was also surprised to find there was no other Cleopatra present; it seemed such an obvious choice.

'Drink?' Crispin offered, and one of the slave girls passing by knelt, offering a tray of glasses brimming with wine.

Susie took one and so did Hugh, who immediately turned away from her, speaking to the man again in low tones. Susie was too enthralled to be as annoyed as she would otherwise have been, and instead gazed around the room, letting the tiny camera take in the scene. Because Hugh could point his more accurately and switch it on and off his would be the most vital pictures of the evening, and hers would be there as backup. At least that's how he explained it. What he really meant was that he expected Susie to be too busy to take pictures of any value, and would instead be featuring prominently in his.

The room was busy, quite full, at least a hundred people, she thought, maybe more, perhaps even double that. She let her gaze wander slowly from one to the next, trying to get faces on camera. But it wasn't easy to concentrate on work because she felt so much a part of the atmosphere, and was shocked at how easy it was to fall into the mood of the event so quickly.

As the man with Hugh – he'd still not been introduced to Susie by name – led them through the room between the tall pillars and the tables laden with delicacies, she saw the kind of things that probably hadn't been seen by anybody in two thousand years. On a couch in the far corner a man was feeding a woman grapes with one hand, while his other groped around inside her toga, toying with her ample breasts as his growing arousal tented the front of his short tunic. It looked to Susie like a scene from a film of ancient Rome, or a painting come to life.

Grand double doors led out into the peaceful evening, to

an elevated patio with ornate stone balustrades and views across to distant, dark rolling hills. The small grottos around the vast gardens, the illuminated ribbed pillars and the white statues rising elegantly from hedges and shrubs – all of it looked as though it might easily have been there for two thousand years, that nothing had changed in this outpost of an empire synonymous with style, decadence and depravity.

Wondering if the setting and the atmosphere had the same surreal effect on the rest of the assembled company as it did on her, Susie eventually asked, 'Where are all these guests from?' She was utterly enthralled by what she'd seen so far, and that fuelled her natural inquisitive nature. 'Who are they all?'

Crispin looked at her for a while, and then eventually answered, 'Friends,' the tone in his voice unable to mask a natural caution. 'Some are friends who share a mutual interest in the full enjoyment of life, in a similar way to you. In fact,' he went on, 'exactly like you, really.'

Susie felt a little embarrassed, remembering how intimately he knew her, as he continued. 'There's always one who does and one who watches,' he said. 'And it has long been apparent that whilst both of them think they're getting the most out of the arrangement, in fact there is always one who benefits the most. But as long as neither of them really knows, then they are happy to visit us on these occasions as pleasure seekers.'

'And the others?' she asked.

'The staff.' He gazed around the terrace at the people quietly milling about, some laughing lightly, some drinking and eating. 'My family has owned this estate for hundreds of years. Most who work here also live on the estate, and their families have done so for hundreds of years. Their great-grandfathers worked for my great-grandfather and so on back through the generations. In that sense, and in the fact that their loyalty to this house and this family is unquestioning, they are all friends.'

Susie listened politely.

'I know it seems an anachronism to talk like that these days, and a politically incorrect one at that, but I'm afraid it's true. The people who live and work on the estate all feel the same sense of loyalty to the family as their relatives have done for many, many years. Let's be fair, not much has changed in that time – not in this part of Norfolk, at least.' As if he could see the questions forming in Susie's mind and on her lips, he swept them away with several more broad strokes of his opinionated brush. 'Hard for outsiders to believe it, I'm afraid, but nonetheless true. There are some people on the estate who've hardly ever left it. Take him, for example,' he gestured towards a Roman soldier with a weathered face and grey hair, resolutely guarding a table of food from unseen adversaries. 'Old Marshal's typical. He went into Norwich on the bus once, in the fifties. Said it was too noisy and he couldn't walk without bumping into people, so he's never been back. His wife took his word for it and she's never been there at all.'

Susie considered the possibility that in this modern day there could be entire villages of people who had never expanded their horizons beyond the one that was physically visible, and found it hard to accept.

'I know, I know.' The man smiled his superior smile. 'But there it is.'

'And the guests?'

'Like yourself, my dear,' he said, somewhat condescendingly. 'They range from friends and acquaintances, to people with a common interest, something to offer, something to give in exchange for a taste of the good life, however brief.' He saw the look on Susie's face.

'Oh yes, we have no illusions here. We have a certain style, a certain level of luxury and people want to be a part of it, they want to belong, to enjoy. And most of them will do anything in exchange. Anything.' He'd chosen the word carefully, she could see. 'They'll abandon their principles, their morals, they'll set aside discomfort, displeasure and even disgust, if it gets them what they want. Greed is a far more powerful motivator than those not in a position to exploit it would believe.'

Even if Susie hadn't seen enough of life already to know that most people were capable of most things, his casually assured manner would have convinced her he was speaking the truth – and speaking from experience.

'Take Rosanna, there,' he continued, waving a languid finger in the direction of a pretty girl drifting towards them. 'She's the daughter of a business acquaintance. The family is financially comfortable but not, well, not excessively rich.' He smiled confidently to indicate that he himself was indeed, well, excessively rich. 'Certainly not rich enough for her tastes,' he went on. 'She wants the lifestyle, the parties, the yachts, the holidays, the fit young polo players, but she hasn't the money to partake. On the other hand, she does have a certain... currency. Everything has a price, and so does everybody.' He smiled as the girl brushed past them with a sparkle in her eyes and an inscrutable smile dancing on her lips, that suggested an awareness of being talked about, and loving it.

'My dear,' he said, and she paused and smiled angelically at him. 'This is *Caroline*.' His inflection had Susie concerned that he knew it wasn't her real name, but Rosanna clearly read it differently, apparently assuming Susie to be competition, for she cast a fierce glare back at Susie as she smoothly, arrogantly moved on towards another chattering group... and straight into a Roman soldier,

139

knocking the silver tray of drinks he was holding clanging and crashing to the flagstones.

'Stupid man!' Rosanna hissed at the poor individual as he instinctively started to bend towards the carnage of wine and glass. 'Look what you've done!' Her hand lashed out, landing flat across the side of his face with a slap that silenced any conversation that lingered following the clatter of the tray hitting stone. 'Don't just stand there like an idiot, you great ox! Clear it up!' Her hand lashed out again and the soldier stood impassive as her hand struck across his face again.

'Tie her,' someone calmly interceded. It was an urbane, silver-haired man of evident authority, and the burly soldier immediately grabbed the indignant girl's arms, another swiftly moving to assist him, Susie barely able to believe it was the same haughty female she was watching, her snooty expression and demeanour evaporating dramatically. Cringing away from the two soldiers as if afraid of having her slaps returned, she was unable to conceal genuine trepidation or the tears that threatened to spill forth, the high and mighty exterior visibly melting.

'Tie her,' the man calmly repeated, and the soldiers obeyed, manhandling her against a large pillar, facing it. She was sobbing quite openly now, desperately straining to look over her shoulder for help or support or a friendly face, but finding none in the crowd that gathered, muttering and nodding sagely with a strange look in their eyes and a slightly ragged edge to their muted comments.

The two soldiers pulled her arms around the pillar and tied her wrists with a leather strap, which appeared to be part of their uniforms. Her cheek was against the column of stone, her pale face turned towards the side where Susie was standing. Her eyes were screwed shut and she was sobbing gently.

'Hold this,' said the man, passing his wine to the soldier beside him, who had already unbuckled his sword belt and was offering the leather strap in exchange.

Taking it in a determined grip he moved closer and lifted the hem of the girl's short dress, revealing a pair of firm, naked, perfectly rounded buttocks.

The men in the growing crowd murmured with appreciation, but their whispers were silenced by the whistle of the leather belt through the air and the flat crack as it licked across the exposed buttocks, making them quiver as the girl squealed in shock and surprise. The blotchy red line had only just started to appear when the belt lashed down again, making her wail once more, and the man paused, waiting for the next welt to appear while the girl sobbed, biting her lip against the pain she felt and the sting she expected.

The man raised his arm and lashed out again, using all his strength. Fortunately for her he was quite elderly and his blows were not as powerful as they could have been, but it was still a cruel blow, landing straight across both buttocks and making the hapless girl wail for the third time.

Chest heaving from the exertion, the man surveyed his handiwork with obvious relish before turning to the soldier beside him and holding out the borrowed belt. Susie battled to control her thundering heart and rapid breathing, provoked by the sudden eroticism of the scene. The instant dispensing of punishment, the lovely naked bottom whipped mercilessly, and the growing marks that signalled the sentence had been expedited, all left her breathless with excitement.

'Take her,' the man said between ragged breaths, and the girl tugged on her bonds, shaking her head when she heard the words. Puzzled, Susie watched as the two soldiers released the girl and dragged her away.

The host's face was an implacable mask as he watched everything, and Susie struggled to control the butterfly dog-fight in her stomach and the molten heat between her legs, stoked to new intensity by the look on the girl's face, who clearly knew what sort of fate awaited her. Susie could only guess what that might be, but the anguished expression left her in little doubt about the nature of the punishment that awaited the poor girl.

And though Susie had fought for self-control she knew her bright eyes and flushed cheeks revealed to all who cared to look that the scene had affected her considerably.

'Another enthusiastic guest playing her role to the full,' the host mused as he led Susie back inside. 'And loving every moment she was too.'

But Susie, who'd interpreted the reaction of the girl differently, didn't believe him even slightly. Which was probably a good thing, because it meant she and Hugh might very well be on to something. On the other hand, if they were on to something they would have to be extremely careful not to let their guard slip.

Without a watch to measure the passing time, Susie didn't know if her camera was still sending its pictures to the recorder outside in the car, but she hoped so, because so far nothing truly exciting had occurred, and what they needed was a collection of genuinely scurrilous pictures, preferably of known people doing things they shouldn't. But her thoughts were suddenly interrupted by the clapping of hands and the host calling for silence and close attention from everyone, which he received immediately, the bustle and murmur dying away quickly to leave a tense air of expectation.

Politely he thanked one and all for their attendance and participation, reminding them that taking part to the full was what made the evening such a success. 'I hope you

will continue to enjoy yourselves for the rest of the night.'
His smile left no doubt about the meaning of his words and
induced a few knowing mumbles, bawdy sniggers, and
raised glasses. 'So with that in mind,' he continued, 'it's
time for the games to begin.' Again he clapped his hands,
twice, and the partygoers looked around eagerly to see
where and how the entertainment would commence.

'No feast would be complete without a sporting contest,'
he said, 'and we begin with the traditional entertainment of
our time. Two males will now demonstrate their strength
and agility as they wrestle for us.' As he spoke two lean
young men appeared by his side, and Susie joined in the
collective gasp that was almost exclusively drawn from
the women in the room, for the two men were handsome,
glistening with oil, and utterly naked.

'The bout ends when one of the contestants is unable to
continue for any reason,' announced the host, explaining
the rules. 'They may not use any weapon, but they can use
hands and feet in any way they choose. The loser gets only
the accolade of taking part. The winner, as always, receives
a prize, and tonight I'm glad to say that our members have
donated a total of five thousand pounds.' Nods of heads,
comments of approval and a ripple of restrained applause,
which Susie joined in with, accompanied this news. But
five thousand pounds! This was no demonstration contest,
this was going to be a real battle and she felt a little clutch
of nervous fear in her tummy – and warmth radiating
between her thighs, reminding her that she was still
simmering with arousal.

Everyone moved out to the gardens, Susie going with
them, and formed a circle on the perfectly manicured,
sheltered lawn. They separated to create a narrow path to
let Crispin through, and he took his place on a small platform
overlooking the small arena the encircled bodies created.

Susie looked around for Hugh but there was no sign of him, and now she thought about it, she couldn't really recall the last time she had seen him. But there was no time to worry because the crowd was cheering as the wrestlers faced each other, prowling warily before they rushed together, grappling for a hold on oiled muscle and flesh, slipping and falling, and an animalistic roar of enthusiasm marked first blood, a fine spray from an assaulted nose, smearing over both glistening bodies in their sweaty embrace.

As the two young men rocked and punched and kicked the crowd yelled and cheered and clapped, many of the women more animated than the men, screaming louder, waving their arms as they encouraged the fighters, whose combat grew increasingly vicious and bloody. Susie had never been a fan of boxing or wrestling, but she'd seen women by the ringside and knew the carnal effect that violence could have on even the most refined of them, and she was seeing it now as the veneer slipped away and passions quickly surfaced. Encouraged, no doubt by the whole escapist atmosphere of the evening, modern standards of behaviour vanished and Susie was looking at scenes that hadn't been observed since the days of the Roman circus, when the poorer boys of the city would make it a point to sit next to a woman of wealth and breeding, in the hope of being able to touch them when the bloodlust created near hysteria. They were successful more often than not, and many were rewarded with fiercely quick couplings under the dark colonnades. Now, in modern England, it was just the same, hands everywhere, the older men fondling the young slave girls and the young men making free with whichever woman was near – in some cases two, Susie noticed, one young man with a hand thrust into the togas of the women on either side of him as they cheered the battle raging in the small grass arena. The host seemed not to notice, eyes watching the fighters intently, completely absorbed.

Then a powerful kick landed on a jaw and sent one of the fighters tumbling backwards, spraying blood from nose and mouth, spattering the women nearest him, but they apparently neither noticed nor cared. Caught up in the frenzied moment Susie cheered as well, and then stopped, feeling foolish, but no one was paying attention to her. There were more cheers as the victim rose unsteadily to his feet, the rabid crowd clearly delighted the fight was not yet over, clearly aroused at the prospect of more blood and more violence. One of those, an attractive woman, was leaning forward slightly, and Susie realised her toga was rucked up at the back and an enterprising male was screwing her from behind, clinging on desperately, trying to stay inside her until he finished what he'd started.

And he was not the only one, Susie realised. Over in some bushes, away from the light of the small arena and only partly visible in the dark, a male bottom rose and fell and clearly there was a supine female beneath it, though it was hard to discern features in the tangle of robes and undergrowth. And there was a woman on her knees, head beneath the tunic of a soldier who stood impassively on guard by one of the elaborate statues, trying to remain stoic and conceal his delight as the head below his waist bobbed faster and faster.

Everyone was so totally absorbed in the violence of the fight or the indulgence of sexual gratification that Susie was sure she'd not be missed, so she began to slip slowly backwards through the debauched throng and headed back inside, relieved to see that the large hall was deserted; she'd worried that she'd been too involved outside and left it too late, that there would be too many people milling about.

But luckily there weren't.

If anyone asked she was searching for the toilet, but really she was looking for the girl who'd been whipped earlier, to see if she had truly been an enthusiastic guest or if – as Susie suspected – something more sinister was going on. The girl's tears had been real, Susie was certain, as had her whole reaction to the punishment, but more significant was her reaction to what was going to happen out of sight of the gathered guests and servants. She'd been genuinely frightened by that threat, Susie knew.

And Susie was determined to find out why.

Chapter Twelve

The doorway to the kitchen gave easily at her touch, opening onto stone steps that curved down and away to the right. Hoping that everyone who should be working was outside watching the violent entertainment, Susie crept silently down the steps, and as the sounds from above faded they were replaced by sounds from below; sounds that made the hairs on the back of her neck stand up and made her doubly aware of the anxiety in the pit of her stomach. Standing in gloomy shadow and peering carefully around the corner at the foot of the steps, the sounds louder now, she knew that the girl had not been acting. Whatever happened upstairs *may* have been for entertainment's sake, but this was definitely different. This was no playacting. This was real.

A group of men stood in a loose circle. At their centre was the girl, still pinioned by her arms, still crying softly. In front of her stood the older man who had meted out the public punishment.

'I'm glad you're not really my daughter,' he said with genuine menace. 'I'd be ashamed to own up to it if you were.' His voice was calm and even, despite the deep breathing which gave away the full extent of his anger. But his icy demeanour was more unnerving than a tantrum would have been, thought Susie. A man with self-control like his might be capable of anything, but her thoughts were interrupted.

'Now it's time you learned some humility, my girl,' he said.

'No,' she pleaded through her tears.

'Well past the time,' he confirmed, scorning her with his eyes as well as his tone. 'You've been running about the place acting like you own everyone and everything, and now you'll just have to learn the truth the hard way.'

This obviously had nothing to do with what had happened earlier with the tray of drinks and the unwarranted assault on the soldier, thought Susie, holding her breath and peering carefully around the stonework. The man had his back to her so she couldn't read his expression, but it was frightening enough to keep the girl in tears.

'Please,' she begged quietly, genuine fear and pleading in her voice, and Susie thought he must release her now that she'd been punished enough. The soldiers thought so too, judging by their uncertain looks, but they brightened visibly when the man slowly shook his head, the silver hair shiny under the lights that hung down from the dark ceiling above.

'You can come home with me now if you like,' he said, and the smiles faded. 'But if you do you will pack your bags tomorrow morning and leave. Forever. I want you to leave home and leave me alone. Leave me in peace with my memories of your mother, before you spoil those as well by growing to look like her. And as of Monday, when I have spoken to my solicitor, I shall change my will so you get precisely what you deserve... nothing.'

The girl looked at him, shock mingling with the fear on her face.

'Or you can remain here and show these men just how much you regret your arrogant, petulant, spoilt little girl temper tantrums.'

'No,' she gasped, disbelief written momentarily in her eyes before the fear took control of her expression once again.

The man shrugged. 'As you wish,' he said wearily. 'But

the choice was yours. Remember that always; the choice was yours.'

The look of horror was eloquent of her inner struggle as she compared the loss of current and future financial security against the price of keeping it: staying and appeasing the men whom she'd flagrantly and frequently abused and belittled, hiding behind her station over theirs. Susie felt a delicious spasm of apprehension as she put herself in the girl's place, imagining what it would be like for her to be left to the mercies of the leering, grudge-bearing group of men, and then hoped fervently that she made the right choice.

'Very well... I'll stay.' The girl's voice was almost inaudible, but Susie felt her heart leap when she heard it.

'I beg your pardon, Rosanna?' He inclined his head slightly forward.

'I said very well,' Rosanna repeated, lifting her chin resolutely, speaking more firmly, 'I'll stay.'

'Say it to them,' he commanded. 'They're the ones you've wronged with your attitude. Tell them you want to apologise for your behaviour. Tell them you want to wipe the slate clean by giving them the only thing you can really call your own. Tell them to enjoy themselves, that it's your gift to them.'

The expressions on those faces Susie could see from where she was hiding showed how popular these last words were, except with Rosanna, whose face was a mask of despair.

But then the trembling lip stilled and her chin jutted forward defiantly. 'No!' she said, almost stamping her foot. 'I've changed my mind. I won't do what you say.'

The man did not looked surprised by the mini rebellion. 'Goodbye, then,' was all he said, turning to leave the kitchen, and that was enough to finally defeat her for her resolve collapsed and she slumped, crying again. 'All right, all right,' she sobbed feebly. 'I will do what you say.'

'Then tell them.'

Susie thought he was relentless.

'I'll stay,' Rosanna confirmed, her shoulders trembling.

'No,' he pressed, 'tell them it's what you want. Ask them if they would like that. Maybe they don't want you here, and who could blame them after the way you've behaved? Ask them.'

Suddenly confronted by the realisation that her entire future depended on a group of men whom she had consistently treated like dirt brought fresh tears flooding. Clearly Rosanna realised that life as she knew it depended not just on their goodwill, but on their desire to enjoy her favours – and she might just have treated them badly enough for long enough to find they'd rather deprive her of everything than give themselves a few moments of entertainment. And worst of all, she knew that whatever decision they made, she was not going to enjoy it.

Susie read all these conflicting thoughts in Rosanna's face in fleeting seconds, before the poor girl's expression settled as she realised there was only one choice she could make. And she realised that they knew it too. She was going to have to beg them to have their fun with her, and they might just scorn the offer as she had scorned them so many times. But in the end, after they'd made her grovel they would accept, and then they would have their fun and their revenge.

Rosanna hung her head, clearly not able to look at them, and said softly but clearly, 'I want to stay, if you will let me.'

It was a brave act, but it didn't satisfy the older man. 'Ask nicely,' he said coldly. 'Always remember your manners.'

'Please?' she asked meekly, and the men's lusty looks

more than told Susie what their response would be. It was the one she had wanted to hear as well, and a glowing warmth spread between her legs.

'Good.' The older man nodded his satisfaction. 'Then make the most of your evening. Try to learn something from it.' He scanned the semicircle of faces and nodded at each. 'You heard what Rosanna asked you; she wants you to teach her some manners. Please do as she requested.'

Without another flicker of emotion he turned to walk away, and Susie saw his face, still pale, still impassive, an icy detachment in his eyes. They were truly unsettling, cold beyond belief, penetrating and all seeing, and her heart and breathing stopped as they bored into the darkness, locking onto hers...

Had he seen her? Had he sensed her presence? Time stood still for Susie, her pulse pounding in her temples, the tension making her nipples stiffen slightly and her palms clammy with perspiration.

He was leaving the kitchen, and he was therefore heading in her direction! Susie knew that if she didn't move fast she would be discovered spying, skulking in the shadows, and then, and then she didn't quite know what, but the prospect of being caught by Rosanna's austere stepfather carried more fear than just messing up a good story.

Knowing she had better move or suffer the consequences, Susie ducked agilely out of sight behind the stone wall and scurried up the steps as fast and as silently as she could, as if the devil himself and all the hounds of hell were on her tail, looking for the small door she'd seen near the top, opening it quickly but quietly and slipping into a tiny store cupboard full of crockery and iron pots.

She waited, crouching in the darkness, not daring to breath, convinced he would hear her if she did, convinced she heard the rustle of his toga as he passed the door on his way back up to the party. And moments later she thought she heard the door at the top of the steps open and close, but she wasn't certain.

She stayed still, trying to control her breathing, waiting. She ought to go and find Hugh, she knew. The girl, Rosanna, should be rescued from the men below in the kitchen, even if she was a snotty cow.

Five minutes must have passed while she hid in the dark, listening for any indication that the man was still lurking out on the steps. But she heard nothing more. He must have gone, returned to the party, leaving Rosanna to the mercy of those men. In her place, Susie knew she'd be desperate for someone to help her.

She carefully opened the door and crept out of the tiny store cupboard, her heart hammering. In the murkiness she glanced up at the door a few steps above, the way back to the revelry. But she hesitated, and then turned and started back down, alone.

Chapter Thirteen

Susie could hear Rosanna before she saw her; a whimpering that slowly changed and grew louder, becoming a wail of distress. And as she got closer, carefully descending step by step, something else too came to her ears, a regular slapping and urgent grunting which Susie recognised only too well, and she knew what to expect as she peered around the rough edge of the stone wall into the vast kitchens.

Barely twenty feet away, Rosanna was lashed face down across a large table, wrists and ankles tied to its stout wooden legs with leather belts. Unable to escape her tormentors she was crying again, tears catching the light as they meandered across her cheeks and soaked onto the scrubbed wooden surface. And one of her tormentors was naked with his tunic bunched around his ankles, a portly man who looked old enough to be her grandfather, rutting away with an erection that was as red in flesh and blue in vein as his face and temples, his rotund gut creating the slapping sound against he raised buttocks every time he lunged forward, impaling her on his cock.

Rosanna was gasping with each inward thrust as her traitorous body responded to the physical stimulation of the intruding shaft. The wriggling attempts at escape had slowed, but she was still moving, the slow rise and fall of her firm bottom now in time with the man's efforts as she lost the battle to control her reactions. Unable to prevent her body's response, each gasping sigh was matched by a jerk of her hips and followed by a small cry of anguish.

The scene was raw and primeval, and produced a

paralysing arousal in Susie, who was frozen still in her hiding place, unable to do anything but watch. The other men, waiting their turn, were likewise motionless, but not silent. As Rosanna's response became increasingly evident, the murmurs of appreciation became increasingly bawdy.

'Not got yer nose stuck up in the air now, young madam,' observed one of them, with simple but accurate profundity.

'Yeah, toffee-nosed cow,' agreed another.

'Think yer too good for the likes of us, do you?' asked another.

'Not any more she don't, she'm not too good for us now.'

'Arr, yer happy enough to have a good bit of Norfolk up yer fanny now. Yer like that well enough.'

'Reckon she does.'

Susie reckoned she did as well. She was only too familiar with the number of ways in which a girl could be betrayed by a body that understood nothing more than instinct, and had no time for the niceties of etiquette or the formalities of a proper introduction. And, judging by her actions, it appeared that Rosanna's body worked on the same principle.

'Go on, you ol' fucker,' urged one, in the rich lowland burr of Norfolk, but 'the ol' fucker' needed no encouragement, for he was already at the point of no return, his face changing from bright red to deep purple as he pumped doggedly back and forth. And it was all getting too much for Rosanna, whose moans were almost completely absorbed into the steady grunts that accompanied the rapid thrusting as he gave her everything he'd got and her body began to move against his, showing him the tempo of her own need.

'Go on then, Rosanna,' goaded another, as the girl tightened her thigh muscles and tilted her striped bottom upwards even more, opening her body to the old man as her fingers tightened their grip on the edge of the table.

Watching from the shadows, Susie wondered what to do. She knew she should act, do something to help the girl on the table, but on the other hand if she did it would give the game away completely and probably not achieve very much except get her into the same predicament as Rosanna.

That was the rational decision for inaction, but a part of her knew there was another reason – the real reason – and it was deep between her legs where an aching fire of excitement raged furiously.

Not often before had she seen anything so intensely sensual and arousing as the scene before her; partly because it was sex at its most basic level, and she could feel the smouldering heat of it from where she hid, and partly because the of the choreography of it, with the girl bent over the table, the red stripes of a beating still imprinted on her buttocks, her tormentor turning her on and threatening to draw forth an orgasm despite her revulsion of him. This was the defining image of Susie's own sexuality, the image that had started with Miss Piggy at school and for some reason reoccurred at critical moments since then. It was impossible for Susie to look at the scene without seeing herself bent over the table, without feeling the leather straps burning across her buttocks, without feeling the penetration and arousal of her own body, without feeling the slow build-up of bliss, becoming needful, rising inevitably to the final betrayal of an explosive climax.

But there was more.

Clutching between her thighs, feeling her mound under her palm and fingers, feeling the warmth and wetness through her dress, the welcoming furrow as her fingers slid between slippery folds; it was the powerless arousal of the girl, this was what fired Susie's own excitement.

Rosanna's hips were moving faster, pushing her bottom

up to meet the man's thrusts, her sighs now gasps and sobs and pleading, an overpowering image of sexuality that was impossible to resist, and Susie was clearly not alone in finding it irresistible.

'Aaarrrrgghhh!' the man suddenly gargled, eyes bulging wider than ever as he bent back and stared up at the ceiling, his groin glued to her punished bottom, his fingers clamping savagely into her buttocks as she tensed, remained utterly still for long seconds, and then went slack on the tabletop.

When he eventually withdrew and bent jadedly to retrieve his tunic Susie wondered again whether to intervene, but once again convinced herself that, outnumbered as she was, it would be better to stay hidden. After all, Rosanna had agreed to stay, had asked to stay, in fact. Her stepfather had made quite sure of that.

'Turn her over,' said a gruff voice, interrupting Susie's thoughts, and as eager hands unbuckled the leather bindings Rosanna started struggling, trying to get away, but it was a vain hope as the lusty men grabbed her by wrists and ankles, pulling her to the floor, holding her while she twisted and floundered.

'Go on then, my pretty,' chuckled a man with bushy sideburns and ratty features. 'You know you'm been wanting this 'un.' As he spoke he pulled the shapely ankle he was holding, parting her thighs. His counterpart followed suit, spreading her legs wide. Her eyes widened as well, watching a younger one pull his tunic over his head to expose admirable muscles. He stood over her, toned torso planted on trim hips and sturdy legs, watching her, staring greedily between her legs, and as he looked Susie saw Rosanna's eyes widen even more... and then she saw why.

Oh my, she thought, and felt the sudden rush of warmth between her own thighs. Neither girl could take their eyes off it, like a young sapling thrusting up from below his waist, pulsing slowly from side to side, rearing ten inches or more into the air.

Rosanna shook her head in denial and squirmed, trying to get away from the advancing erection as he knelt, but leering soldiers held her arms and legs tightly.

'No...' she wailed as he rested it against her, guiding it downwards with one hand, spreading her glistening wet lips around the bulbous helmet.

'Arr,' he croaked happily as he felt the warmth and wetness of her, and leaned closer.

'Aaahhh...' she cried as he filled her, slowly, inexorably.

'Arr,' he mumbled again as he sank contentedly, deeper into the welcoming tightness.

Susie remained stock still, riveted to the spot, watching as he pressed himself home, inch by breathtaking inch.

'Mmmerrgh...' gasped Rosanna as he gradually came to a stop, with all his weight resting on her and all his incredible length inside her. The other men let go of her arms and legs and he watched, impassive, as her wriggles and gasps slowed until she was just rocking beneath his weight, gentle movements that slid her pussy up and down his column.

The sight was unbearably arousing, and Susie felt the slippery heat beneath her fingertips, soaking into the front of her dress, felt the knickers wet and slithery, material against material, the deep dark warmth of her body opening to the pressure of her touch.

'Uh!' grunted the youth, still motionless, resting against the slender shape beneath him.

'Mmmmm...' Rosanna rocked against him, easing him in and out of her body. 'Mmm... mmm...' she mumbled each time he sank deeper. Her hands, fingers outstretched, were on his chest, just resting there. Her knees rose as she drew her heels back against her bottom, opening herself and pushing harder against him.

Unaware that her hand had been pulling her hemline higher, Susie felt fingers on her thigh and moved her feet apart, giving her access to the soaking gusset that stretched over her seething desire. Resting one hand on the stone wall for support she raised a foot, placing it one step higher than the other, so her hand could reach deep between her parted legs as she watched Rosanna fucking the youth's huge cock.

Her hands had slid around and down, pausing briefly on the small of his back, but then she gripped his muscled buttocks in desperate need, grinding against him, gasps of pleasure punctuating the urgent slapping of flesh upon flesh.

Susie felt her fingers pushing deeper, a pale imitation of the solid thickness filling Rosanna as she heaved faster and faster and finally the youth could be still no more and Rosanna wailed in pleasure as he started moving, clenching muscles in his bottom driving him up and down, thrusting in and out as Rosanna raised her knees higher until she wrapped her legs around his, lifting to meet him, crying out over and over again. 'Aah... aah... aah... aah!'

Susie's fingers flew back and forth between her own legs in unison with his lunges, Rosanna gasping as he fucked her soundly, Susie pulling her knickers down and stepping out of one leg so she could push into herself as the boy pushed into the girl who had her head thrown back as she cried encouragement, opening herself to him, giving control of her body to the needs of her climax, urging him to give her what she wanted, hands on his hips, nails digging his buttocks, and suddenly he gasped as if he'd been punched and froze, immobile while she clung to him, hands and knees clutching as he pumped, slowing to a stop, panting as if she'd run a marathon and lost, sucking in air, gasps that turned to moans and then tears, because she'd given herself away, revealed everything and gained nothing in return.

'Good boy,' said one of the onlookers. 'But I wish you'd waited. I'll never follow that.'

'Me neither,' said another.

Nor me, thought Susie, who had also been close to a climax when the youth had erupted inside Rosanna, but not close enough.

'I can't either. But I'm going to fuck her anyway.' Standing on the fringe of the group an old man stripped off his tunic, revealing a body so thin it made his modest erection look impressive by comparison.

He shuffled between Rosanna's thighs and lay on top of her, and she barely stirred as he took his erection in one hand and guided it between her soft sex lips.

'No,' she murmured quietly as she felt him enter her, but that was all, and she lay quite still as he started to rut away with little finesse. Although old he was energetic and thorough and her body reacted at once, lifting her knees, clutching his hollowed buttocks and pulling him deeper with a series of inward tugs.

There was complete silence apart from the breath hissing through his dry lips as he pumped, and the sweet sighs in her throat announcing her growing pleasure. Her face wincing with delight, her eyes closed, nipples as hard as little red buds she gripped him, pulling him deeper, guiding him as he fucked her.

Susie was holding her dress higher, hand busy, two fingers penetrating the soft, syrupy tunnel, thumb pressing into the top of the wet furrow, tickling the button that stood hard and sensitive as she tried to make herself climax with Rosanna, just as the old man made a gasping, wheezing, spluttering sound and slumped on top of the lovely supine girl.

Rosanna whimpered in frustration, not quite reaching her

goal in time, but it was too late and he rolled aside, lying on his back, chest heaving as he waited for his breathing to stabilise and the strength to return to his frail frame.

Fingers still moving, but slower now, Susie was almost as disappointed as Rosanna, who now lay motionless, breasts gently rising and falling as she breathed, legs apart, the glistening pinkness ready between them.

'Come on,' said one of the others, lifting the elderly man with ease, 'you come and have a rest over here. Looks like you could do with it.'

'Thass about killed the old boy, that has,' observed another.

'But what a way to go,' another chuckled.

'Yerrs,' growled a deeper voice, 'and not just for him. I wouldn't mind dying on a job like that myself. How often do you get the chance for a posh, beautiful fuck like 'er? Not offen, if ever.'

'More to the point, how often do *you* get the chance to fuck anything that don't have four legs?' one of them mocked, and they all laughed raucously.

Chapter Fourteen

Susie suddenly felt a compelling need to look behind her, and a hand flew to her mouth to suppress the gasp of shock, alert enough to smother any noise that might betray her presence to the mob in the kitchen.

There, a few feet away, stood a tall, slim, dark and handsome man, like the archetypal vampire in a dark cloak, almost completely hidden in the shadows apart from the pale smile and the eyes; burning gold in the dark, like a wild feline.

Suddenly Susie realised what she must look like, her skirt around her waist, legs apart, knickers dangling from one ankle, fingers deep between her thighs. But before she could compose herself he held up a warning hand.

He smiled, although his lips didn't move. But she was bathed in the warmth of his smile nonetheless, which radiated from his eyes. The golden gaze left her spellbound face and crept lower, where she felt it as a physical warmth, and knew he was staring at her breasts, lingering appreciatively, and then creeping lower still, between her legs. Then he looked at her face again, deep into her eyes, staring into her soul, and he nodded. She knew it was okay, that it was acceptable for her to be watching Rosanna and to be touching herself, to be enjoying the intense scene. She knew he wanted her to carry on, wanted to watch her watching.

As her hand began to move again she somehow knew he wasn't just a voyeur looking for cheap thrills, but that he wanted to enjoy the beauty of her arousal for its own sake.

She knew that the purity of her lust was part of his understanding and that his admiration and pleasure while watching her touch herself didn't cheapen her actions, but gave them grace and elegance.

Leaning back against the wall she put one foot on the next step up and lifted her skirt higher, making sure he could see as her hand moved steadily and her fingers stretched and spread. She knew he could see her body opening around the slippery digits, see perfectly well in the dark, and she felt the heat of his smile increase, bathing her in his pleasure.

His eyes flickered over her shoulder and hers followed his command, knowing he wanted her to look, and at once she knew that he too understood the emotions created by the primeval urgency of raw sex that was being enacted on the flagstone floor of the kitchen.

Another of the men was screwing Rosanna, and she hissed each time he dropped his hips like a piston. 'Yes... yes... yes... yes!' she gasped again and again, and Susie felt herself driven by the same need, fingers moving firmly and steadily, enjoying him watching her, enjoying him seeing her respond in a similar way to how Rosanna was responding.

And then the entwined couple squeezed each other and came together, and Susie was gripped by something too, something that had been eluding her for quite some time and was now making her tremble as waves of tension gripped her being, and she turned to make sure he was still watching her at that moment of orgasm, baring her body and soul, her mouth opening in a silent scream as he looked down into her with that penetrating golden gaze that saw everything, understood everything, and knew everything.

The stranger made no effort to move closer, as she expected him to. He stood motionless, eyes glowing with a fire of sexual arousal that could not be misunderstood. But he did not move closer.

Rosanna squealed as she was mounted yet again, distracting Susie, who glanced with diminishing interest at the ragged group, but when she dreamily glanced back the stranger was gone.

The big hall was deserted, and outside the noise of the crowd was far more subdued than it had been earlier during the fight. Susie stood on the raised patio area and gazed out into the night, over the lawns, witnessing a scene of flagrant depravity. The evening had descended into one mass orgy, naked bodies entwined like a heaving, living carpet before her astonished eyes, and as she wondered where the beautiful stranger had vanished to, and then if Hugh was somewhere in that writhing contortion of bodies, someone started molesting her bottom through her dress.

'Hey...' she objected, but the hands started lifting the hem anyway, mauling the backs of her thighs, pressing between her buttocks, reminding her shamefully that she'd left her discarded knickers on the kitchen floor, and then without any further preliminaries, spread her open and slipped steadily up between her moist sex lips, wriggling into her wetness without the courtesy of seeking permission first. But, as was usual for Susie, she gave in to the demands of her body without thinking, and her feet inched apart as the man pushed her shoulder and she was forced to support herself on the ornate stone balustrade overlooking the gardens.

Her dress was held up around her waist, there was a little urgent fumbling against her bottom, and then with one long stab the fingers were hastily replaced by a fat penis, as though its owner didn't want to give her the opportunity to change her mind, making her hunch her shoulders and gasp with the suddenness of the penetration. Her held lolled back and her eyes half closed, but in the reflection of the large French doors to their side she saw them in profile, and saw her lover, and it wasn't the dreamy stranger she'd assumed it to be, but a plump man with sweaty jowls and a bald head. His eyes were closed in grim concentration as he held her hips, his ruddy complexion raised to the night skies overhead, his feet planted resolutely wide as he leaned back from the waist for maximum penetration, and he rutted feverishly against her bent elegance as though it was the highpoint of his miserable life and he was going to make the absolute most of it before anything or anyone could come and snatch it away from him. And so Susie braced herself against his rabid onslaught, and closed her eyes fully as her treacherous body once again succumbed to the stimulus.

High up in the rear elevation of the building a small window closed slowly on a darkened room, the golden eyes which had been watching so intently through the narrow slit blazed momentarily, and the sound of a contented snarl was drowned by the decadent revelry below.

Chapter Fifteen

Wrestling with his conscience had been a relatively new experience for Hugh, so new that even though the area of his brain given over to such esoteric matters was minuscule, the fight had been long and hard.

But in the end the rewards were simply too enormous, and he'd accepted the offer put forward by the group's *real* leader, not Crispin, the host of the photo shoot and the orgy, whom Susie thought of as the leader because she didn't know any better. Not that Hugh had any inkling of the truth until it was explained to him. The real leader was so important he seldom appeared at any of the gatherings, although he was usually there, on the premises, observing but not participating. He looked familiar to Hugh, and he was certain that he was in the presence of a VIP of some sort, although politics was not normally a subject that gained much of his attention. In the end it was the voice that triggered his memory, and for a moment he started to pay attention until he realised the subject was every bit as dull as he'd thought.

The topic of conversation was, boringly enough, not sex and swingers, not sin and swapping in high places, nor even straightforward shagging. Hugh's hopes of being the man who filmed a top politician spanking his secretary or whipping up support from some young constituency wives in an altogether too literal manner faded from view as the man droned on and on.

And on... and on.

Politics was all it was – boring, everyday politics. After

a while Hugh gave up wondering if he wore black stockings and suspenders under his three-piece pinstripe, and as the fellow went droning on about how to use the power of the mind to give yourself power over people, Hugh lost interest completely, to the point at which he was on the brink of leaving, walking out, going back to the house and nailing the rest of them with one well-aimed front page spread, was just about to go when the leader – the real one – sensed his mood and piqued his interest with a well chosen sentence.

'In order to achieve our aims, I need to perform a major ritual and I need a very special kind of girl to assist me in that. And I want Susie to be that girl.'

Hugh only heard two words out of that lot – *ritual* and *Susie*. Whatever was required of her he would make sure she did it, if only for the pleasure of watching her performing in a *ritual*. He was already growing hard when several thoughts collided in his brain, all with different effects. The idea that the leader of the group thought Susie was Hugh's to give away delighted him, and completed the stiffening in his trousers. The idea that the ritual would involve some form of – preferably – perverse sexual activity sent the blood roaring even faster through his veins. And the knowledge that the leader wanted something from him gave Hugh a little bit of power over a very highly placed politician. Which was a novelty he determined to savour in full.

'Well…' he said, stalling for time and trying to appear as disinterested as possible in the proposition.

'I realise it's a lot to ask,' the man continued, 'but I can offer a great deal in return. In particular, I can give you complete power over as many other women as you wish.'

'You mean…'

'You won't get her back.' He stared, waiting and watching

for a reaction, but Hugh was so dumbfounded by the remark he couldn't think of anything to say, and so the man explained further. 'I never allow my girls to be given to others,' he said coldly. 'It gives me no pleasure at all. Once she becomes mine, she remains mine. Forever.'

Well at least knowing she'd be around for a good long while removed the awful possibility that Hugh had actually been contemplating. He thought carefully. He'd grown used to Susie, grown used to his power over her, making her do whatever he wanted, whenever he wanted, and giving that up was not an idea he was particularly comfortable with. Typically he gave no consideration whatsoever to what her opinion on the subject might be, or whether she would relish becoming the lifetime property of a man she had never met. Likewise, it apparently did not occur to the man to wonder whether Susie would agree to such a trade, or even if she considered herself to be Hugh's to trade.

Breaking the silence, the man emphasised his incentive. 'The power I can show you will provide you with a hundred Susies, a thousand. You can live in a world full of Susies.'

'So why do you want her, if there are so many others available?'

'Because she's different things to you and me. To you she's just another girl who thinks she's too good for you, one you can reduce to your own level by putting your hand in her pants. Yes?' He didn't wait for confirmation of his assessment. 'What you like about Susie is that she's all airs and graces and you – just you – know how to make her drop them as fast as she drops her knickers. You just like the power your knowledge of her true nature gives you.'

Hugh didn't say anything, because there was nothing to say. The man was spot on.

'I can show you how to be that powerful all the time. Give me Susie and I'll give you the power to make any female behave like Susie.'

'But if you can make any female you want do what you want – that *is* what you're saying, isn't it?' he asked, and continued when the man nodded. 'Then why don't you just make another girl do whatever it is you want? Why must it be Susie?'

'I could do that,' he acknowledged, 'just as I can show you how to make any woman behave like her. But what I cannot do is make them think and feel like her. Many would be acting against their instincts, against their better judgement.' Hugh felt himself stiffen even more at the very idea, moving in his seat to conceal the evidence as the man continued. 'But I'm not looking for just any girl. I need,' he sighed deeply, 'someone special. Someone like Susie. Only there are very few like her, and I simply don't have the time to continue searching. And why should I, when the lovely Susie is available now?'

'Well just find one and make her do whatever it is you want,' persisted Hugh, getting even harder at the prospect.

'I could do that too. But I need her to do certain things of her own free will, and I'm sure you understand that I'm talking about the kind of things most girls would never even contemplate doing. As you know, Susie is one of a rare few who are capable of extremes, and I believe she will do what I need out of curiosity and sheer sexual greed. That she performs her task willingly is what's important to my purpose and makes no difference to yours. In fact,' he added slyly, 'I think the idea of making women do things against their better judgement is probably even more appealing to you than the idea of watching Susie do what comes naturally to her.'

Good point, Hugh privately acknowledged, and though he didn't say so, from that moment the decision was made, and they were only arguing about the details – most of which were as exciting to Hugh as they were surprising and shocking.

'They're what?' Susie struggled to contain her anger.

'Fucked,' Hugh said. 'The pictures are fucked.'

'How did that happen?' she asked acidly, suspecting quite correctly that Hugh was lying, but believing quite erroneously that his reason was simply that he would find it highly entertaining to make her go through another evening like the previous one all over again, just for the fun of it. His fun.

'It's just one of those things,' he said. 'This new digital stuff is so sensitive. No one can guarantee results every time.

'You messed it up,' she accused.

'Okay, maybe I did,' he conceded, taking her by surprise. 'But either way, we have to go back.'

'*Have* to?' she said.

'Have to,' Hugh insisted. 'The editor—'

'Will have your balls on a plate by lunchtime,' she interrupted vehemently, sensing that this at last was payback time. 'And when he does, you needn't expect me to help you out.'

But with an untypical degree of finesse, Hugh played his trump card like a gentleman.

'He already knows,' he said. 'And he wants us to go back.' He slumped down in his chair as he spoke and Susie could see at once that he was telling the truth – he'd already had the ear bashing.

It had almost been the hardest part of keeping his end of the bargain, but he'd done it, and now that he had everything else would be easy.

'Last night was a bit of a washout, I'm afraid,' he'd said in his early morning phone call. Taking the bull by the horns was the only way he could deal with the editor, and he knew that soft-soaping just didn't work at all. The direct approach was always the best and he'd gone straight to the point, owning up to the fact that Susie's camera had been transmitting to a recorder in the car outside and it had sent hash instead of the beautiful clear pictures he'd collected while testing it in the house before they went. He didn't mention how easy it had been to make sure of this, any more than he mentioned the second recorder in the boot, which *had* recorded everything, perfectly, although the tape ran out just as she descended the steps to the kitchen.

'What about the other one?' the editor demanded angrily.

'You've seen the stills.' Hugh had sent some freeze-frames from his own camera by email.

'That was just a fancy dress party with two blokes wrestling naked. Like a scene from a surreal movie. It was old hat twenty years ago.'

'I know.'

'Where's the scandal? Where's the upper-class porno? Where are the rich and famous getting their rocks off with people they shouldn't?'

'They were there.' Hugh embarked on a little heavy but accurate namedropping. 'We just haven't got pictures. Only a story.'

'You know how it works,' barked the editor, 'and it only works with pictures. No pics, no story, no front page splash, no sell-out. And no job,' he added darkly.

After that it became easier, and eventually he had the editor's backing for another try. No, that wasn't quite true – the editor *demanded* another try. He was so angry he'd forgotten to be considerate and hadn't asked if Susie wanted to try again or not. He'd ordered it.

'Must have seen the expenses,' Hugh said apologetically,

but Susie remained unconvinced. 'We've still got my story and a few pictures of people behaving badly,' she persisted. 'We've run stories with less evidence than this before.'

'Not people like these, we haven't,' Hugh argued. 'This is heavy stuff. This one has to be watertight or we'll all need a watertight bum-hole.' He was echoing the editor's own words, and they tolled the awful ring of truth in Susie's ears.

'And?' she asked wearily, beginning to accept the inevitable.

'While you were sleeping I went round to see Crispin.' He let the words hang, waiting until she was hooked. 'And he introduced me to the *real* man at the top.'

Susie remained silent, which meant she was curious.

'He's not just any old local MP. He's a *much* bigger fish than that.'

'Shit!'

'Exactly. The boss wants this one very badly.'

'I bet he does.'

'And he wants us to be sure.'

'Yes, he would. But that's your department, isn't it?'

'Yes, and it's going to be harder than ever now.'

'Oh?'

'Well, think about it; he won't be at one of their sleazy photo shoots, will he?'

'No, I suppose not.' She almost smiled, because Hugh had got them into this fix and there didn't seem to be a way out. Not the blue-eyed boy today, she thought, pleased he was in trouble at last and the editor was beginning to see what he was really like.

'But he won't have to be.' Susie's smile faded; smug Hugh was back, business as usual. 'I've fixed up a better deal for you – for us, I mean.'

'Oh yes?'

'Yes. A private party. They're looking for pretty girls to attend as…'

'As what exactly, Hugh?' Susie wasn't sure she really wanted to know.

'As willing guests.'

'Willing?'

'Willing.'

He was making her ask because he enjoyed it. She knew that, but she had to ask. So hating herself, and him, she asked. 'What sort of willing?'

Triumph flickered in his smile. 'Well, like the servant girls at the Roman bash; you know, dress up a bit, playacting a bit.'

Susie thought of Rosanna and the orgy. 'Playacting?' she asked.

'Yes, pretending a bit at first, and then… well, you know the rest, I'm sure.' He stared, devouring the look on her face, the slightly open mouth, tongue tracing the edges of those even white teeth, and the eyes, most of all the eyes, wide and white with large pupils. He didn't need to hear her speak or see her chest rise with her suddenly rapid breathing to know she was excited by the adventure he was proposing, to know there was a damp warmth in her knickers. With a sudden lurch in his own underpants he wondered what they were like. White, he imagined, because Susie preferred virgin white, very tight, and revealing in the way they clung to the smooth curves of her perfect body. She was such a little temptress; he couldn't resist goading her some more. 'Look, it's the usual thing, no holds barred. Entertaining the male guests… letting them have their fun. You know the ropes…'

'Yes, I do,' said Susie, because she did.

'They asked if my wife would be interested.'

Susie allowed a smile at the success of their ploy. 'He

bought it then?'

'Lock, stock, and wedding ring,' Hugh said. 'Actually, he asked if I would be interested in being present while my wife entertained him and his guests – some extremely top-class people.'

'Okay.' She agreed, but she had to. It was the story of her life; giving in to the demands of her adulterous body, but it was also the story of a lifetime. After this she could write a best-selling book about sex and scandal in high places and go and live in the country. Kingscombe, she thought. It was Kingscombe again, sidling into her thoughts when she least expected it. Because the peace and quiet concealed so much about a place that was seething with clandestine activities. Just as her own everyday exterior concealed insatiable sexual undercurrents, so the outward calm of the pretty west country village was a curtain which overlaid a melting pot of frenzied coupling between people who should not be coupling with each other. She and Kingscombe were two of a kind, and she knew she'd always be able to find there peace or pleasure in whatever mix and quantity she needed it.

There was just one more thing to get out of the way, one more evening being groped and slobbered over by some stranger – or strangers. As she turned to the stairs, heading back up to her bedroom, Susie tried to ignore the warm wet sensation between her legs as her body anticipated the night ahead with an eagerness that her mind tried to deny, but could not.

Hugh watched her go, and then headed towards the room he privately thought of as mission control, where his cameras awaited his guidance. He knew he had to be quick, because he'd seen the twinkle in her eyes and knew she would start at once, and he did not want to miss even one second of the entertainment.

Chapter Sixteen

A pale silver disc floated above the city, drifting between the clouds, brushing the spire of the cathedral with a luminous glow and painting the cobbles white before plunging the narrow lanes into darkness. In the deep recesses of the quiet streets it seemed nothing had changed in hundreds of years. There were no outward signs of the modern world, and all lay quiet under the glare of the full moon, unchanged and unchanging.

Seeing that everything was as it should be, he snapped closed the curtains of the narrow room overlooking the square patch of ground on which the church had tortured and burnt so many souls in the name of peace and love, and looked down at the book, the hand-lettered words on the crinkled pages still visible in the shadows.

Carefully he turned the pages one by one, using the time to prepare himself, building the concentration and energy as he pressed the pages flat at the place he sought, reading the words, remembering.

The process required the softening of his target by making her behave in a loose and licentious way. It was no good his subject doing that because she chose to; it had to be at his bidding, and after the previous day this first part of his ritual was complete. His finger moved down the page, and he began to hum softly as he read.

The bare boards of the room were overlaid with a large black sheet, and on it were described the lines and curves of the pentagram, stark white, even in the soft glow of the dark candles that flickered from tall iron stands, one at each corner of the black cloth square.

Music hummed, low and deep, the tones of a church organ, swelling from the cassette player in the corner as he turned and sprayed the air with scent from a bottle, taking care to make certain that a fine mist of perfume drifted and settled on the naked girl who lay motionless in the centre of the pentagram. Replacing the bottle on the small table, he pressed the book open once more, though he knew the words by heart and had no need of reminders.

Picking up the heavy pewter chalice he turned to face the pentagram with its motionless form, swirling the pungent liquor with slow sweeps of his hand.

'Here now I drink the lifeblood of Satan. Through this indulgence He gives me the power to call forth the Minions of the Infernal Pit. My flesh burns in ecstasy. Riding upon the energies of my venomous fluids are the fantasies I now cast into the slumbering mind, which is absent of thoughts of the obscenities I crave. Hail Pan! Shemhamforash! Hail Satan!'

He raised the chalice and drank, long deep swallows until it was tilted almost vertical, and empty. He replaced it carefully and looked down at the girl. She seemed to be lying on a pillow of gold, but it was her long blonde hair that surrounded her head like a cloud, glowing in the candlelight. Her breasts were young enough to be firm even against the pull of gravity, and the nipples were stark tips, hardened by the caress of the cool evening air, or maybe it was anticipation that made them tighten and rise. Her stomach was flat, her sex mound pink and smooth, split by the shadowed crease into which his eyes now bored.

From within his robes he produced a small scrap of white cloth and raised it to his face, covering his nose and mouth, inhaling the musk deeply. His other hand plucked open his robe and his erection swung heavily in front of him. It was the sign and the girl remembered her lesson well, obediently parting her legs. She was wet and ready, as the ritual required, the earlier caning having made her so.

She had cried, of course, as they always did at first, and then she simply moaned as he caned her, explaining as he did so exactly what he was going to do to her now the correct moment had arrived. The words on the old pages explaining the ritual were bare and stark: *Now let the sex or masturbation begin*, it said. But he had gone into specific detail, telling her when to open her thighs, telling her she must put him in her body, telling her he must ejaculate inside her. And all the time the cane lashed across her squirming buttocks and he fought the impulse to plunge his virulent stiffness into her slippery tightness, knowing he needed her pure and clean for the ritual itself.

Now she showed the value of the whipping, doing exactly as he'd instructed, opening her legs to him and reaching up gingerly to take him in one hand, spreading the tight lips apart with the other and positioning him against her entrance.

As he felt the heat enclose the end of his penis he closed his eyes, visualising his purpose, seeing the projections of his mind like a silver stream of liquid shooting from the window and up into the sky, turning into a gaseous ephemeral creature, a phantom thought that raced across the sky in a perfect arc towards the small house where his chosen target lay sleeping.

He moved at lightning speed through the skies, taking only a fraction of a second to arrive at his destination, passing through the roof of the small house, lowering through the bedroom ceiling to where she lay on her back, arms and legs flung wide under the covers, as if waiting. As he watched, one hand reached down between her legs and as he merged into and through the light sheet as easily as he had filtered through the roof he saw she was holding herself open, waiting for him, and he grasped her breasts in his hands as he lowered the tip of his erection between her outstretched fingers.

In his palms the girl's nipples were as stiff as berries too, and he squeezed them, his mind seeing the sleeping figure arch and gasp in surprise and pleasure. He was resting against the opening, feeling its warmth around the tip of his erection, welcoming, opening to his pressure. His sharp downward thrust was accompanied by a delightful squeal from the girl, and his mind saw another girl writhing as he pierced her heated wetness.

He let his mind embrace the distant figure, let the tendrils of his thoughts wrap themselves around her until they were absorbed through her skin, her eyes, her nose, her mouth and her ears, until she was thinking his thoughts and seeing the future he wanted for her, seeing it as her body rose to full arousal, seeing it as the sexual tensions drummed through her groin, seeing it as she rose to a climax and forever thinking of it as a source of excitement and orgasm, wanting it, just as he did, needing it to feed her newly implanted desires.

The moans in his ears were real as well as imagined, and his fierce thrusting was driving the girl beneath him towards a sexual frenzy of her own. She was young, tender and sweet, but very ripe, and the clinging embrace of that hot wet flesh was a pleasure he'd been denying himself for too long. He knew there were only seconds left in which to enjoy her, and he let his eyes drink in the reality, let his mind feast on the sensations of her juices, slick beneath his fingertips as he grasped her firm buttocks and pulled himself deeper, deeper, and felt her buck beneath his thrusts until he knew the moment was now.

Closing his eyes he concentrated on the image of his victim, who likewise squirmed and moaned under the phantom assault, seeing her face and body, remembering it as she had screamed and moaned and writhed as he came and came and came, and though others entered her and ravished her it was at his bidding and his command, and he was the source of her arousal, the cause of her frenzy and now the object of her desire, and he clenched his buttocks and pushed his pelvis forward, spraying inside the girl, rich emissions of fluid that oozed thickly inside her, knowing that far across the silver-spired nightscape of the city, Susie could feel his ejaculation pumping inside her.

He let go of the material clenched in the knotted fingers of his left hand, and the tiny white knickers he had retrieved from the kitchen of the big house dropped limply to the floor, their purpose more than served.

The visualisation should end when the effects of the orgasm cease. That was the delightful final instruction in the book. Delightful, because it left him free to concentrate on the matter in hand, and the matter in hand was a newly deflowered girl whose clinging warmth was already making him stiff once more.

Chapter Seventeen

'Just go along with it,' Hugh told Susie. 'Whatever happens, just go along with it.'

'Why?' she asked curiously. 'What's going to happen?'

'Well, you know what they were like last week.'

She knew. Better than Hugh did, she thought. He hadn't been screwed senseless by what had felt like half the men in Norfolk. But it was hard to believe a whole week had passed since they were at the Roman orgy.

The time had passed in a blur of days and nights, days when she could seldom think about anything except the basement kitchen at the big house, Rosanna's lithe body and the endless succession of rampant penises. And of course the man with the golden eyes, who'd bathed her soul with understanding and her pussy with a fire that could not be doused, no matter what she did or how often she did it.

She'd been so aroused and so unable to satisfy that desire that she'd even contemplated asking Hugh if he'd help her out with a stiff prick, which was the only thing she hadn't tried, but that was only a short-lived idea that occurred to her just the once after a particularly restless night.

Her nights had been tormented by dreams and she slept only fitfully, but she'd awake not able to remember the dreams that had troubled her, but with her body on fire, refusing to be subdued as her fingers caressed then penetrated as she sought different ways of relieving a pressure she couldn't understand.

By day she was lethargic, almost dazed by fatigue, taking

advantage of the sunshine to sit in the rear garden of the house and let her mind wander. But every time it drifted off it conjured up vivid memories of the party at the big house, of the orgy in the garden and of a beautiful girl, naked on a wooden table, her body taut as a bow as man after man entered and ravished her as she rose to unbearable heights of sexual ecstasy, wracked by climax after climax and still unsatisfied.

In her mind Susie watched each intense orgasm, sharing the sensations of pleasure and feeling the sorrow of continuing need just as strongly as the tormented figure on the table. And it was only gradually that she realised the figure was blonde, not dark. It was two or three days in which she'd seen these mental images night and day before she drew close enough to look down into the girl's eyes and find she was staring at her own, that it was her, Susie, stretched out on the table.

Once she knew what she'd always known without admitting it, the images grew stronger and more vivid, and the needs of her body grew as the idea of being held for the pleasure of numerous men filled her with yearning and she began to welcome the daydreams and the brutal men started beating her, grunting with effort as they lashed her buttocks with whips, with belts and canes, each one firing her to dizzy heights before thrusting fiercely into her, dripping sweat onto her tender body as they ejaculated aggressively, and then moved aside for the next one, and the next, each man beating her first before releasing their sexual tension by fucking her.

The images always faded as she looked down into her own face, and then she would climb the stairs to satisfy her cravings with nimble fingers, unaware of the mechanical eyes that watched her every move and relayed each trembling gesture to the room where Hugh watched, recording everything, second by second, gasp by gasp.

Then one night she woke in a lather as usual, unable to remember the dream that had disturbed her sleep but knowing it was even more arousing than the dream she had by day, but failing once again to claw its images back from the fringes of her subconscious, though it was always agonisingly close.

This time she thought her desperate pussy was on fire, so hot was the syrupy wetness as her fingers gently slipped inside, beginning the caresses that would lead her towards the momentary release of an orgasm.

As she stroked between her thighs she felt a strange coldness in the room, and drew the sheet over herself even though the night was warm and close, and for a moment or two she felt as if she wasn't alone, as if there was someone standing close, watching as she stroked her restless body.

But the door was locked, making sure Hugh could not creep in and catch her while she was busy with her fingers, and she knew she was alone.

But the cold was tangible, almost a physical presence that pressed her down against the mattress, catching in her throat and making it hard to breathe, and as she slid two fingers downwards and spread her pink lips apart she gasped as the cold air filled her like a phantom penis, and she could almost feel it thicken and jerk, ejaculating inside her body where the muscles clenched around it as she came as well.

Susie's breath hung ragged in the dark and she slumped back on the mattress, fully relaxed for the first time in days, feeling the energy draining from her body as she drifted on an undulating stream of semiconscious thought, slowly falling asleep, drained of all emotion and strength, and as she closed her eyes she thought for a moment that two small pinpricks of gold flared in the darkness above her – like the blinking eyes of a cat.

It was dusk when they arrived at the big house Susie remembered so well, and as they crunched along the gravel drive elongated shadows reached out towards her like clutching fingers, making her shiver with a sudden clutch of fear. As she felt the familiar and instant response in her knickers she almost smiled to herself, because by now she knew there was nothing to fear. She already knew the worst that could happen, and that didn't frighten her at all. In fact she felt her spirits lifting slightly as she considered the prospect of laying herself bare to another crowd of onlookers before they closed in and began to feed off her beauty and vibrancy...

'Please, do come in,' Crispin greeted with an oily smile, and though he was speaking only to Hugh, ignoring Susie completely, she sensed a difference in him, and realised that this was not his usual demeanour. Instead of being distant and superior, he seemed more relaxed, more normal. Certainly he wasn't obsequious or ingratiating, but clearly he was no longer so sure of his authority, no longer acting as if nothing and no one mattered except him. He was being polite, but because he had to be not because he chose to be. Which meant that somewhere in the big house was someone who ranked above him in whatever hierarchy he subscribed to.

He showed them into a large room with alcoves full of books and small sculptures, twisted shapes in rough bronze and smooth marble. And sitting in a large wingback leather chair, in semi-shadow despite the lamp on the table beside him, was a man she recognised at once, and now the barbed shockwave that jangled her nerves was definitely fear.

'Welcome,' said the man who had given his stepdaughter

182

to the group of men down in the kitchen of this very house. 'My dear.' He acknowledged Susie with a slight inclination of his head, but he barely looked at her, and she almost shuddered with relief as she began to breathe again.

He was already speaking to Hugh, who was smiling and nodding agreement, and Susie couldn't really hear more than the occasional words until he asked a little louder, 'And she is dressed as we discussed?' to which Hugh nodded again.

It wasn't such an obviously stupid question, even though anyone with eyes could see for themselves exactly how Susie was dressed; in a simple black dress, not too long, not too short, not too tight; just tastefully stylish.

'Let me see,' the man said to Hugh.

'Susie, lift your skirt up,' said her accomplice, watching her hesitate. 'Susie, lift your skirt up,' he repeated, and knowing it had to be done, she plucked the hemline and lifted it to her waist, exposing her slender thighs but not, she hoped, her traitorously damp underwear.

'Higher.' Hugh's tone was stern and she did as he demanded, standing with her skirt around her middle so the three men could admire the knickers she'd chosen so carefully. Plain, simple and white, they dipped from the hip to a small triangle that clung snugly to the slight swell of her pubis, tight between her soft lips and gently separating them, and the silence that fell on the room fully justified her choice, the breathless sensuality of the vision intensified by the fact that they were clearly damp with the lush juices of arousal, a shadowy wetness that revealed the soft folds of the smoothness within.

Crispin was the first to speak. 'May I?' he enquired, without taking his eyes from Susie's knickers, and the sitting man murmured assent. He stepped forward and cupped Susie, his fingers between her thighs, his palm cosseting the warm moist material with just enough pressure to separate the two lips a little further. 'Perfect,' he breathed, talking to the sitting man, though staring down to where his hand was wedged snugly between Susie's thighs.

'Through there,' the silver-haired man said to Hugh, indicating a doorway.

Hugh moved a pace nearer. 'Through there,' he echoed. 'You'll find some clothes. Put them on, but keep your knickers on.'

Blushing as she extricated herself from the upturned hand, knowing she'd left a trace of her damp arousal on it, Susie went through to a small cloakroom, with a table and a chair, upon which lay the clothes Hugh had mentioned, although it seemed a grand description for what appeared to be little more than a flimsy white veil. But there was a sort of clasp arrangement along one edge, and Susie guessed it was meant to fasten around her like a drape. She slipped off her dress and shoes, took off her bra, and wrapped herself in the silky perfection, a delight against her skin. Shivering, and knowing it was in some ways more revealing than being naked, especially where it clung to her firm breasts and kissed the dark nipples into proud erectness, she was about to return to the library when, at the ajar door, she heard the three men discussing something.

'…Major ritual ahead, as I explained…'

Holding her breath, with her ear to the slight gap, Susie heard the silver-haired man addressing the other two, and strained to hear more.

'…Always need a special altar for something this important… but…' she lost some of his next words. '…Lucky to have one as ripe as this…'

'…Thought you needed virgins…' she heard Hugh respond, and the other two chuckled.

'…Desperate for it, so much better for our needs…

184

Rarely lucky enough to find one as perfect as her…'

Susie strained closer to hear.

'…Your reward for presenting us with… will be membership, and of course the gift of control.'

Susie froze, afraid to even breathe in case she missed more of the conversation than she was already missing.

'Have you chosen someone… as your first…?'

'Oh yes.' The smug satisfaction in Hugh's voice was evident, and as she heard his oily tones Susie could picture the precise expression on his face. As she imagined the eyes narrowing calculatingly, as they did when he was making someone do something they didn't want to do, she shivered as the memories came flooding back. She'd seen that look and heard that tone before, and an image of Sophie came to mind, filling her with dread.

'Oh no,' she whispered the vow determinedly, prepared to do battle with Hugh and the world if it was necessary to keep Sophie from falling into his miserable clutches once more, 'you'll never get your hands on her again.'

And then, with back straight and eyes blazing, she pulled the door wider and walked into the library.

The room was now dark and at first her eyes struggled to see anything at all, but as she got used to the gloom the vague shapes she could see settled into more definite outlines, but fear made her feel dizzy.

And that fear was intensified by the fact that she could see little or nothing of what lay ahead, making her take hesitant steps, and the drifting smoke added an extra element of foreboding and hidden danger. And her senses were being attacked at once; the air thick with a cloying perfume, her ears filled by insistent chords of classical music that resonated from speakers she couldn't see, but which had a bass presence she could feel.

A hand pressed on her shoulder, urging her forward, and

185

she obeyed, conscious of the warm wetness between her legs as her body moved a half pace and stopped.

The floor was soft under her bare feet, deep dark carpet with a complex pattern of white lines crisscrossing each other inside a circle; it could have been writing, but Susie couldn't make any sense of it. And anyway, she was too preoccupied with what else was happening. Now her eyes had grown used to the gloom she could see a group of figures standing in a semicircle around a large table, which had been draped in black cloth and placed in the centre of the room – and the centre of the pattern, which she could now see was circular. In the corners were four small tables, upon each of which burned a tall black candle.

With increasing anxiety she felt like she was in a scene from a horror film, and she was the dozy innocent girl who walked naively into the heart of it all while the audience willed her to turn and run before it was too late. But Susie knew it was already too late, and there was no escape from whatever lay ahead.

'Go on, then.' Hugh's hissed instruction together with a sharp prod between her shoulders actually restored an element of normality. Knowing he was still there, still the grubby little mortal she knew and disliked made her feel safer and better somehow, as she did as he said and took another tentative step.

The figures around her were all men, she judged from their size and the loom of their outlines as she drew nearer, facing them across the table. All were draped in dark robes with hoods, like macabre, medieval monks, and with another clutch of fear she saw that Hugh was also dressed like that, meaning he was much more a part of it all than she realised, as her shimmering veil of transparent white made her stand out amongst them like a beacon.

With her eyes gradually becoming more accustomed to

the dim light she could see more detail, although the faces of the men around her were hidden in the shadows of their hoods. In front of her, above the table, a single picture hung on the wall, a complex arrangement of an animal head inside a pattern similar to that on the floor, but even as a student of Sunday newspaper Satanism, Susie failed completely to recognise it, or understand its significance in the setting.

One man, who she assumed to be him with the silver hair, took up a position in front of the table, midway from either end. Another stood nearby while everyone else gathered around in a semicircle, leaving just Susie and Hugh alone in the middle of the room.

'It is time,' he said. 'Are you prepared?'

'I am prepared, master,' replied Hugh in a monotone, and stepped forward. The second man, who seemed to have assumed the role of assistant, picked something from a table crowded with objects large and small, and silently passed it to the man Hugh had addressed as 'master'. He in turn handed it gravely to Hugh, and as it glinted in the candlelight Susie saw with real horror that it was a knife. And the horror increased as Hugh turned towards her, raising his arms, and for a moment she thought...

As the scream formed soundlessly in lungs paralysed with fear, Hugh pushed back one baggy sleeve and extended a naked forearm. From assistant to the master came a large silver chalice, held out beneath Hugh's outstretched arm.

In a shaky voice at first, but with growing confidence, Hugh began to speak. 'I renounce Christ,' he said quietly. 'I give myself to the Prince of Darkness.'

Then, with a quick slash that made Susie gasp and flinch as though she felt it physically, he cut himself on the soft inside of his arm and let the blood dribble into the cup the master was holding for him.

Susie whimpered in anxious terror, but the quiet chanting drowned the sound. Behind her and all around her in the darkness the other men were muttering the same rhythmic words. Holding the chalice of Hugh's blood high in one hand and Hugh's bleeding wrist in the other, the master stepped forward.

'Tonight we celebrate a new member into our fold,' he announced, 'a new soldier for our master. Hail Satan!'

From all around her came answering calls. 'Hail Satan!' the men chanted together. 'Hail Satan!'

Susie was petrified, too scared to shout, scream, or flee. Frozen to the spot she awaited the next development with increasing disbelief, because the master had turned to her and she knew that whatever he – they – had planned for her, this was the moment they'd planned it for.

He took her arm and repositioned her slightly, facing the semicircle of hooded figures. One of them she knew was Hugh, and the surge of anger she felt towards him as she imagined his self-satisfied smugness somehow made her feel better by introducing an element of normality. After all, this was just another one of Hugh's games to get her knickers off, and she reminded herself with relief that if Hugh was involved in the planning then the worst that would happen was that she'd have to let the group of weirdoes take it in turns. So everything was going to be okay. She was ready for them now.

As she did a swift check around the room she counted thirteen, which made a sort of sense, she supposed, in black magic terms.

'Oh,' she gasped, as the master made a gesture and they crowded around closer, taking her arms and then fastening straps around her wrists and ankles, which were connected to ropes fixed to the floor and ceiling, so that as they were steadily pulled her body was drawn into a star shape, arms and legs wide apart, forming a human cross in the centre of the dank room. And when she was tightly secured they shuffled back into the shadows a little, leaving her with only the hideous image glaring down from the wall above the table. Horns, long tail, hind legs with hooves, he was the archetypal image of the devil with which schoolchildren and horror movie buffs are familiar. Her eyes were drawn to the huge erection that speared from his woolly groin – long, curved and gnarled with veins.

A movement caught her eye and provided a distraction from that chain of thought that at first she thought was welcome. The master's assistant had begun arranging things on the table and she strained to see what he was doing – and then wished she hadn't.

In a neat row he had placed several strange objects: the large silver chalice, the wicked knife, a stick of incense ready for burning, an unlit black candle, a small bowl of water and another that seemed to contain earth or sand. And finally, a tall stout object that she recognised at once. Black and shiny with a proud head, thick veins and a broad girth that grew wider towards its base, it was an alarming copy of the phallus that sprouted from the groin of the man-goat in the image on the wall before her.

With a mixture of fear and arousal simmering between her thighs, Susie knew at once who it was for, and she was horrified to find herself circling slowly, her hips rotating as reflexes tensed the muscles in her thighs and buttocks as if it was already there, touching her, spreading, entering…

Then the ringing of a hand bell broke the spell. It was held by one of the dark figures, moving into each corner of the room and ringing it briefly before moving on. Then he moved to the table and rang it in front of the picture before placing it with the other items and turning away, melting

189

again into the shadows.

The master nodded to the unseen men grouped behind Susie, and immediately she felt the touch of their hands on her shoulders; hands that knew how the diaphanous veil unfastened, and suddenly the misty white cloud of delicate material was gone, and she stood naked but for her white knickers.

Now the master pointed to the knife behind him on the table, and the assistant handed it to him. Turning his back on Susie and unaware of the sudden sigh of relief that made her shudder, he pointed with the sharp tip towards the picture of the man-goat and spoke. 'In nomine Dei nostri Satanas Luciferi excelsi!' he shouted and Susie jumped, startled not by the words or the unexpected volume but just because no one else had spoken for so long she'd grown accustomed to the silence.

A shadowy figure detached itself from the group that gathered in the darkness behind her and stepped forward to the table, and the assistant handed him something which Susie didn't see or recognise until the figure turned towards her, holding a short-handled scourge in his right hand, countless leather fronds dangling from the shaft. He then drifted out of her field of vision, making her desperately turn her head from side to side in a vain attempt to keep her eye on him.

'In the name of Satan, the Ruler of the earth, the King of the world, I command the forces of Darkness to bestow their Infernal power upon me!' The voice came from behind her, and was followed, as she knew it would be, by the hiss of the leather fronds whistling through the air before they landed with a *crack!* across her bottom, making her gasp and wince.

'Open wide the gates of Hell and come forth from the abyss to greet me as your brother!' proclaimed the voice, and the leather whispered through the air again. *Smack!* She swayed under the impact and her buttocks clenched in response.

'Grant me the power to bless this sacred altar erected to you, Lord Satan.'

Crack! Numerous leather strands curled between her legs to flick the half-moon of white silk, taut and wet, the acute sensations exploding like a firework.

'I have taken thy name as a part of myself!'

Whip! Again the leather tips stung right between her legs, kissing the tight wet material with thin lines of fire into the flowering folds of a body that was opening, ready.

'I live as the beasts of the field, rejoicing in the fleshly life!' *Whip!*

'I favour the just and curse the rotten!' *Whip!*

Susie moaned instinctively, but not in distress, trying to lean forward in her bonds, trying to bend her waist and stick out her pert rump, offering the rounded globes to the lash, offering the wet opening to its sharp caress.

'By all the Gods of the Pit, I command the unholy darkness, the blackest of magics shall be made manifest in this altar!' *Whip!*

'Come forth and answer to your names by manifesting my desire!' *Whip!*

Her arousal was almost unbearable now.

There was shuffling and she saw the shadows move on the wall, flitting in the candlelight as one by one the rest of the group moved to stand behind her with the whip and do as ordered, calling out a name and then lashing the leather strands across her bottom, hard enough to mark her with thin red lines, hard enough to sting, hard enough to start the endorphins in her bloodstream, hard enough to kiss between her thighs like a snake tongue flickering over the wet gusset of her delicate knickers where it stretched across a soft opening that was burning with need and desire.

'Oh hear the names.' *Whip!*

Susie hardly needed the spur of fear to add to her arousal but that was present as well, the cold clutch of the unknown turning her on long before the lashes of the whip had started. Five or six of them had stood behind and called out a strange name before dispensing the stinging blow that aroused as much as it hurt.

'Abaddon the destroyer!' *Whip!*

She had a chance to regain her breath as they changed places, each man handing the whip to his successor.

'Amon, god of life and reproduction!' *Whip!* And Susie felt the trickle on the insides of her thighs as her juices leaked.

'Astaroth, lascivious goddess of lust!' *Whip!*

Even in the subdued candlelight she could see the wetness of her knickers when she gazed down through tousled hair, but still she strained at the ropes, spreading her legs as wide as she could, thrusting her scalded bottom back, offering her helpless body to the creepy throng.

'Beelzebub, Lord of the Flies!' *Lash!* That blow was harder and struck deeper, tight in the cleft of her buttocks where the wet silk was being absorbed into a body that trembled with need.

'Euronymous, prince of death!' *Whip!* Gentler, but lower and right on target, leather fronds kissed the exposed pinkness that peeped wetly around the edges of the white silk. She knew just what she looked like from behind, with her rounded cheeks thrust out, as the white curve became a narrow slash that was disappearing into her, and she knew they could see the wetness of her desperate need, see how much she wanted what must surely follow the beating.

'Hecate, goddess of witchcraft!' *Crack!* And as her body trembled at the blow another small pearl of moisture leaked from the silky gusset onto her tensed thigh.

'Lilith, she-devil!' *Whip!*

'Namah, devil of seduction!' *Whip!* Susie moaned, a long deep moan of pleasure and yearning.

But that was the last of them, and in the enshrouding silence the master turned his back on everyone and, facing the image of the man-goat, raised the silver chalice and drank from it, calling out more names between each sip, naming Satan, Lucifer, Baal and Leviathan.

And as he did, another figure stepped forward to receive the silver knife from the assistant, and turned again, standing directly in front of Susie, and she was about to whimper with fear when he took the elasticated waist of her knickers in his free hand and slashed it with the knife, the scrap of wet cloth sliding down her leg and bunching around her bound ankle.

The master stepped forward, holding an open book in his hands, and stood motionless waiting for the assistant, who approached holding something long and shiny in his hand. It wasn't the knife. It was tall, thick, black and gnarled.

'Oooh…' she gasped when it touched her between the thighs. Not from surprise, because she'd watched it aiming straight at the soft wet centre of her body. But it was cold and heavy, as though turned from a lump of solid metal.

'See, oh minions of eternal darkness, through this altar I maketh a gate of entrance.' The master was reading from the book, and his assistant suited action to the words, pushing the huge cold shaft up into Susie's body, making her squeal again as it spread her open.

'Oooh… ah…' she cried as he pushed some more, pressing it higher and deeper.

'Ye slimy beasts who rest beyond time, awaken now to the beat of the noiseless sound which cometh from this shrine.'

There was a wet sound as the metal monster was pulled out of Susie's body.

'Built to Thy Mighty Lord, oh Prince of Darkness, ye who casts the gloom of knowledge which springeth forth from the All Seeing Eye, that wisdom which sees the flaws of mankind.'

'Aah...' she moaned as it eased up inside her again.

'Blessed are the children of Thy wing, tooth and claw, and make blessed the centre of their sanctuary, oh Baal!'

Susie moaned again as the assistant pulled the phallus halfway from her and suddenly thrust it deep again.

'Behold, we make this a place of blasphemy against the cursed one!' She gasped again as he pulled and pushed, plunging the thick shaft into her.

'Now this is a place of immoral practices, a double-edged sword which shall mend the strong or render death to weakling numb in mind.'

'Ah – ah!' Susie squealed as the assistant began to thrust the thing in and out at a steady pace.

'A place dedicated to the one true god, moving within our flesh and sinews – Satan!'

'Ah... ah... ah!' She writhed and twisted, flexing her hips as she eased down against the shaft, pushing her body as far onto it as the ropes that bound her would allow.

'Manifest oh dark creatures!'

'Yes, yes.' Susie's soft moans punctuated the ritual she hardly heard as the moving phallus sent familiar waves of pleasure rippling through her body, spreading out from the centre where it penetrated as if her whole body was made of liquid fire.

'Now come with spike, horn and tail, wing and hoofed foot and cast all manor of decadent sin upon thy chamber piece.'

'Mm... mmm...' She was almost there now, revelling in

the sensations as she rose towards the edge of heaven, suddenly aware that the thick metal shaft that spread her and filled her was no longer cold, but burning with a heat that matched her own.

'Whosoever voices thy wish before this altar, being that this child is worthy of Your kiss, shall have thy reality stretched before him. Shemhamforash! Hail Satan!'

'Aaah... oh!' Susie wailed as her climax shook her body from head to toe and her hips jerked as the spasms pulled at every muscle, clenching the soft pink tunnel around the shaft in an iron grip that held it inside her until the final shudders had died away.

The master watched her carefully, eyes glinting inside the shadowy hood as her body relaxed and her weight slumped against the ropes that held her. His eyes never left her face as the assistant pulled the thing out of her and laid it on the table. Then he lit a black candle and let its hot wax drip and dribble over her breasts, the sudden heat making her wince wearily, the wax hardening on her soft flesh like streaks of congealed blood.

Then he placed the candle on the floor by her foot, and in the flickering light she watched, amazed, as he raised his black robe and lifted it above his waist, wrapping it around and tying a knot so it remained there, uncovering a stout erection that speared prominently from the shadows of his groin into the flitting candlelight.

Silently he stepped closer, grasping himself in one hand, directing it between Susie's legs, nudging up between her sex lips, still swollen and wet from her climax. Then he flexed his hips and slid swiftly into her, pushing all the way up so that he almost lifted her off her feet as his thighs wedged between hers.

'Ooh!' she gasped jadedly.

'With the fires of Satan I bless this unholy altar,' said the master, and Susie's head lolled as she felt the assistant withdraw and then thrust back in, hard and thick.

'Oh…' she gasped again, and the man began to fuck her with aggressive, staccato thrusts that made her sigh in unison with his movements, and the ropes that bound her creak quietly but audibly.

The master took the bowl of water from the table and sprinkled it over their joined bodies, intoning, 'With the breath of Lucifer I bless this unholy altar.'

'Ah…' she gasped midway through his blessing, as the assistant pumped in and out with a steady rhythm.

The master picked up the other bowl and sprinkled them with earth. 'With the body of Baal I bless this unholy altar,' he chanted, and Susie pressed against the hooded man between her thighs, panting and gasping as his speed outran hers and she knew she was losing him, knew he was ahead of her, and then he grunted and she felt him erupt deep inside – once, twice, and again.

'So it is done!' he exclaimed through gritted teeth, his voice strained, his thrusts gradually slowing.

And together the cloaked and hooded figures chorused, 'Hail Satan!'

As the chants and music died away, leaving Susie's slowly undulating body, the disturbing music, and the quietly creaking ropes that held her as the only sounds and movement in the room, the master's assistant slowly straightened his back and legs, pulling himself out of her. Unwinding his black robe from around his waist he let it fall to conceal the wet and shiny penis that was still semi-erect, and turned away, leaving Susie alone in the shimmering circle of light cast from the black candle by her feet.

With eyes partly closed, mouth slightly open, she was

still fully aroused and teetering on the brink of release, unable to do anything about it because of the bindings at each wrist. Denied any relief she moaned as she tensed against the ropes that held her. But the moans were soft and the movement languid, completely at odds with the fire of arousal deep in her stomach.

'Now we have consecrated a new altar we are able to make high magic,' announced the master, 'and this is the main purpose of our ceremonies this evening.' As his voice died away he nodded towards his assistant, who motioned to the shadows in the darkness and figures emerged again, hands undoing the ropes at her wrists and ankles, easing her down, laying her carefully on the floor amid the confusion of white lines and whorls that made up the pentagram pattern, aligning her in perfect parallel with the table and the wall, with its staring picture of the man-goat and his fearsome erection.

The smoke from the joss-sticks still drifted around the murky room, pungent mist that seemed to move with the sonorous tones of the organ music, as if making each of the chords visible to the eye, revealing the actual shapes of its powerful underlying rhythm, like a slow heartbeat.

When Susie was perfectly arranged and the surrounding figures had drawn back to the outside edges of the circular white pattern, the master approached and placed a photograph on the floor above her head. She couldn't see who it was, but she saw enough to know it was a portrait of a man, like a PR handout, a familiar image and one she was sure she ought to recognise. But her train of thought was interrupted as the master spoke again.

'I place this here so I can look into your eyes,' he said, appearing to speak directly over Susie's head as if he was actually talking to the photograph, and shrugged off his dark cloak, standing at Susie's feet, not naked like his assistant had been, but fully clothed, towering over her in black trousers and a black silk shirt.

But there was no comfort for Susie in that, for without hesitation he undid the waist of the trousers with a flick of his wrist and then opened them, drawing out a penis that was thick and long, semi-hard already, either from watching the assistant violating their victim, or perhaps just from contemplating what he was about to do to her himself.

A little shudder of expectation rippled through her body, and if those watching her so carefully hadn't noticed the subtle puckering of her nipples, they might have been forgiven for thinking she was suddenly afraid. And indeed it might have been fear that started the insistent moistness once again, but the master's eyes narrowed as he saw the tender petals of her body opening, sparkling with dewdrops of wetness, and at his waist a dark shadow thickened and grew.

Holding it loosely in his hand he began to massage it in time with the music, staring once again above Susie's head at the picture he had placed there. And then his voice began again, sultry and monotone. 'It has been long and hard that I have waited for your tongue to speak my words,' he said, but Susie was hardly aware of the words, staring as the thing he was holding began to thicken and swell.

'From across the plateaus of your consciousness I grasp the essence of your mind!' he intoned, and slowly his grip expanded to accommodate the increasing thickness of his own flesh, and Susie felt her body expanding too, making itself ready.

'I am within you, now your soul, now your mind! I hath chosen you as my slave, and from the ninth tower of Hell I call to thee!'

It was stiff and straight now, a rod of solid flesh with a shiny purple tip that was revealed each time he pulled back on it. From where she lay on the floor gazing up with wide, spellbound eyes, the thing seemed magnified, huge.

'You speak in defiance of my ways, then stop as the great dogs bay at your very presence, and wonder why your life is spared.'

Still massaging himself, long, slow, luxurious strokes, his knees began to bend, and Susie felt hands come out from the darkness, pulling her ankles apart, spreading her legs so he could kneel between them.

'I am the life moving through the vessels of your beating heart, Sir Richard, and your saviour.'

If Susie had not been so fascinated by the small drip of pearly-white fluid forming on the bulbous tip of his erection she might have realised who Sir Richard was and connected the name and the photograph together. But she wasn't thinking about what she could hear, only what she could see and feel – and she could feel herself opening wider, the soft petals hot and wet as her hips lifted slightly in supplication.

'You have my mark now, and serve under me! In the fruitless hour of your chained spirit and mind I am your movements and thoughts; I am your one and only lord!'

His fist was clenched firmly around the rigid shaft and was pumping faster and faster, pulling the foreskin right back to expose the rounded end and then smoothing it forward, hooding it again.

'I could have let you die by my hand or crushed you underfoot, so do my will and answer to my commands!'

Instinct and reflex were taking control of Susie, and as her body began the slow undulation that rocked her hips, her hands cupped her breasts, lifting them in a display of invitation before smoothing their way down over her flat stomach, pressing against her hips as they rose a few inches into the air, begging for penetration of the soft lips that her fingers now spread apart, showing him the way.

'Thoth becomes the strings of my marionette!' he called, and her flingers slid into the warm tunnel. Almost at once the hands that were still holding her ankles and pulling her legs apart were joined by others that merged out of the darkness and grasped her wrists, tugging her hands away from a body that was aching with need.

'I am working the magic of existence, carving it into your flesh that burns with a hopeless dream of escape!'

His eyes had glazed and his attention wandered away from his subject. He looked down at Susie's widespread body, the cherry-tipped breasts that defied gravity with a mouth-wateringly youthful firmness. His fist moving steadily up and down the length of his erection, he looked down between her legs, below the small blonde tuft to the humid wetness of her arousal, the flowering lips that opened in desire.

'My mere thoughts are hot red coals searing the tissues of your brain!'

Her hips were moving in a slow, sensual circle, instinctively lifting higher, Susie begging to be touched, to be stroked and spread and filled and penetrated.

'I beckon you now to my side. The vines of my power are wrapped around you a thousand times!'

His hand was moving quickly, dropping tiny droplets of pre-issue, shimmering as they arced downwards to land on her taut belly, where they lay glistening in the candlelight as she moaned her frustration. 'Fuck me,' she pleaded softly, pulling against the grip of the hands around her wrists and ankles, lifting her sex towards him. 'Fuck me,' she begged again, wishing they would let her go so she could grab him and push herself onto his impressive erection.

'The thorns hold sway over your every twitch! Come now to the bosom of my desires, Sir Richard, and watch your reason denied!'

Incredibly Susie saw his erection swelling to even greater dimensions, longer and thicker and stiffer in his hand, and she knew he had reached his peak. Then, just as it began to pulse and the eye opened to spit creamy jets into the air, he yelled, 'Hail Satan!' and plunged into her. The first hot emission splashed into the hollow of her tummy, there was another splattering of warmth between her legs, on the insides of her thighs and the soft pink wetness of her sex lips, and then he was invading her. Huge and heavy as it spread and sank deeper and deeper, she felt it throbbing as his mighty ejaculation finally ebbed.

'Hail Satan!' he called again. 'The pig is mine!' and he pulled his dripping shaft out of her heaving body, leaving her still unsatisfied, still desperately writhing on the floor.

He rose to his feet, tucking his flaccid wet penis into his trousers. As he began to fasten them he nodded another silent command, and at once an obedient cloaked and hooded figure emerged from the darkness and stood beside him, and without seeing his face Susie knew him at once by the way he stood, the set of his shoulders and the angle of his head; it was Hugh.

And she saw that he too held a photograph. Dropping to one knee between Susie's legs, which were still being held apart by unyielding hands, Hugh leant over her to place his picture on the floor above her head, bringing his face close to hers, allowing her the chance to speak.

'What are you up to, you bastard?' she hissed in his ear. The vehemence of the question made him pull away, but he continued to straighten, rising silently from her, his eyes diverted as he stared at the picture on the floor by her head, and the relentless grip on her wrists and ankles prevented her from moving enough to manage even the briefest glimpse at it. But she knew enough about Hugh to suspect that she wouldn't like the significance, no matter who was in the picture; probably her, she suspected, or Sophie.

Gravely, Hugh lifted his robe around his hips to reveal his erection, looking about ready to erupt over the shapely body pinned to the floor before him. Grasping himself in one hand he began to recite, reading the words from a book held open for him by another cloaked figure.

'From across the plateaus of your consciousness I grasp the essence of your mind,' he quoted rather clumsily.

'I hath chosen you as my slave,' he seemed to be getting a little more assured of himself, 'and from the ninth tower of Hell I call to thee!

'You speak in defiance of my ways,' he went on, and she sighed as her disloyal body began to undulate on the floor again. Her thighs tensed, the tendons strained and her knees bent a little as she lifted, bottom rising clear of the floor as she shamefully offered herself to him, silently begging for relief, in whatever form, no matter it would be provided by a man she disliked and didn't trust.

'I am the life moving through the vessels of your beating heart,' he read, 'and your saviour.'

'Please,' she gasped breathlessly. 'Please.' Transfixed, she ground her hips sensuously, willing him to hurry through the rest of the words and fuck her, and she knew deep down he was winning another battle in their longstanding feud. Silently she cursed, because it always seemed to come to this with Hugh, no matter how good her plans or determined her intentions. Somehow she always seemed to end up on her back with her legs apart, begging him to fuck her and hating herself for loving it when he did.

'Come now to the bosom of my desires, Sophie, and watch your reason denied.'

Susie whimpered as the first viscous drops splattered across her breasts, and before her first cry had died away he covered her and sank inside her, ejaculating still, making her sob loudly as her sudden climax wracked every muscle, every sinew, every nerve, and her sex clutched his cock, squeezing and releasing.

'Hail Satan!' the feverish gathering chanted. 'The pig is yours!' and Susie began to cry as another robed figure loomed out of the darkness to take Hugh's place on his knees between her thighs. He too put something on the floor above her head and then, deftly flinging the black cloth over his shoulder to expose a hairy torso with a pot belly above a stubby penis that was already rigid, he began to rub himself slowly as he chanted the opening words of the familiar ritual. Through tear-filled eyes Susie watched as he stroked himself, quoted the litany, and lunged forward, impaling her, swiftly filling her with a thickness that took her breath away, and again Susie found her perfidious body had taken control and let her down.

Chapter Eighteen

'Bastard!' she yelled, and her flat-handed swing would
have floored him if it had ever connected with the side of
his face, but Hugh caught her wrist easily and held it,
unable to conceal the faint traces of that familiar
triumphant smirk.

Without that Susie would probably have believed him,
would have accepted his explanations, but all the time she
listened to his words her mind kept focusing on the tiny
lifting at the corners of his mouth and the arrogant gleam
in his eyes, almost as if he was taunting her, admitting the
whole thing was a pack of lies and daring her to challenge
him. As if he knew that in the end it didn't matter, because
she would always do what he told her to do – especially if
his instructions required her to drop her silk underwear,
spread her legs and allow whoever it was next to do
whatever it was they wanted.

'I was just going along with it, like they wanted me to,'
he insisted. 'I had to think of someone, a name, real quick,
and Sophie just sprang to mind. It doesn't *mean* anything,
it's just a game, part of the show, for fun. I just went
along with them so as not to arouse their suspicions.' But
she didn't believe that, not even remotely. She definitely
did believe, though, that as usual Hugh had been an
enthusiastic participant, and took complete advantage of
her being held and unable to stop him getting exactly what
he wanted, and equally unable to stop herself responding
as he did. And she knew that was high on Hugh's list of
pleasures; not just having his way with her, but doing so

despite her reticence and enjoying the traitorous response of her body as it overpowered her conscious mind and forced her to welcome him and induce her to climax.

After the rituals ended, when all the hooded figures had shuffled away anonymously, when Susie had showered and dressed again in her black dress, they had tea with the silver-haired man in a comfortable lounge. Once again urbane and civilised in an expensive suit, hair neatly brushed and voice gently soothing, she couldn't think of him as the master any more, but as an experienced individual with nothing more sinister in his background than a private fondness for sexual excesses he couldn't satisfy at home.

'We'd like to do the same again in a week's time,' he said to Hugh, continuing to ignore Susie, just as he had earlier.

'Of course,' said Hugh, infuriating Susie with the way he was so quick to make major decisions involving her for her, but she suppressed her annoyance, for now was not the time to lose her cool and spoil the weeks of patient and covert hard work.

'This evening was a fairly low key affair,' the man continued, 'and we do have a much, um…' he searched somewhere in the air above Hugh's head for the word, '…much more *lavish* performance in mind, but we've been waiting for the right person. As you know, we find that the presence of an outsider can be very beneficial, and especially so if that person has the right qualities. The ritual we have in mind is the most significant we have ever attempted. In fact, very few people have ever tried it, and its importance makes the finding of exactly the right person even more crucial. For this to succeed the female we require must be obedient – no, more than obedient, submissive, even subservient, and willing to do as instructed by a master, which we all know is a very prominent character trait in Susie.'

Ignoring her completely, Hugh agreed this to be true.

'And as you know, the myth that we need virgins is just that – a myth. Oh, we need purity sometimes, and though it's hard to find we always manage.'

Hugh raised an inquisitive eyebrow.

'When we need someone new, someone pure and fresh,' the man explained, 'we simply find a new member for the group, someone who wants something we can give and is willing to trade it for something he has that *we* want.'

Again the raised eyebrow from Hugh.

'A female – a daughter, a niece, a young bride. They don't have to be virgins, but of course it's favourable if they are. But for the very special occasions we need someone equally very special. Obedient but passionate, because sexual energy is vital to the ceremony, and the more energy that's released the more successful the ceremony will be. And as we've all noticed, Susie appears to be just such a passionate girl.'

Again Hugh agreed. 'Indeed,' he concurred with oily deference, 'she is absolutely perfect for your requirements,' and he unhesitatingly promised that she would do anything she was told to do. 'Anything,' he emphasised, without even casting a glance in her direction, and once again she felt the annoyance surge, but also a warmth of anticipation between her primly closed thighs that thrilled her with anticipation.

But as soon as they were safely back at the rented house in Norwich she lashed out with her palm, and now stood in the kitchen trying to suppress the anger stoked by the thought of what she faced, and that it was devious Hugh who was making such major decisions for her, and that for the sake of their undercover work, she had to go along with it all.

Which made the editor's phone call a formality. He, and Susie, knew that he couldn't really ask more of her than she'd already given, but his enthusiasm for the next step along the investigative path was almost tangible down the telephone line, and Susie knew she couldn't start thinking about backing out now.

One of the problems that meant their work had to continue, was that Hugh's latest secret pictures were good, but not good enough. The shapes and the actions were visible, especially when silhouetted against the pale shape of Susie's nakedness. But the faces were blurred and indistinct, each participant's identity hidden in the shadows of a black hood.

But Hugh had recognised one or two and the editor was desperate to nail them properly, especially when Hugh told him that he'd managed to ascertain that a VIP guest of significant importance was expected to attend. So, desperate for Susie's co-operation, the editor promised to speak with the local police chief and arrange for surveillance from the boys in blue on the night. He assured her the mention of secret occult rituals involving local patricians, politicians and dignitaries would be more than enough to guarantee their involvement. Susie was less than overwhelmed with relief at the thought, but at least it meant their work would be over at the weekend, come what may, and so she agreed.

Two days later she and Hugh were in an office at the county police headquarters on the outskirts of the city, planning the details of the coming Saturday night's events with three senior officers, all male, who regarded her with overt, condescending interest, staring openly, examining her legs, her breasts and her bottom. That, plus the way they too addressed Hugh the whole time, ignoring her, made her feel they weren't much different to or better than the people they were setting out to entrap.

About the only thing of interest to emerge from the meeting – at least as far as Susie was concerned – was the discovery that devil worship, even when genuine rather than feigned, is in itself not illegal. Later that evening, alone in her bedroom, Susie made sure the door was safely locked against the snide bastard Hugh. She wouldn't have been a bit surprised if he'd taken their engineered congress of the other evening to mean he could make free with her any time he chose, and just come in and help himself. But with the door locked he couldn't, and Susie sprawled on her bed with her laptop, and after a swift e-mail check to make certain that Sophie was still safe at university and a hundred miles away, she began trawling the net, looking for information about devil worshippers.

She found out a little very quickly and then not much more. The first thing she discovered was that Satanists are not to be confused with witches, who are usually female and are adherents of the pagan religion of Wicca, the left hand path or whatever, and generally speaking are – in most cases outside popular fiction – little more than benevolent loonies.

But genuine Satanists are a very different bucket of giblets altogether, being mostly male and generally gripped by an unpleasant ambition for power and wealth, both material and sexual. And beyond them are the devil worshippers proper, who believe in chaos, destruction, lust and wickedness, with the ultimate goal of restoring Lucifer, Prince of Darkness, to his throne, ruling the world. Conjuring up the devil himself is the greatest and most difficult piece of magic to which a true believer can aspire, and they dedicate their lives to study of the black arts in order to become capable of this feat. Luckily, thought Susie as she read, it didn't seem to have happened yet, probably because all those lovely virgins sidetracked them so easily.

The genuine devil worshipper has no qualms, scruples, morals nor regrets and regards all humans who are not likeminded as nothing more than useful fodder. However, and perhaps luckily for the bulk of humanity which does not share this ambition, true Satanism is not an organised religion, and there is no central authority or ruling body, no structure nor any kind of organisation at all. Anyone who wants to can just set up in business as a devil worshipper and invite whomever he or she chooses to join in with him. Satanists are almost exclusively men, as Susie had already discovered at first hand, but many practicing worshippers involve their wives, girlfriends and female family members, who are usually attached to the group as sort of official hangers-on known as Sisters of Light.

Susie clicked to another site. They have women so they can have sex, not Sisters, she thought, and felt the seam in the groin of her jeans separate the soft flesh as her body moistened in her knickers. 'Typical men,' she murmured, and suddenly Satanists weren't so sinister after all. 'Just a bunch of blokes dressing up in silly costumes and poncing around in the dark so they can trick gullible girls into opening their legs.' She saw the picture in the back of her mind and opened her own legs, easing the seam and feeling the moist heat under her fingertips.

The nature of Satanism itself, and the people it attracts, is such that it encourages domination and control of others, she read, and is based on imposition of the will, forcing others to subject themselves to humiliation and degradation either in pure subservience or in the quest for greater riches. Which is more or less what the master had said, though not so bluntly, making Susie think that maybe he *was* serious about it after all. Or maybe that was just his sales pitch, she thought, her mind dwelling on the best phrases – *humiliation and degradation*, she thought, feeling the dampness through the denim as her fingers rested more firmly on the softness beneath the curve. *Pure subservience*, she said softly, pressing her fingers inwards.

In order to demonstrate subservience the Sisters of Light are regularly required to submit to flagellation and punishment at the hands of one or all the members of the group, again something Susie had found out the hard way, and she closed her eyes to relive the moment, picturing the scene from outside herself, seeing from a distance the spread-eagled nakedness, the firm flesh quivering as each stinging lash landed, hearing the crack of the whip and feeling again the warm glow spreading hot and wet into the white silk of her knickers.

Somehow or other her nimble fingers had undone her jeans and were feeling the real heat and wetness as it soaked into white cotton, and she rolled away from the laptop, lying on her back to push her jeans down her thighs, kicking one leg free so she could part them and savour the wetness of the material, the tingling delight as it slithered across the pink smoothness beneath, shrinking until it was just a stark white line bisecting her and her fingers had vanished on either side, sliding luxuriously deeper into the welcoming warmth.

Plucking gently at her nipples with her free hand, Susie closed her eyes, and as she continued her slow, soothing movements, her mind saw the pictures with pin-sharp clarity. No longer tied, she was using the scourge on the trim buttocks of a slender virgin girl. Full breasts quivered as her body swung in the ropes from which she hung, star-shaped, and the full roundness of her panties was ripe with a luscious juiciness which darkened and dampened the material.

Susie plucked the wet material from her own sex and held it aside, allowing the fingers of her other hand to spread and penetrate freely, stroking, teasing and plunging as she continued to play the scene in her mind.

With the wicked silver dagger Susie cut the girl's knickers free, and then with her fingers she explored the plump pussy that leaked warm moisture, tight and hot. 'She's ready,' she whispered over her shoulder to the master, and reluctantly stood aside as he placed himself at the entrance to the girl's body and thrust, and witnessed a rush of sensation in her own sex and sighed a whimper of delight that matched the girl's shriek of surprise.

Flat on her back, knees raised and parted, Susie presented herself directly into the lens of Hugh's favourite bedpost camera. When she stiffened and froze, and the neat pink lips clutched at the fingers inside her, Hugh almost changed his mind about letting her go.

The master was right. She was definitely something special, and it was easy to see why he wanted her for his spell. Hugh had been convinced it was virgins he needed, but the master had very quietly informed him that in order to conjure up the Prince of Darkness it would be necessary to offer him something valuable in return. Customarily he would be offered a bride, and it was immediately clear that Susie was intended to fill that role, and become a bride of Lucifer.

Had she scrolled down one more page on the website she was logged on to, Susie might have read all of this for herself, but her laptop had been forgotten as soon as her fingers began their ministrations in her knickers, and the website was now forgotten.

Not even the insistent beeping as its batteries went flat distracted her enough to switch it off, and as the calls for attention grew fainter and fainter, the slow rhythm of Susie's hips grew stronger and stronger. The girl was kneeling now on all fours, and Susie was beside her, taking each successive man in her hand, guiding him to the girl, spreading the soft lips with two fingers and feeding each new erection inside, revelling in the sensations in her fingertips as she shared the pleasure of both parties, feeling the girl moisten and spread, feeling the men thicken and throb.

On her knees with her bottom raised, reaching back between her legs, Susie had all but pressed her own juicy body against the lens of Hugh's camera as her fingers worked. The image filled Hugh's monitor and it was all too much for him. Hastily he unzipped his trousers, clutching the stiff column that sprang free, not wanting her to reach her approaching climax without him.

Chapter Nineteen

'Right then, all set?' Hugh beamed what he fondly imagined to be his friendly, encouraging smile in Susie's direction. Bitter experience had taught her it was in reality his smarmiest and most triumphant grin, and that Hugh not only knew exactly what the next few hours held in store, but was looking forward to them immensely. Which in turn meant that he had something planned for Susie, something that would almost certainly involve her submitting to the unwanted attentions of strangers. Hugh's enjoyment came from the power of making Susie do whatever it was, and from knowing that she wasn't particularly relishing the prospect. Thus the warm wetness already leaking into her knickers was her private victory over Hugh's unpleasantness. The secret knowledge that being cajoled into questionable activities with people she didn't know or like filled her with liquid delight enabled her to face Hugh without slapping him around the face and wiping that sanctimonious smile into the middle of next week.

Hugh was wearing his wristwatch camera, set to a wider aperture that, he explained, would allow in more light and hopefully let them distinguish faces this time, but Susie wasn't taking any chances. Although privately quivering with sexual anticipation, she still didn't plan on having to go through it all again because of some technical 'hitch' that Hugh had engineered just so he could watch her being fucked by men in fancy dress every Saturday night for the next month.

So, as he flicked the switch that primed the recorder hidden on the back seat of the car, to which his wristwatch would send the images that should incriminate the night's participants, Susie merely settled her handbag more carefully over her shoulder, her own tiny camera secreted inside, which she could hopefully switch on later at the right moment.

She got out of the car, waiting for Hugh so they could climb the stone steps up to the big house together. Once again Susie had followed his very precise instructions about how she should prepare for the evening; he said they were relayed from the one who got a kick out of playing the role of master, but Susie was more inclined to believe that Hugh just enjoyed telling her what to do and wear and having her obey.

So, as ordered, she was freshly bathed and carefully shaved, leaving just a neat blonde triangle, the curved fullness of her pink lips smooth and soft, filling the sheer white silk with a delicate bulge of visible promise.

As they walked up the steps Susie's mind was already roaming across an uncharted plain of potential sexual abandonment, and she was startled when the large front door opened even before they reached it. 'Good evening,' said the enigmatic man called the master, smiling politely. 'I'm glad you're so punctual, because we have a slight change of plan. It's nothing serious, just a different venue for this evening. I'm afraid this house isn't really the right place for the, um, the ritual we've planned, so we'll be going elsewhere. No, no,' he went on as Hugh reached for his car keys, 'don't worry about that. Leave it here and pick it up later. There's plenty of room for us in my car, and it'll be so much more convenient. Come with me, both of you.'

Hugh's face was blank. Susie tried to read something

into it but saw nothing, and in the end concluded that he too was surprised by the change of venue. If he'd been expecting it then he would have enjoyed her discomfort far too much to keep the smirk off his face.

As a chauffeur opened the door of a big black Mercedes and they climbed in, Susie began to feel more than a little worried, because this unexpected development would scotch the plans for police back up. It would also render Hugh's camera useless.

'Where are we going?' she asked as the car swung out of the drive and turned eastwards.

'Not far,' the man said. 'Just a few minutes' drive.'

Silently Susie thanked her foresight in bringing the handbag camera with her. Now she just had to hope there would be an opportunity to switch it on and put it somewhere it could see enough of what was happening to get the story finished. But whatever it saw, she knew she would be at the centre of it.

They drove in silence. Hugh had settled now, seemingly unperturbed by the change of plans, and once again Susie was tempted to speculate that it was good acting on his part, that he actually did know something she didn't. Fear of the unknown mingled with her excited anticipation, provoking the inevitable result between her legs, and the silky material of her damp knickers hugged her smooth, freshly-shaven pussy, and slid slightly against the soft leather of the rear seat.

After only a short journey the car slowed and the three passengers turned their attention to the outside; on one side of the road the corn stood tall, on the other side a brick wall parted at a gateway now missing its gates. Clearly the entrance to an imposing house, it guided them onto a wide sweeping drive, but Susie could see at once that it was all wrong. Not just because of the missing gates, but also because of the wild undergrowth that encroached over the edges of the deeply rutted gravel drive like Triffids waiting to attack.

There was a morbid air of decay, the distant house derelict and forlorn in the darkening countryside. It was an eerie feeling and Susie shivered as cold fear gripped the pit of her stomach, and as they emerged from under a copse of trees the house loomed over them, even more creepy than its ghostly silhouette had been from a distance.

Susie gasped, and even Hugh looked a little disconcerted as the car crunched to a halt in front of what had once been a magnificent front entrance. It still was, in masonry terms at least, but without the woodwork of even the frame, never mind the double doors, it was a stark hole that led into a dark, foreboding interior. Derelict was indeed the word; there was not a piece of surviving woodwork anywhere. No doors, no window frames, no roof. Just a huge, empty shell of ornately laid stone, as if it had been at some time in its history gutted by fire, leaving only the triangular gables and the slab front, with its gothic window arches silhouetted against the sky.

'Right then,' the man said briskly, and in the shadows of the back seat Susie had the presence of mind to reach into her bag and set the camera running, just before the rear door was opened by the chauffeur.

Susie and Hugh followed the man, his footsteps crunching on loose gravel as he skirted the steps up to the yawning black entrance, and instead chose a narrow flight going down, leading into the ruin from below ground level. Conscious of the shortness of her skirt and the damp warmth in her knickers, Susie felt vulnerable, easily violated, and the sensation only added to her plight as her body flowered. The steps were dank and slimy with dark green moss, and led into what had been the basement of the huge mansion. Now it was a flat, grassy plain, surrounded on all four sides by the towering walls of the ruined house, their ghostly emptiness heightened by the sharp beams of moonlight that picked their way through every window and the open roof.

But what alarmed Susie more and made her gasp with apprehension were the silent ranks of black-robed figures, rows and rows of them forming a sinister square. There must have been more than a hundred people there, and for a moment Susie feared she'd have to fuck them all, until she noticed that some of the black robes were shorter than others, long shirts in fact, and the legs of those figures, visible in the pale light of the moon, were definitely female. The Sisters of Light, she guessed, and she estimated they made up at least a third of the assembly, maybe more. Certainly there were more than enough of them to make the evening less daunting.

In the centre of the grass area was a large black square of black cloth, clearly marked with the circular and angular pattern she recognised from the other evening, and which the Internet had told her was the pentagram revered by Satanists and witches everywhere. At the far end stood the black covered altar, adorned with black candles at either end, flanking an inverted crucifix, and scattered in apparently random disarray were the various accoutrements of magic ritual, with which she was now more than familiar. Her research had also informed her that the picture hanging on the crumbling wall above the altar, which had been present at the other house, was the Baphomet of Eliphas Levi, the eighteenth-century representation of the devil himself, as half man, half goat, with cloven hooves, pointed tail and horned, goat-like head.

As Susie, and Hugh she noticed, stared around the bizarre

scene, their silver-haired companion removed his robes from a leather briefcase offered by his chauffeur, and slipped them over his head as the driver did likewise. Pulling up the hood, and taking up the chalice, dagger, and large leather-bound book, he became the master once more, moving purposefully to stand with his back to the altar, facing his congregation, who began to shuffle closer, herding Hugh and Susie in towards the centre, until they stood alone in the middle of the pentagram, the horseshoe of black-clad worshippers watching them intently.

Holding a sputtering black candle in one hand the chauffeur, now transformed into a robed assistant, walked around the ruin, ringing a bell in all four corners, and then to some other predetermined pattern Susie didn't understand. All the time low music droned soothingly, and the incense burners around the perimeter of the grass area wafted spirals of pungent white smoke.

Susie felt increasingly vulnerable. The air of expectancy that had been omnipresent within the stark remains intensified as the silent multitude drew closer, almost as if they were focusing their energy in Susie's direction, so that now the tension was a palpable presence, as if the air itself had thickened and was pressing against her. Still unsure of what lay ahead, apart from the certainty that it involved sex, Susie shivered apprehensively, and she could feel the heat from her pussy encased snugly in her knickers.

The bell ringing ceased, and there was a long silence during which no one moved or made a sound. Hugh refused to look at her, and she wondered why he was beside her.

Eventually the master took up the large book, opened it at a marked page and began to read in hushed tones, the words indistinguishable from each other, just like the vicar in church on a Sunday when Susie was a young girl.

Except he read from the holy bible, whereas the leather-bound tome laying open across the master's hands was named *Grimoire*, or something like that, from what she could just make out.

Susie heard footfalls on the grass and felt hands on her wrists; female hands that held her while others took her bag... no, not her bag! The hands holding her wrists stopped her from doing anything but watch in despair as the bag with its precious contents was carried away. So disturbed was she by the loss of her secret camera, she hardly noticed as fingers lowered the zip at the back of her dress and brushed the garment from her shoulders. One hand released her wrist to remove it completely and the dress fell at her feet, leaving her standing in the moonlight, naked but for her white knickers. For a moment she neither noticed nor cared; her bag had been placed in a niche about six feet off the ground. Some beam or joist or something had been slotted there when the house was complete, but now it made a safe resting place for her bag – which was, by an incredible piece of luck, facing the right way, its tiny hidden eye watching all that took place.

Greatly relieved, Susie turned her attention back to her immediate surroundings. A breeze wafted across her nipples, making them rise for all to see. Then knowing hands were at her waist, gently pulling her panties down and off.

The women were young, and dressed only in short black shifts she'd earlier thought were cloaks, and now she could see they were made of a diaphanous satin, so that their shadowy breasts could be seen swaying provocatively in the moonlight.

They held her naked, and then the unexpected warmth of sweet-smelling oil being poured on her shoulders followed a soft liquid sound behind her. The viscous stream oozed down onto her breasts and into her deep cleavage, and then further, leaving a trail over her flat tummy and trickling into the neat triangle of shaped blonde curls.

Almost before she had the chance to enjoy the sensations the hands were massaging her shoulders, rubbing the sweet-scented oil into her skin. It seemed to tingle softly as it soaked into her, burning gently with just a little more heat than its natural warmth would have created, and somehow it seemed to make her flesh come alive. Now she could feel the caress of the cool night air on her shoulders and breasts, cooling the tips of her nipples, contrasting with the unexpected warmth of the fragrant ointment. And as the sure hands circled her shoulders and slithered lower, cupping her breasts, lifting and smoothing, she could feel the texture of the girls' skin, and feel the ridges and whorls in the fingertips that brushed her so softly. Her nipples strained, so hard she thought they would burst, but the gentle hands came only close enough to tantalise, never allowing the relief she sought by touching her where she needed to be touch.

'Ah...' A soft moan escaped Susie's lips and her shoulders moved slightly as she tried to manoeuvre herself into the path of the slowly pleasing hands, but to no avail. Then there was more oil, dribbling its incandescent path down her thighs, over her bottom, trickling across the smooth globes and into the narrow valley that separated them, running faster down the back of her legs as the hands sank lower, across her tummy on either side, kneading the malleable flesh of her buttocks. The hands moved in concert but belonged to different girls, the timing slightly different as they caressed and massaged, separating her buttocks, squeezing and dividing, tugging gently at the soft pinkness that nestled below.

Her feet moved apart a little, a slight but definite invitation, but the hands passed on, smoothing the backs of her thighs, leaving only the memory of their closeness to that part of her which now burned with a searing heat of its own. Two hands on each of her legs, the Sisters of Light massaged steadily downwards to her ankles and then began to climb again, warm circles of sensation that set her calves on fire first, then her thighs, higher and higher, fingers brushing up between her legs. Their steady rise was a command that she could not ignore, and she moved her feet again, opening her thighs, waiting for the touch between them, straining forward, hardly breathing as she tensed for the first finger that would slither between her waiting lips and sink so easily into the hot darkness there.

But the touch never came. Instead the hands continued to massage her thighs, circle her buttocks and run smooth traces across her tummy, all but touching the light blonde curls that appeared almost white in the moonlight, but never quite reaching her centre. The girls paused, watching the master, who suddenly interrupted the dreamlike quality of the night.

'Hail Satan,' he said, quietly but firmly, and from all around Susie countless voices echoed his call.

Solemnly, the master took the silver chalice from his robed assistant and raised it to his lips, taking a long draught, which he swallowed reverently. Then he passed the heavy goblet to Hugh, who lowered his head in salute before drinking an equal amount of the contents, before handing it back. Eyes shining expectantly he watched with a self-satisfied smile as the master stood in front of Susie, whose naked body was glowing with the scented oil that still tingled on her flesh. The chalice contained a dark, sweet-smelling liquid, like mulled wine, thought Susie, as the master placed the rim against her lips and tilted it, pouring the contents into her mouth so she had little choice but to swallow, although not fast enough and the overflow spilled from the corners of her mouth, running dark red down her chin and dripping on her breasts.

The drink was spicy and not at all unpleasant, but it was warm, and seemed to burn with the same kind of glow as the massage oil. So now there was an inner warmth too, spreading through her veins, radiating from her centre to her outspread extremities. Already alight with arousal thanks to the gentle hands that still attended her, Susie felt herself also beginning to burn with a desire that urgently demanded immediate fulfilment.

Her head felt light, and as the mist swirled in the moonlight it seemed to her that everyone was floating, drifting in the night, and indeed she did feel lighter than air, as if she could fly. If the hands holding her wrists and ankles slackened their grip she would simply glide away into the night, and be looking down at the scene from somewhere high in the clouds.

The master was reciting another litany of devil worship, but though she could hear the individual words quite clearly she couldn't understand what they meant, or what he was saying, until he paused and looked deep into her eyes with an undisguised greed, the intensity of which she had rarely seen before. And then when he spoke the words rang clearly in the night.

'Who gives this woman?'

'I do,' said Hugh, and at once two of the Sisters of Light took him by the arms and, one on either side, led him forward to the altar, and Susie immediately understood that once again Hugh had known more about what the evening entailed than he'd admitted to her. But the warmth of the oil on her flesh and the relaxing heat of the drink

222

seemed to suspend both reality and normality, and it was impossible to be angry. There was just a pleasant relaxed sensation that filled her entire being.

'Let it be so.' The master looked only briefly at Hugh as two robed figures loomed out of the mist and took him by the arms, but although he made no resistance as they held him, she thought she saw fear in his eyes, real fear, and the realisation was like a wave of cold water as she understood that something was wrong, but the understanding subsided as quickly as it had come and before she could even think about reacting to it. But as more shapes emerged from the mists and she saw they were more Sisters of Light, he appeared to relax again, looking assured once more.

Still reading from his book in a subdued monotone that made the stream of words still more difficult to interpret, the master turned to the altar, holding the book out so his assistant could place the gleaming dagger on its open pages. Turning back he faced Hugh, whose eyes flickered wildly once again; he'd seen the dagger before, when he'd given blood to become a member of the sect and he clearly wasn't happy to see it again. And he looked even less happy as another cloaked figure lifted it from its resting place on the pages and turned to face him.

Susie saw his face change, the expression quite clearly one of fear as the dark figure leaned towards him, hand outstretched, silver blade glinting in the night air. After a brief pause, during which Hugh held his breath and Susie was conscious of the steady thumping of her pulse, it descended slowly, the tip slipping under the collar of Hugh's shirt. Then with one aggressive swipe it sliced down, shredding it to the waist.

Hugh gasped, a mixture of shock and relief, and then gasped again as the knife was inserted into the waistband of his trousers. There was another sound of razor-sharp steel slicing through material and the figure stooped in front of Hugh, cutting down one leg, then the other, silver blade glinting in the moonlight as the rest of his clothes were quickly and efficiently cut away, leaving him pale and shivering in the drifting light of the moon, the look on his face one which Susie could only perceive as terror. Hugh was genuinely frightened, and Susie couldn't help enjoying the moment even though it meant events had definitely passed out of his control, if they were ever in it, which could be ominous for both of them.

But with a mixture of relief and regret she saw his fear was once again only momentary, and the avaricious expression she knew so well was soon back in his eyes, the reason only too clear as two Sisters of Light advanced to stand beside him, reaching out with the small bowls, and as the warm oil dribbled across his shoulders he began to relax. As the skilled hands smoothed the aromatic oil into his arms, his chest, his buttocks and his thighs, Hugh began to rise proudly to the occasion. The chanting masses gathered in a semicircle behind the tableau at the altar appeared not to notice, continuing their mantra in unison. But the Sisters of Light whose ministrations had produced the reaction saw at once. Unashamed and unhurried their fingers, slippery with perfumed oil, wrapped around his shaft as it reared up, and began to rub it slowly. Behind him other hands massaged the oil into glistening buttocks, deep between the firm cheeks until one probing finger sank inside him, and with a jerk his erection was complete.

In the same instant several dark figures detached themselves from the throng and moved close, some bending to the foot of the altar, grabbing coils of rope which lay there and others grabbing Hugh by the arms and lifting and laying him on the altar, tying the rope around his legs and arms, binding him firmly in place with his erect penis spearing up into the night.

Susie understood at once; the other ends of the ropes had already been tied around the sturdy wooden legs of the altar in preparation for this moment, so that lashing Hugh in place took only seconds. Once he was pinned down one of the sisters who had administered to him earlier stepped forward and poured more of the pungent oil onto his now wilting erection, letting it trickle over his testicles and down between the cheeks of his bottom. Her other hand massaged the shaft back into life, thickening and straightening again as the fingers soothed his tightening sac. In one smooth movement the woman straightened her finger and sank it slowly but firmly between his cheeks again, making him whimper pathetically, although his erection stiffened further and pulsed with involuntary spasms.

Though everything was becoming increasingly surreal and blurry as the drink robbed her of coherent thought and movement, even of the ability to focus her eyes properly, Susie felt her own arousal grow as the woman massaged Hugh's erection. It seemed that they – Susie and Hugh – were going to be the centrepiece of the night's entertainment, and the idea of having him inside her seemed a lot more appealing now than it had done only a few hours earlier. In fact, she could feel the same old telltale warmth between her legs just looking at that glistening column of rigid flesh.

The proud tip was purple, the shaft straining hard and straight, painfully erect, as the sister moved away. For a moment Hugh was a stark white form on the black altar until, still reading from the tome, the master stepped into her place, waiting while she raised his robe waist high, revealing his white thighs and buttocks and his own erection protruding in front of him. Pouring a generous splash of warm oil from her jug the sister massaged the master's erection, spreading the fluid and completing his growth with half a dozen steady strokes. He stood, reading constantly, as she guided him into place and with one smooth thrust he impaled Hugh to the hilt, spearing him between the buttocks and forcing himself roughly deeper and deeper. Hugh inhaled deeply and squealed, but the master continued his litany, thrusting into Hugh's bucking body until the ritual ended with the familiar call of, 'Hail Satan!' and this time it was the master's buttocks that quivered and clenched, and incredibly as his back straightened to push forward during climax, the silhouette of Hugh's erection jerked and thick jets of semen arced across his torso, splattering powerfully and audibly onto his chest.

Strangely and intensely aroused by the utterly bizarre image of Hugh there, being fucked by another man on an altar, Susie pulled against the arms holding her as the crowd gathered closer in the darkness and matched the master's call, hailing Satan in a regular, hypnotic chant. And even in her stupor she realised that their eyes were all turning on her, and the sisters were back, their hands spreading the warm oil into her skin, making it radiate as the fingers dipped lower and lower, caressing between her legs, the slippery smoothness of the unguent mixing with her own hot juices in a blazing cocktail of need.

She gasped as two fingers spread her, holding her open, and two more slid inside, slithering around, carrying the aromatic lubricant deeper so she was smouldering inside and out, no longer able to tell her own lust from the heat of the oil.

'She's ready, master,' said one of the women beside her, fingers squirming deeper into the slippery wetness and making her gasp an audible confirmation.

She was still writhing as the master began to wave his arms as wraiths of mist crawled through the gaping windows, carrying the sharp tang of pasture and woodland as they rolled across the grass and the smell mixed with the heady incense and the oil to make Susie think it might all be a dream and she was about to wake up, safe in her bed in Norwich with her hand buried between her legs, searching the warm darkness for the source of all that moisture. Because she was very wet, again or still, she was no longer sure of anything except the growing urgency of her need to be filled. The heady scent of the incense was burning her nostrils, her skin was aflame with the heat from the oil the possessive hands smoothed knowingly across buttock and thigh, squeezing breast and nipple and slithering in a tantalising wave of wetness between her legs. The drink had gone to her head, and her eyes seemed unable to focus on anything more than a few feet away, and what she could see fell into two sharply contrasting halves of impenetrable gloom in the distance and fuzzy brightness nearby, as the glow from a thousand candles lit the misty air and fringed every shape with their light, so that her world seemed to have been painted by an artist in the impressionist style.

Now more figures were coming forward, joining the master in the mist, and the hands that held her pulled her downwards, laying her across the pentagram. Ropes were placed around her wrists and ankles and pulled roughly tight. There was a sudden coarse hammering, and Susie saw wooden spikes being driven into the ground, to which the ropes that held her wrists were tied. Then there was pressure as the bindings at her ankles were pulled tight, dragging her legs wide apart, so she was spread out on the ground, a pale white star against the black cloth.

Then the music and chanting rose to a new and higher level as the crowd gathered around in a semicircle, looking expectantly beyond the altar into the mist, thickest and most volatile around the dark hole in the ground, the staircase that opened down into the disused cellar. And it seemed as if the cellar was the source of the mist, that it emanated from below ground instead of the surrounding cornfields, billowing upwards in thick swirls that seemed to be lit from within by a deep, reddish glow.

As the light grew brighter the music swelled and the chanting grew louder still. "Hail Satan!" they repeated, over and over again, and as Susie looked around at them, their faces rapt and intent, she almost believed that they almost believed. And then the chant became a crescendo as they flung themselves down as one, kneeling on the ground, heads bowed, still chanting into the night, and Susie turned her head to see what had prompted their fervent actions.

At first she could see nothing but light and shadow, but then… then there was something, a shadow, a figure in the night. Through the swirling mist it moved, swaying as it walked, as if it was having difficulty standing upright, lurching slightly from side to side. At first she thought it must just be the picture of the man-goat being carried towards her, but even allowing for her woozy condition and the swirling mists and smoke, she quickly realised it was something more than that, far more sinister than that, growing bigger and rising higher until it was taller and broader than the master, and then she saw its eyes were glowing red and faint wisps of mist trailed around the head as it breathed from nostrils that glistened as if they were as damp as those of a sweating bull.

And then it opened its mouth to let a long, sinuous tongue loll sideways, and Susie felt her body freeze and her heart stop because it was alive, and it couldn't walk properly because it was hard for a goat to walk upright on its hind legs, swaying unsteadily on cloven hooves, long, arrow-pointed tail swishing angrily from side to side.

But it wasn't a goat because though it had horns and pointed furry ears, the face was a hideous mixture of animal and human, with blazing red eyes under a low forehead, an evil, pointed snout and a drooling mouth full of sharp teeth. More man than goat, it was still a beast, though as it slouched towards her through the mist she could see it had human arms and a broad, hairy chest. And beneath a narrow waist it was all masculine again. Between its legs – its animal legs – swung a pair of heavy testicles and a thick pole of dark, leathery skin.

The sheath had drawn back and a pink tip trailed dribbles of viscous fluid, long strands that dangled towards the ground and meandering rivulets that trickled down the shaft, making it glisten in the glow of the candles. It was standing over Susie, nostrils dilating as it sniffed her, and when it detected the musk of her arousal small dribbles of semen splashed across her stomach, hot and thick and sticky.

Still feeling as though she was floating, surrounded by the hypnotic music and the encircling mist and smoke, warmed by the incense, the oil and the strange liquid from the chalice, Susie's perceptions were blurred but her instincts were on full alert; as she looked through narrowed eyes, trying to hold the scene in focus, she felt a familiar grabbing lurch between her legs as her body yearned to be filled.

Feeling dazed and uncertain of what was reality and what wasn't, Susie lay still and silent as the creature raised its head, and as its mouth opened the ground shook with the power of its ferocious roar and a wave of stinking breath carried the foul smell of sewage and rotting compost into the night air that parted before it and closed in again afterwards, long, curling tendrils of white mist.

There was complete and utter silence from the assembled throng as the creature crouched awkwardly above her, arms stretching out to take the weight of its body as its back legs, unable to kneel, bent backwards, bringing the huge black stalk down between her thighs, lower and lower, closer and closer until it finally rested against her. As soon as it sensed the heated wetness of her open sex the creature snarled and lunged, sinking its shaft inside her.

A cold shaft, Susie realised with shock, cold like a piece of metal or stone, it was soft and flexible like flesh, but frozen like ice. And enormous, she realised with a shock as it moved deeper, spreading her squirming body wider and wider, stretching and pulling at the tender pinkness, deeper and deeper until she feared she could take no more.

At last it stopped and she was full, long and thick and cold, pushed into her like a skewer of ice that not even the heat of her body could warm, still less melt. Yet she could feel herself clinging to it, feel it freezing her where it penetrated, but still warm and wet so the obscene thing could slide easily in and out as the figure began to fuck her, stabbing thrusts in a frantic dance of carnal lust with no thought for rhythm or style. This was simply animal need, a pounding race to the finish with only one objective in mind. And as the thought occurred the creature lifted its head and roared another savage call of triumph and lunged even deeper into Susie. Somewhere inside she felt as though a steaming geyser had erupted, filled by a continual stream of liquid heat that oozed back around its base and leaked down between her buttocks, where it seeped outward into the black cloth on which she lay.

Chapter Twenty

Even after the time that had elapsed Susie was still seething with anger. It wasn't like it was a surprise. She'd expected Hugh to behave like a bastard right from the start, and he had. But the confirmation that he was a bigger creep than even she'd imagined fuelled her anger just the same. 'So let me get this right – Hugh did a deal with lord what's-his-name, Crispin, and sold me down the river?' she said indignantly.

'More or less, I'm afraid, yes.' The editor was suitably abashed. After all, it was his idea to give Hugh the job in the first place, and Susie had maintained right from the start that he was untrustworthy.

'And he didn't just sell me down the river, right? I mean, he made loads of money, had another crack at my sister, and in return he told them I'd be the local bike for a bunch of loonies in black cloaks. Yes?'

'Welllll…'

'Well yes, you mean. He told them I'd do whatever he said because it was my job. So they knew from the minute I went there that I'd go along with their stupid pantomime and let anything with a dick shag me senseless.'

'It was along those lines, I'm afraid, yes.'

'*And* he made sure that no one came to help?'

'Erm, yes,' confirmed the editor, uncomfortably, 'something like that must have happened.'

Susie raised an accusing eyebrow, and the dark-suited man beside her as she faced the editor across his desk shuffled his papers in a threatening manner.

'Well,' continued the editor, 'I mean, we know he did some sort of a deal with Crispin, and he definitely warned him about the proposed police activities on Saturday night. And he was definitely promised all the riches and preferment that are the supposed benefits of Satanism. Which, I suppose, included Sophie, your erm, well, if the, ah, enchantment actually *worked*, that is…'

'He thought it was going to, though, didn't he?'

'Um, yes, no doubt about that, he believed.' The editor coughed quietly. 'Having spoken to him at, um, some length on the phone, there's no doubt in my mind that he thought there was some kind of truth in it all.'

'So when he joined them, with the knife and blood and everything, he really became a proper Satanist?'

'Well now, Susie,' began the editor paternally, and then snapped back into businesslike mode as the suit leaned forward, a shark scenting blood. 'Well, there's no such thing, really. It seems to be mostly a load of bunkum, manipulated by certain people and groups mostly so they can have sex with girls who'd otherwise turn their nose up at them.' He had the good grace to look down at his desktop as he made the point, and Susie tried to blush, but failed.

The solicitor cast a sidelong glance at her and shifted uncomfortably in his seat, placing his paperwork over his lap.

'But the master, he tricked him?' demanded Susie.

'Oh yes. Hugh wasn't planning on being a sexual participant that night, and certainly not in the way it turned out, at least. No, definitely not.'

'Glad he was, though,' Susie said appreciatively, and opened the newspaper at the centre pages so she could enjoy the pictures all over again. There was no doubt that the improvised handbag-cam had been a great success and, thanks to the bright light of the full moon, the pictures were pin sharp and crystal clear despite being captured from video, the moonlight almost as good as a proper flash. The largest of the pictures showed the master in the act of buggering Hugh across the altar, and though his face was contorted, beyond any doubt at the exact moment of ejaculation, there was equally no doubt about his identity. Not just a local MP, but also the leader of his parliamentary party and therefore a candidate for Prime Minister in the next election – which was doubtless the prize he was seeking to obtain through his magic rituals.

And the chauffeur was actually the chief superintendent of the police force in a neighbouring county, and was also clearly recognisable. Several more of the participants proved to be local businessmen and politicians, and a number of the Sisters of Light had also been identified. Most were the wives of the men involved, but one was the mayoress of a nearby town; her husband hadn't been present and was even now waxing lyrical outrage on every radio and television news bulletin that could find room for him.

From the newspaper's point of view the story was an entirely satisfactory conclusion to the affair. Everyone who had been positively identified was named in the article, and there had already been radio and television news stories about resignations and marriage break-ups. Circulation had outstripped supply despite an extra run, and part two of the story, due the following week, had already increased orders still further.

From Susie's point of view things had indeed gone horribly wrong at the end, but her memories of the night were as blurred as her vision had been at the time, so the horror of it all was slightly distanced. Furthermore, she'd once had sex in the course of duty with a man in an alien costume, and the fancy dress creature who laid across her that night in Norfolk had not been much different to the special effects monster in north London. Except perhaps that this one had entered her with his costume dildo rather than the real thing, and she recalled its roughness and vast girth and length with a shudder of mixed dread and delight.

But even better than the triumph of the story, when the editor found out all he'd done he fired Hugh immediately, so some good had come of it all. And then, since he was no longer a member of staff, Susie argued, there was no reason not to use his picture in the feature. Thus justice had finally been done, in the shape of the large image of him on the front page, and the even larger one on the centrespread, in which everybody was clearly recognisable, including Hugh, unmistakeably being buggered in both pictures with every indication of actually enjoying it.

At last Susie had her revenge on Hugh, in full; his starring role on the front page ensuring that he would never trouble her or Sophie ever again.

But she was in the paper too, and though her face was, as always, blurred or cropped, the story yet again had her by-line and it was hard for any intelligent reader to ignore the fact that she had been the central figure on that night and on previous occasions described in lurid detail that week, and the next... and the week after, if the editor could arrange it.

'Now then,' she said, with more confidence than she felt, 'about the terms.'

The solicitor snapped into action, funnelling paperwork from his narrow briefcase, fanning it across the editor's desk and also laying sheaves of it on top of his case.

'I have one or two problems with a couple of details,'

the editor began, balancing his reading glasses on his nose, but got no further.

'Not negotiable,' snapped the suit, through a shark-like mouth.

'You don't know what they are yet,' began the editor importantly, and once again got no further.

'Not interested. Not negotiable.' He waved a handful of bony fingers across the fan of paperwork. 'None of it's negotiable. All or nothing.'

'But—'

'No, but nothing.'

The editor glared at him and was glared back at in return, so switched his glare to Susie. Cold fingers of fear iced her spine, and as she crossed her legs she cursed the sudden warmth in her knickers. Always when she was scared, she thought, but then it reminded her why she had to stand firm, not to back down. Because if she didn't the sudden seepage of wetness prompted by fear, by curiosity or by sheer uncontrollable need, would always get the better of her better nature.

'Sorry,' she said as calmly as she could, heart pounding, juices leaking insistently warm into the gusset of her knickers, 'not negotiable,' she finished.

'It's the film…'

'Not negotiable,' snapped the suit, who had now assumed the appearance of a great white, all teeth and anger.

'Do you mind, could I…?' the editor persisted, giving the legal man a cold stare. 'Susie, look, let me speak to your lawyer in private a moment.'

She hesitated only a fraction of a second before agreeing; the solicitor had asked for far more than she would have ever considered, so even if he was bought off or backed down she'd still get a great deal more than she had wanted, so what was there to lose?

'I'll wait outside,' she said, and left the office, padding quietly down the grey-carpeted corridor, heading straight for the door she remembered. She'd gone in there the first day, when she was just a frightened job applicant waiting to see the editor, sat on that very oval of white plastic and felt the same hot wetness creeping from her soft pink lips.

Skirt up, legs parted, Susie held her knickers to one side with one hand and let the fingers of her other stroke and soothe her to a long, slow climax, feeling herself relax as the shuddering pulled at the toned muscles in her shapely thighs.

They were waiting for her when she got back, and her lawyer ushered her silently back inside the editor's office. He looked somehow different, she thought; red-faced and somewhat flustered, like a boy who'd been caught scrumping, or peeping through the window of a girls' changing room. He'd been looking at pictures, she thought with a sudden flash. Pictures of her. He wouldn't meet her eye, but he couldn't look away when she crossed her elegant legs, letting the smooth whisper of nylon stimulate his eardrums, and he began to search aimlessly through his paperwork, taking a good ten seconds to regain his concentration.

'Right, Susie,' he started, 'I, um, we've agreed – that is to say…'

'There's no film,' snapped the editor, obviously back in control of the meeting. 'I ordered it to be destroyed after we'd scanned it.'

Susie was gob-smacked by the news. 'But—'

'I beat Special Branch by about thirty seconds. They shouted and stamped their feet but we didn't have a tape to give them. I told them they could buy the paper to see the only pictures we'd got. Didn't like it, but what could they do?' He shrugged happily. 'So they went away empty-handed.'

'And the rest?'

'All agreed,' said the editor and the suit in unison.

'Fine.' Susie nodded her agreement.

'Bank transfers today, paperwork in a few days.' The editor smiled a regretful smile. 'We're sorry to lose you, of course, but I can understand why. And I'm sure you'll feel much better after you've spent a couple of years in the country, recuperating.'

Susie did her best to smile a regretful smile, but inside she was whooping with joy. Not only was she relatively wealthy now, since the editor had agreed a very generous severance payment in view of her hardship, but for the first time since she'd left college and started work at the paper, she knew exactly where she was going and what she was going to do.

The editor watched her and the suit leave before he picked up the phone and dialled the three-digit number that rang in the proprietor's penthouse upstairs. 'All done,' he said heavily. 'No, no fuss. I told her it had been destroyed and she believed me. I still think we should burn it.'

He cocked his head away from the phone and listened to ten seconds of angry diatribe followed by a loud click as the other end was slammed down.

'Ignorant bastard,' he said to himself, and dropped the phone onto its cradle, turning to look out of the window to where Susie and the solicitor were crossing the car park two floors below. No one at the paper had told her that the final minutes of the videotape showed her lying on the makeshift altar, legs apart, moonlight shining between them, apparently in the throes of a multiple orgasm that seemed to go on and on and on.

Apart from the shadowy figures at each corner of the altar, and the master with his assistant on the far side, watching intently, there was no one else to be seen near her; no man, no woman, and definitely no large goat-like creature like the one she described.

'It looks as if she's being…' the solicitor's voice had tailed away as he watched the film in the editor's office after Susie had been asked to leave.

'Exactly,' said the editor.

'But there's no one else in the picture…'

'Don't you mean *nothing* else?' the editor asked carefully.

The solicitor's mouth flapped a bit, but no sound came forth.

'The official line,' said the editor ponderously, 'is that it was all an hallucination brought on by the drink, and that in a trancelike state she actually had a multiple orgasm.'

'Lasting seven minutes?'

'Quite so. However, Special Branch informs me that there can be no question that a member of parliament was able to conjure up Lucifer, Prince of Darkness, nor that Susie was ever forced to have sex with him… it… whatever. And anyone who suggests such a thing will be prosecuted within an inch of their life and never work in this town again. Etcetera, etcetera.'

'Aha…' the solicitor said slowly, contemplating the meaning of those words.

'Precisely. And whatever the truth, I don't believe Susie really wants this tape for herself.'

The solicitor had agreed on Susie's behalf to accept the editor's word that the tape had been destroyed, and had also agreed to listen most carefully to a fellow solicitor's brief in the matter of an impending libel case in which he would certainly represent the newspaper to the best of his considerable and expensive capabilities.

And so he sat in a wine bar over lunch, trying not to look up Susie's skirt and failing; trying not to remember what she looked like naked with her thighs apart and knees drawn up; trying not to imagine what it would be like to fuck the blonde beauty, and failing dismally.

Susie was wondering whether to let him take her home and do something about the insistent wetness in her knickers, or whether to go home and do it herself. He wasn't that good-looking, or that nice. But he was a man, and he was there, and she was a girl, and she was feeling wet. Very wet, from sheer pleasure, not fear.

In her handbag was a copy of a publishing contract for a book provisionally entitled, *The Kingscombe Wives*, by Susie Wills. She could recall the blurb almost word for word. *Beneath the outwardly quiet and peaceful tributary of village life* – it said – *flows all the passion, lust and desire you'd find in a big city, maybe even more so. In a series of frank and open conversations with award winning journalist Susie Wills, the wives, girlfriends, lovers and mistresses of this outwardly respectable and isolated rural community reveal what really goes on behind closed doors.*

Of course, they hadn't agreed to speak to her yet, but they would, she knew they would. If she couldn't persuade them, she reasoned, no one could. And remembering the soft flesh glowing in the firelight of the vicar's study, and the rustle of expensive underwear, she felt a delightful warm trickle and let her legs open beneath the table, and then again, just a little bit more, just enough for the solicitor's searching hand to ease between them and brush the small strip of wet silk aside. He really did have long fingers, Susie thought luxuriously, opening her thighs a little more as she felt the beginnings of a small but exquisite climax.

'Get the bill,' she whispered huskily, closing her thighs and trapping his hand for a moment. 'It's time to go home.'